HOW HUGE THE NIGHT

A Novel

Heather Munn and Lydia Munn

How Huge the Night: A Novel

Published by Kregel Publications, a division of Kregel, Inc., P.O. Box 2607, Grand Rapids, MI 49501.

Apart from certain historical and public figures and historic facts, the persons and events portrayed in this work are the creations of the authors, and any resemblance to persons living or dead is purely coincidental.

Library of Congress Cataloging-in-Publication Data

ISBN 978-0-8254-3310-8

Printed in the United States of America

11 12 13 14 15 / 5 4 3 2 1

To Ted and Betty Lennox and Grace Lennox Schuler,
I was a stranger, and you welcomed me.

Chapter 1

Not in Paris Anymore

"Isn't that beautiful, Julien?"

"No."

Even without looking, he knew he had hurt his father. He shoved his hands in his pockets and stood there at the top of the hill, looking at the so-called view. A few hills with trees on them and cow pastures in between and, tumbled down the hillside like blocks some giant kid had spilled, the houses of Papa's hometown.

Papa thought he'd given Julien a great present. Taken all his happy boyhood memories and wrapped them in a brown paper package and tied it up with string. *Papa. I know where I'm not wanted.* While Mama and Magali unpacked the boxes, he'd gone down into town and seen the flat, cold eyes of the guys his age. The stares that told him not to come closer. Not to say hi. He'd lost his way and wandered narrow dirt and cobblestone streets, not daring to speak to anyone. He passed old men in cloth caps, cigarette stubs in their dirty fingers, laughing; he heard one say something about "*les estivants*," and his friend reply, "At least they'll leave." *Les estivants.* The summer people. *No, see, I live here. Unfortunately.*

"I know you miss Paris, Julien. But Tanieux is a very special town."

There was a tightness in Julien's chest. *I tried so hard to lie to you, Papa. I can't do it anymore.*

"I hate it here."

"Julien." His father's voice was sharp. "You know nothing about this town. Do you know what it's called when you hate something you know nothing about? It's called prejudice."

"I know something. I know *they* hate *me*."

"Julien, what basis can you possibly have—"

Day before yesterday on his way through town, Julien had seen a soldier in full uniform—a Third Armored Company uniform, brown leather jacket. A tank driver—*man* he'd wanted to talk to that guy—holding the hand of this beautiful girl in a white dress, with all these guys Julien's age clustered round, and everyone going on about something he couldn't quite hear—blah blah *Germany*, something something *Hitler*, blah blah blah *army, get 'em*, loud shouts of *Yeah* and laughter, and then the girl shouting, *It's not funny, it's not funny, you could get killed!*

Julien had stood there, riveted by that beautiful girl shouting at her soldier, and a hot whisper had run through his veins: *It's war—isn't it.* And he'd taken one step into the street, to cross, to ask *What happened? What did Hitler do?*—and the soldier had turned to him with a flat, outraged stare. And then the others, one by one—like he was a cat that had peed on the carpet. The girl in the white dress didn't look at him at all. He could still feel it. It burned.

"That pastor promised you this job in his new school, and now it's not even opening and now you have to teach at the public boys' school. Why do *you* like it here?"

"The new school will open next year, and I will teach there. As you know." Papa's voice was hard now. Yeah. He knew. He knew next week he would have to walk through the school gate and face those guys who'd looked at him like he was something they'd found under a rock. He would have to walk through that gate beside some skinny Jewish kid with glasses—some kid with parents from *Germany*—their new *boarder*, who was going to get the empty room across from his in a few days so they could be the *two* new boys from Paris, together.

"You also know that there is going to be a war. So aside from *why I like it here*, you could try considering what other reasons your mother and I might have had for moving south."

He'd come home, the day he'd seen the soldier, to find his sister cooking supper. Burning supper. To find that Hitler had invaded Poland and his mother and father were in their bedroom with the door closed. His mother hadn't come out.

There was silence for a moment. Julien thrust his hands into his pockets and contemplated the dull gray slate roofs of beautiful, beautiful Tanieux.

"You see this bush?"

Julien glanced up. Papa was pointing at a green, scrubby thing that looked like an uneven, upside-down broom. He didn't look mad. Apparently they were moving on to botany. "Do you know what it's called?"

"No."

"It's a *genêt*. Around here we used to call them *balais*." *Brooms*, how brilliant. "You could use them for a broom if you didn't have one. You could burn them for winter fuel when there wasn't enough wood."

Or tie them on your feet for snowshoes. For walking to school uphill both ways.

"We did that during the Great War. There wasn't enough of anything then."

Julien looked at the bush, its skeletal green fingers all pointing up at the sky. Dozens like it, all down the hillside, dotted the cow pastures. They didn't look like anything the cows would want to eat. They didn't look like they would burn either.

"I don't know what the next few years hold, Julien. But the people who live on this land—they know how to survive." Papa looked out over the hills. "You don't know how deep your roots go till you need them."

Julien said nothing. His father sighed, and turned, and led the way on down the road to Grandpa's farm.

They had come here every Christmas since Julien was a kid; he could see it without even shutting his eyes, what it looked like in winter. Snow blowing over rock-hard wheel ruts frozen in the mud, the bitter wind cutting through your clothes: the *burle*, a wind so harsh it had a name. That was Tanieux to him: a winter town, a cold, stone village huddled on its hillside, Grandpa's kitchen its one welcoming place. He'd loved that kitchen, golden with firelight, warm with the steam of a pot-au-feu on the stove.

Now it was hot and bright and dusty, and the garden was a vast green jungle, and his back hurt worse than it ever had in his life, and he was less than halfway done with his row of beans. Mama was in the kitchen, her eyes red and her black hair plastered to her forehead, canning the three buckets he'd already picked, with Magali, his younger sister, stoking the woodstove. And Mama wasn't singing; she was working and not singing. It wasn't right.

Mama was *good*. She should have been an opera singer; there'd never been a day in Paris that she didn't sing. Thinking of it, the sound of it, he was visited with a sudden, painful image of happiness: looking out their kitchen window, down into the little courtyard with the sun shining through the leaves of the tree he'd climbed as a kid, looking at his cousin Vincent standing down there with his brown leather soccer ball under his arm, calling, "Come on, Julien. Let's go!"

And instead, he'd go home tonight and sit with an aching back, alone in his room, and tomorrow he'd wake up and look out the window and see not his own street but the jumbled rooftops of Tanieux, where nobody wanted him. From the window of his room, he could see all the way down to the boys' school, a square gray block with a low stone wall around it, standing alone on the other side of the river. It looked like a prison from where he was standing. He'd be starting in a week.

He walked away. Suddenly, and fast.

He didn't know where he was going. Away. A feverish energy drove his feet: they kicked at the dirt between the rows, they moved like there was someplace to go to get rid of that aching knot behind his breastbone. Between the edge of the garden and the woods was a long, low stack of graying firewood, and an ax stuck in a piece of log.

He looked around. No one. He tugged on the ax, and it came free. He had seen this before: you lifted it up over your shoulder, and then you swung, and it–

Bounced.

It bounced so hard it nearly jerked his arms out of their sockets. He looked quickly around. Then at the wood: there was a mark, a little line cut in its surface. That was what he'd done.

He raised the ax up again–*Oh yeah? This is for Tanieux*–and smashed it down into the log. It bounced again. He set his jaw.

This is for that soldier yesterday. And that girl–that girl ignoring me. Wham! The ax bounced higher than before, almost over his head, and at the end of its bounce, he bore down wildly and brought it crashing down again with a resounding *whack* as the ax head hit the log side-on, its blade not even touching the wood. "Aaaah!" Julien roared, and kicked the log over and the ax with it.

"Julien!"

He jerked around so fast the tree line blurred. Grandpa. Grandpa standing with his seamed and weathered face set hard as stone. He had *never* seen Grandpa look like that.

"Do you know what one of those things can do to you?"

Julien looked down at the ax, and kept on looking at it.

"Look at me. Do you know?"

Julien looked at him. It kind of hurt. "No."

"It can put a deep enough cut in your foot to lame you for life. It can put a deep enough cut elsewhere to bleed you to death. *Especially*," he said in a sharp voice, "if no one is with you when you do it."

"I'm sorry, Grandpa. I'm really sorry."

"You're the only grandson I've got, Julien."

"Yes, sir."

"And I'd like to keep you. If I may." His voice had the slightest tremble in it. "I know I never forbade you to touch my maul without asking, but I didn't think I needed to."

"Your what?"

Grandpa gestured at the ax. "What did you think that was?"

"An ax."

Grandpa's mouth twitched. A web of smile wrinkles began to break out around his eyes. "Let me show you what an ax looks like."

The ax was thin and sharp, for felling trees; the maul was wedge shaped, for splitting them. At least he'd been using it for the right job. Grandpa showed him how to set his log on a base; how to aim along the grain and keep his eye on it; how to try again. And again. And again. Then showed him how to start with the maul as far back behind his head as he could reach. Since he wasn't strong enough to do it the normal way. Grandpa didn't say that part. He didn't have to.

I'm going to get you, log.

Julien lifted his maul into position and sighted; then sudden as lightning, he went into the swing with every ounce of strength he had, feeling the power of it, the earth pulling with him as the heavy maul fell—and glanced off hard to the right as the log tumbled off the base and Julien stumbled forward and cracked his shin on it, painfully. He stood there, his teeth clenched on a curse word, blinking fast against the sting of tears.

"The first time I tried to split wood," said Grandpa's voice from behind him, "my brother asked if I was trying to dig a hole. 'Cause he'd never thought of using a maul, but it seemed to be working."

Julien tried to grin. Grandpa had probably been ten years old. Not fifteen.

"It's not the easiest, moving."

Julien stared at him.

"You're supposed to learn so many things you never knew, and everyone else has known them forever. I only did it once–and I didn't take to it. Came right back home to Tanieux after a year."

Well I don't have that option.

"Looking like a fool. I broke my apprenticeship. That made me officially a failure."

Julien blinked. "So then what did you do?"

"I did what you do when you've failed to better yourself. Became a farmer." He stood silent a moment, his eyes on the hills, and said quietly, "And loved it."

Julien followed his grandfather's gaze out over the long rows of the garden, over the field of oats golden in the sun, to the rounded silhouette of the nearest hill; and suddenly it went all through him again like quiet fire: *War. There's going to be a war.*

"Grandpa? What was the Great War like?"

"We were very hungry."

Hungry? To cover his confusion, Julien picked up the log and set it on the base again.

"The front didn't come anywhere near this far south. You know that, I'm sure. But there weren't enough men to go around here in the hills, and there weren't enough hands to do what needed doing–and even afterward . . ." His eyes were shadowed as he looked at Julien. "It seemed like only half of them came back. And they weren't the same. There was something in them you couldn't understand. I mean," he said slowly, "something *I* couldn't understand. I wasn't there, you know. Your father wasn't either. He was too young." Grandpa glanced away. "Barely."

Julien looked down at the maul, thinking about this. Neither his father nor his grandfather. And Papa said France would declare war within the week. And here he was.

"Your mother, on the other hand—the front passed over her village twice, in Italy. But you know that, I'm sure."

He looked away. Something was tightening in his chest. *Sure. Of course. Except no one ever tells me anything.* He lifted the maul, and his grandfather stepped back; but then he stopped and looked up at the hills and swallowed. "No," he said. "I didn't."

"She didn't tell you?"

"No." He shook his head. "Uncle Giovanni used to tell me and Vincent all about his friends in the prison camp and the crazy escape schemes they cooked up. It took me awhile to figure out there was more to the war than that."

"They just don't want to talk about it," Grandpa murmured. "I suppose we'll never understand."

Julien looked at the maul in his hands and looked at Grandpa. "Maybe I will," he said.

Grandpa's face changed in an instant. "No," he whispered. He was pale. "Julien. Don't say that. You're fifteen, Julien."

"I know." Julien's voice was a whisper too. He didn't know where to look, didn't know what to do with the fire that was rushing through his body. He hefted the maul and swung it suddenly in a fast, tight circle, his eye on the grain of the wood. There was a *thunk*, and the two halves of the log sprang away to either side. They lay on the grass, incredible, their split edges clean as bone.

The lowering sun shone through the big south window as they finished their quiet supper, making patches of gold on the wall.

Julien's back and arms ached. Mama's eyes weren't red anymore, but something about her didn't seem right. She didn't look at any of them. Papa asked how many jars of beans she'd canned, and she answered without looking at him, without looking at anything—except a glance, lightning quick, toward the window. Not at the light. At the radio.

"Mama," said Magali. She tossed her curly black hair. "Hey, Mama."

Mama didn't answer.

"Mama, tell them about the mouse."

Julien watched his mother swallow and turn toward Magali with difficulty, like someone bringing herself out of a trance.

"In the sink?" Magali prompted.

"You tell it, Lili," said Mama softly.

"Well, there was this mouse," Magali started. "Um, in the sink. Except we didn't see it until I'd run the dishwater. And it was alive—I don't know how it got in there, but it was alive, and it was swimming round and round . . . looking . . . y'know . . . kinda scared . . . and then I fished it out and put it outside. It was funny," she finished gamely. She looked at Mama again. Mama didn't seem to see her. She turned on Julien. "Hey, I heard you split a log. In only half an hour."

"Yeah? You wanna try?" growled Julien.

"I bet I could do it."

"Don't bet your life savings." The chime of the grandfather clock by the stairwell door cut through Julien's words, and, a second later, the deep tolling of the church bell in town. Papa and Mama were both on their feet.

Mama stood still, both hands on the table. Papa crossed the room and switched on the radio.

Loud static leapt into the room, a buzzing like an army of bees. Mama went to the radio. Julien and Magali followed. Phrases came through as they leaned in: *a general mobilization. Reinforcements being sent to the Maginot Line. British forces are landing in France to . . . since our nation's declaration of war . . .*

War.

Efforts to persuade Belgium and Holland have failed . . . mmzzzzsh . . . remain neutral. Gallant Poland is no match for the German war machine . . . crack-crack-crack-fzz . . . pushing deep into the countryside . . . ffff . . . no stopping . . . crack-crack-crack-crack!

Papa switched off the radio.

Julien and Magali looked at each other. Magali's eyes were wide.

"Maria," said Papa in a gentle voice. "You get some rest. I'll do the dishes."

Mama nodded, not looking at anything. She walked slowly toward the bedroom door, stumbling on the edge of the rug as if she were blind.

Julien couldn't sleep. His room on the third floor under the eaves was like an oven. His arms ached. His country was at war. He twisted and turned in the sweaty sheets, trying to find a position where his arms didn't hurt.

He got up and opened the window to ragged clouds lit by the half moon. And the faint gleam of the river down at the far edge of town by the school. He turned away.

He slipped out his door, quietly, and down the hall to the stairwell; down the stone stairs, cool on his bare feet, to the second floor where his family lived. The living and dining room was full of moonlight and shadows. He crept to the bathroom door and opened it very quietly. Mama and Papa were asleep in the next room. He'd turn the water on just a trickle, wash the sweat off—

His hand froze on the tap.

"It won't be like that, Maria." His father's voice carried through the thin wall. "We're not in Paris anymore. There's nothing they *want* in Tanieux."

"There was nothing they wanted in Bassano."

He had never heard her voice like that. Bitter.

Papa answered in a low voice Julien could not catch. He put his ear to the wall. He shouldn't listen. He shouldn't.

". . . reasons we're here. And Benjamin—his parents want safety for him more than anything, and *this* is where they chose. Maria, I firmly believe that the Germans cannot get this far south."

"Unless they win." A chill went down Julien's spine, the way she said it. She said it as if they *would*.

He opened the door very slowly, very quietly, listening to his father's murmur in which he caught only the name *Giovanni*, and then *soldier*, and then *Julien's too young*. Then louder: "You will *never* be alone like that again."

"Don't make promises you can't keep." Her voice was flat and terrible.

Julien ran light and silent on his bare feet, through the stairwell door and up the cold stone stairs in the dark, and threw himself into bed, trembling.

He closed his eyes, pictured his street back in Paris, the Rue Bernier: the green grass of the park and Vincent's brown leather soccer ball; the shouts of the guys, Renaud and Gaëtan and Mathieu; Mama leaning out their second-story window, calling him in for supper. Home, Paris, with none of this happening.

This was happening.

He turned over and smashed his face into the pillow. *They cannot get this far south. Unless they win.*

They wouldn't win—they couldn't win. But if they made it into France at all, where would they aim for? Paris—where Vincent and Uncle Giovanni were, and Aunt Nadine and the little girls—that was where. He saw, suddenly, himself and Vincent in brown leather jackets, in two tanks at the mouth of the Rue Bernier, shuddering with the recoil of the guns. *They shall not pass.*

In his history textbook, there'd been a map of the Great War: little red lines, jagged red splashes. Verdun had been a red splash, and no one had told him Verdun was a city where boys played in the park and mothers leaned out second-floor windows to call them in for supper. Bullets broke those windows. He saw the kitchen at home in Paris, the scarred pine table he'd known forever, broken glass and shrapnel among the dishes in the sink. Stupid. So *stupid*. How could he not have known?

He was shaking.

He got out of bed and went to the window. Dark clouds were blowing in over the moon. A breeze touched his face.

A faint sound began to rise from below, a pure and lovely thread of song through the darkness. Mama's voice. From her open bedroom window, just below his, rose the sound of Mama quietly singing the song she had sung in church every year at Easter ever since he could remember. *To you the glory, O risen one.*

The resurrection song.

Julien knelt at the window and listened, lips parted, taking in that pure sound till it ached in his limbs. He leaned his face into his hands and saw her in his mind, standing alone and singing, and it came to him that if he ever became a soldier, it would break her heart. The war would have to last three or four years first, and she could not survive that. And then his going away. Her voice rose easy as a bird to its final line: *No, I fear nothing*. Then stopped.

Julien looked up. The moon was gone, and so were the stars, and he was on his knees. "God," he whispered. His voice was dry. "God. Please don't let them get to Paris. Please keep . . . everybody . . . safe." He sounded like a child—*and God bless Mommy*. When had God ever stopped a war because a teenager asked him to? The image came back, the tanks firing, the recoil, Vincent's face grinning. He could never be a soldier. Never drive a tank.

It was unbearable.

I want to do something. God. Let me do *something. Please.* The word *serve* rose in his mind, the word *protect*, but he couldn't even think them; it sounded stupid. What did he know how to do? Do the dishes, play soccer. Split wood.

The breeze brought the scent of rain in the dark. A drop fell on the windowsill. He got back into bed, pulled the sheet up over himself, and slept.

Chapter 2

Burn

Nina read the words on the pale green card for the last time. *Name:* Nina Krenkel. *Birth date:* 07-08-1924. *Birthplace:* Vienna. *Hair:* brown. *Eyes:* green. *Race:* Jew.

Then she opened the furnace door and put it in.

The flames flared and ate the words in long licks. It was a ghost card of curled ash, the words still visible for a moment, slowly fluttering apart in the wind of the fire's burning. Nina watched, transfixed, as her name fell away into flakes on the glowing coals.

"Nina! You *did it?*"

She whirled to face her younger brother. "I promised. And you promised too."

"But we never got the fake ones!"

"He said we had to do it anyway. We have to, Gustav. We have to do everything he says." Her eyes burned. She stood, pulling herself up by her crutches. "You want to go up there and tell him we're not doing it? And let him die knowing that?"

"But Nina, Uncle Yakov—"

"Uncle Yakov is *wrong!*" she shouted. "Did you hear what he said? He said *crazy*. Is Father crazy, Gustav? Tell me." She looked him in the eye. "Do you honestly think he is crazy?"

Gustav looked at her, his black eyes wide. "I–" He shut his mouth and looked down at his shoes. Shoes that Father had made him. "No," he whispered. "He's not crazy."

"I know it's scary, Gustav. I'm scared too. But he knows." *Just look in his eyes. Did you ever wonder if dying people can see the future? It scares me, Gustav, it scares me so bad, the things he looks like he knows.* "He says we're safer if we go. He knows. So we're going." She stood leaning on her crutches, looking at him; then she held out her hand. He looked back at her for a long time, put his hand in his pocket, and pulled out a pale green card.

She took it and bent again to the furnace door.

Everything was ready. She had packed food, clothes, blankets. She had the key to the drawer with Father's letters in it, his will and the money and the tickets–the drawer where the false identity papers were supposed to have been when they came. They wouldn't come now, Father had told her in his thin, labored voice–he could hardly breathe now. "He cheated me," he'd whispered. "He cheated my children. May he be forgotten." Then he'd swallowed and said, even softer, "Or maybe they caught him. Who knows?"

Father was in his attic bedroom, where he had been for weeks, the room where the doctor had told them he would die. Soon. The sun slanted in through the window; the white-stitched stars on the brown eiderdown shone, and so did Father's eyes, out of the dimness. "Nina. Nina, my daughter." She was still catching her breath from climbing the stairs on her crutches, but he had less breath than she.

"Father, I've done it. I burned mine, and Gustav's too."

His skin was paper thin around his eyes. His breathing rasped. "Good," he whispered. "Nina. I love you so much."

She looked at him. She must not cry. "What should I do next, Father?"

"Your hair." His thin hand came up a little in a helpless movement toward her, as if he would have taken her long, wavy hair in his fingers to feel it. "It's so lovely. So . . . Jewish. It won't be safe. And the world was never safe for a woman alone, Nina. Tell Gustav to cut it now. You think you can do it? Be a boy?"

"I picked myself a name, Father. Niko."

"That's my girl. That's a very smart name." Suddenly a fit of something like coughing took him. Something in between coughing and choking, again and again the head bobbing forward and the wet sound in the throat. She bent over him, mouth open, hands going to him helplessly. Nothing she could do. He swallowed and breathed again. "Soon, Nina," he whispered.

She bit her trembling lip hard.

"You will live, my daughter. You will give me grandchildren. You will find a place where you are safe." *Did you ever wonder if dying people can see the future?* There was a strange light in his eyes.

He was gazing at her, the shimmer of tears growing in his eyes. His voice came out hoarse: "Nina, Nina, I want so much for you to live. Promise you'll do everything I told you, Nina. Niko."

"I promise," she whispered, and bent her head.

Chapter 3

Foreigner

"Julien, this is Benjamin Keller. Benjamin, Julien Losier."

Julien stuck out his hand to shake. Then he stuck it so close to Benjamin's stomach that the guy couldn't miss it even if he *was* looking straight at his highly polished shoes. After a moment, Benjamin gave him limp fingers. He shook them.

"It's such a pleasure to meet you," Julien heard his mother saying behind him. Then Madame Keller, a little breathy, said: "I know you'll take such good care of Benjamin. I can see it in your face." She had a slight German accent. Julien clenched his teeth a little tighter.

"Would anyone like some coffee?" asked his father.

Benjamin stood there, skinny, looking about twelve. All you could see of his face was his nose and the tops of his glasses. A book dangled from his left hand, wrapped around one finger. Julien pictured himself walking through the school gate with him.

"Cream? Sugar?"

I am going to die.

They poured Julien *verveine* tea because, for some reason, fifteen still wasn't old enough for coffee. Benjamin opened his book under the table and began to read. They talked about the new school, and they talked about the history of Tanieux, and they talked about how Monsieur Bernard, the stationmaster, didn't think the pastor should be opening an international school in wartime and how wrong he was. Benjamin's father sipped coffee and said he had heard wonderful things about Tanieux, and the pastor and his wife—a man with piercing blue eyes and a tall, rawboned woman—sat across the table from him and beamed. That pastor. This was all his fault.

Julien knew three things about the pastor: Papa was crazy about him, he was a pacifist, and his real name was César Alexandre. Rumor had it his middle name was Napoleon. Poor guy. That might explain the pacifist thing.

Papa called him Pastor Alex. His new best friend.

"Certainly there is some anti-Jewish sentiment," Monsieur Keller was saying. He had an accent too. "It might not be something a non-Jew would notice, but we feel it is on the rise. And ironically enough, we have started to feel the effects of anti-German sentiment as well."

Anti-German sentiment! In Paris? *Really?*

"I have hopes that Benjamin will find much less prejudice here," said the pastor.

Julien slumped in his chair. *We are* both *going to die.*

They walked the Kellers to the early train. The station was full of people waiting, jostling, talking; farmers in their cloth caps standing by their stacks of crates, live chickens clucking from some of them; kids poking their fingers in and running away, screaming with laughter. And the summer people, the *estivants*. Women in white silk dresses with wide, immaculate straw hats; men in suits, hanging back from the dusty farmers and the grubby kids; their own children scrubbed and ready to go home to Lyon or Dijon or Paris. Where they belonged.

Where he belonged.

A high, far-off whistle, and the children began to yell: "She's coming! *La Galoche!* She's coming!" Madame Keller was shaking Mama's hand again and again; Julien saw with horror that she was beginning to cry. He looked away and saw something he'd never seen before: Benjamin's face. Benjamin, standing straight like a real person, looking at his father, his eyes big and brown and dark. And then the train was steaming round the bend, and some kid was jumping and waving at it, and the stationmaster in his dark blue cap with cold fury on his face was shouting, "Get behind the line, brat!" The kid flinched and fell back, and then the train was steaming into the station, and there was chaos and noise and luggage and boarding, and the Kellers looking through the window at them, their faces up against the glass, and Benjamin looking back at them, and the wheels starting to churn, and the train pulling out with a high, eerie whistle onto its long track between the hills.

And Benjamin, standing by Julien, staring at his feet.

A thick, smothering silence seeped out from Benjamin's room and filled the house. He sat at every meal, looking at the food he was pushing around on his plate, dampening every attempt at conversation. Breakfast would end, and Papa would tell the top of Benjamin's head that they were going out to the farm. Did he want to come? A tiny shake of his head.

Thank you, God.

Out at the farm, there was work to be done: there was harvesting and wood to be split and freedom to be drunk to the last drop. Julien could feel his swing growing truer, his muscles harder, his lungs deeper in the open air. A pleasant ache now ran through his limbs at night, instead of burning.

At home they had the radio, but no news. The *boches*—the Germans—were busy tearing up Poland. In France, nothing moved except reinforcements to the Maginot Line, the massive line of fortifications that would keep the Germans out of France. "*C'est une drôle de guerre*," the announcer said. Funny kind of war. Julien kicked his ball around the little walled backyard in the evening, alone, thinking of Vincent. He'd asked Benjamin if he could teach him a little about soccer. Benjamin had said it wasn't his life's ambition to kick a ball.

Julien kicked his ball, and the wall sent it back to him perfectly, without fail. You couldn't score against a wall. You couldn't tell a wall about how Verdun wasn't just a red splash on a map, or the broken glass in the sink, or how bad you wanted to drive a tank. To *do* something.

Papa got out the big family Bible for Friday night devotions, and Benjamin said his second full sentence. He said, "So this is one of the things I have to do to live here?"

Papa stared at him. He ran his hand through his hair and said, "No. You don't"—Benjamin's chair scraped on the floor—"*but* you will stay seated until I have finished speaking, young man."

Benjamin sat motionless, his chair facing half away from the table.

"We are starting a new book of the Bible today," said Papa. "Genesis."

Benjamin did not move.

Papa outdid himself. He had Julien flip the lights off as he talked about the darkness before the dawn of creation. He talked about the word, and the act, and how the authors of the Bible knew that descriptions of God were nothing compared to showing what he did. In the dark, Julien heard the scrape of a chair on the floor. God's first act, said Papa—the giving of light. And he switched the light back on, and Julien blinked in the sudden blaze. Benjamin was back at the table, looking at Papa with his wide brown eyes.

Monday was Julien's last day on the farm. School started tomorrow. Tomorrow he would try his chances with Benjamin and those guys who'd stared at them in the street. He'd find out where there was some soccer going on. Then they'd see what Julien Losier was made of.

He and Grandpa were digging the last fall potatoes, Grandpa putting a digging fork in the ground and turning up a handful of them all golden for Julien to gather. He'd thought this was a weed patch till Grandpa had showed him the thin, withered stalks in a neat line where the potatoes hid. They worked in silence together, keeping up the rhythm, the only sound the small nourishing *thunk* of potato on potato in the basket.

When the silence had deepened and lengthened between them, Grandpa opened his mouth.

"How's life with Benjamin?"

"Oh," Julien said, and exhaled slowly, his fingers digging into the dirt. His mind was suddenly blank. "It's . . . it's not . . ."

Grandpa turned up another clutch of potatoes, and Julien gathered them with quick fingers. Grandpa planted his fork, put his foot on it, and paused.

"Not so good," said Julien finally.

Grandpa nodded without surprise, and Julien felt the ache in his chest give way a little.

"I don't know, Grandpa, it's just . . ." *Horrible. He makes everything weird, and wrong, and he's German, and I think he hates me.* "I wish . . ."

"What do you wish, Julien?"

"I wish one single thing was the way it used to be."

Grandpa nodded. "You've lost a lot this summer," he said.

A rush of tears filled Julien's eyes, and he blinked fast. He bent down to gather a stray potato.

Grandpa was quiet for a moment, leaning on his fork. Julien looked up and followed his gaze past Tanieux's hill and the farther wooded ridge, on toward low green mountains in the west, with the sun above them.

"The two-headed mountain. See it?" Grandpa pointed with his chin. One of the green peaks was split in two, one part taller than the other. "Her name's Lizieux."

Julien nodded.

"I like to think she's the first thing our ancestors saw of this place on their journey north." He looked at Julien. "Never let them tell you you're not from Tanieux, Julien. You're part of the story Tanieux is most proud of."

"What?"

"You weren't listening when your father and the pastor were talking to the Kellers. You were thinking, 'That's just history.' Julien, history is where we come from." His grandfather's warm eyes were webbed with a thousand smile wrinkles. "Listen now. Our people came up from the south. They came in fear. Because they were Huguenots, and religious freedom had been revoked in France, and the king's soldiers were arresting and torturing any Protestant they could find. They came looking for shelter. Refuge." He looked at the far green mountains. "They came up the Régordane road, the old road beyond those mountains, and I like to think they looked east one morning and saw Lizieux holding up her wounded head and thought, 'Maybe there. Maybe there is a place for us.'"

Grandpa turned to Julien. "They came here. And they were taken in."

Julien looked at the mountains from where he knelt, his hands in the dirt. "I see," he said.

"Oh, Julien, I want to tell you so many stories, if you'll hear them. I want to tell you the stories of Tanieux. The story of how it started. Of Manu and how he built the chapel by the stream—have you seen it? Four hundred years old, that chapel is. Listen. Winter's coming. That's when we tell each other stories here. By the fire, when the *burle* is blowing outside. Come winter, I'll tell you the stories of Tanieux. If you're willing."

"Yeah," said Julien slowly. "That sounds good."

Julien walked home slowly, watching the sun sink over Lizieux behind long bars of white and gold. Thinking of how Grandpa had called the mountain she. Of his people, whoever they were, fleeing north on the old road past the mountains.

Julien had fallen behind the others as he climbed the hill; halfway up, he passed a farmhouse, old stone with a slate roof and a broad orchard in back. A wall around the farmyard. And, leaning on the wrought iron gate, one of the guys who had stared at him in town.

Julien gave him a nod; the ice blue eyes looked right through him as if he wasn't there. It didn't matter whose people had come up the Régordane road; this road, on this hill, was someone else's ground. *That* guy's ground.

Julien gave the cold look back and walked on past with his head high. He'd see him at school tomorrow.

And he would show him.

Chapter 4

Go

Death came for Father in the night.

That was how she thought of it—could not help thinking of it—that something had come and taken him. She hadn't known. He'd been the same as ever when she went to bed. But this morning—She could feel the stillness of his body even from the doorway, even in the dark, and her throat tightened. She tried to keep her hand from shaking as she laid it on his heart to feel for the pulse; his flesh was cold, and for a moment, raw terror touched her.

Death has come, the stranger. Death, the thief.

But as the words rose in her mind, she was already turning away from him and into action. There was only one way to love him now. *Promise you'll do everything I said.*

I want you to leave the instant I die. Take my eiderdown. Unlock the drawer. Take the tickets and the money, put my will and the first letter on the kitchen table. Mail the second letter. Uncle Yakov will get it within the day and come. He'll bury me. Let the dead bury the dead. But you—get out of Austria while you still can. Go to the station, and get on that train.

She had the eiderdown off him and rolled up and the papers out of the drawer, and she was down the stairs before she had time to think, to tell her mind in so many words what had happened. Then she was shaking Gustav, whispering. "Gustav. Gustav. It's time."

She couldn't go up to him again. She knew she should go up with Gustav, kiss Father on the forehead, say goodbye; but she could not. If she let herself do that–if she let herself cry–no. She had to do everything he'd said. Check through the packs, put in the money, the tickets, the letter; put the will on the table with her books and her mother's painting–the only thing she had from her . . . *Please give these things to Heide Müller at my school, and tell her to keep them for me. Do not worry about us. God will take care of us.* She hadn't written that to please Uncle Yakov. It was true.

"There is no God, most likely," Father had told her once, when he was healthy and strong. "And if there is–" He'd stopped, his eyes very sad, and hadn't finished the sentence, even when she asked. But she couldn't believe like him, she couldn't help it. Somehow there just had to be a God. Especially now. Especially–she turned sharply from the letter, to the window; no sign of dawn in the sky. *Oh Gustav, come down.* She began to check through the packs again.

He came down. His eyes were huge in the darkness, looking at her. She held out his pack to him, and he took it. "Are you ready?"

He nodded.

They crept down the stairs and through the dark clutter of the workshop to the back door; Nina unlocked it, and stopped, her heart beating fast. They would walk out this door into the world. Alone. Only God to protect them. "Hear, O Israel," she heard herself murmur, and stopped. She felt Gustav's hand seeking hers, and took it and held it tight; and he joined in. "Hear, O Israel. The Lord our God"–they whispered the Sh'ma into the stillness–"the Lord is one." *Hear, O God. Hear us, help us, oh help.*

Together they slipped out the door into the dark.

Chapter 5

King of France

One day, Julien would have a real soccer ball. But for now, he had what he had: an old volleyball Papa had brought home from his school, with a couple seams Mama had repaired. It wasn't beautiful, but it was his. He couldn't bring it to school; no soccer balls allowed during school hours, just like back home. But there would be a way. There always was.

A single oak tree stood in the schoolyard, smooth dust and trampled grass in its shade; under it lounged a group of guys, and Julien knew them for what they were. At his old school, the broad stone steps were where the in-group of the *troisième* class would be holding court; the kings of the school. Here it was the tree.

In the center, his back against the trunk, sat the cold-eyed boy from yesterday.

Henri Quatre, they were calling him. Henri the Fourth, king of France in fifteen-whatever. King of France, anyway. He got the idea.

He'd lost Benjamin in the crowd before crossing the bridge; at least there was that.

But he was invisible. The twelve-year-olds in *sixième—les petits sixièmes*, he'd been one a lifetime ago—ran and shouted in the sun. Guys stood in groups by the low black stone wall or under the *préau* rain-shelter talking; Benjamin sat on the wall reading; Julien stood a few paces outside the royal court under the tree, and no one saw him. Not one glance.

The bell rang for assembly, and Monsieur Astier, the broad-shouldered principal, announced their fates for the year. Monsieur Matthias for French, Madame Balard for geography, Papa for history. Monsieur Ricot, a skinny frowning character, for physics and as *professeur principal* for the *troisième* class. A groan went up. "Not Cocorico!" someone whispered. Ricot frowned harder and led them away to their homeroom.

They scrambled for seatmates at the heavy double desks—or Julien scrambled; everyone else paired off instantly, leaving him looking at Benjamin across an empty front-row desk. He gritted his teeth and sat down.

Ricot called the roll. Henri Quatre was Henri Bernard. Bernard. Julien had heard that somewhere—the stationmaster with the cold, angry face. Naturally. Henri's seatmate was a bull-necked guy named Pierre Rostin—as in, "Pierre Rostin, sit down!"—who, every time Julien glanced back, was flicking tiny drops of ink onto the neck of Gaston Moriot in front of him. They'd both been under the tree. They'd both been in town that day with the soldier. So had Gilles Perrault, with the light brown hair and the constant smile, and Jérémie, grinning and whispering to him. So had half the class.

And at break it was the same again, and Julien stood outside the circle, hesitant, unseen except for a moment's hostile glance from Henri. They talked. He listened. Getting old Cocorico for homeroom was just their luck. Léon Barre's father had said last week he'd vote for a Communist, and him and Gaston's father had almost gotten into a fistfight. Pierre's brother André, who drove a tank, had left a week ago for the Maginot Line. They were having a soccer game just as soon as they got the field set up. Tomorrow after lunch.

Julien stood still as a statue, an invisible statue on the wrong side of the tree, his blood pounding in his ears. He would be there. Oh yes, he would be there.

A little field lay behind the school, on the other side of the wall. Everyone was there.

Pierre was hacking at a sapling with a hatchet while Henri watched; guys were scraping the touchlines in the grass with hoes. Gilles and a short, solemn-faced guy were standing by a half-constructed goal, deep in discussion. The solemn-faced one glanced over at him, and a corner of his mouth went up.

"Hey," said Julien, "you guys want some help?"

"You know the regulation height of a goal?"

"One-third of the width."

Gilles's eyebrows rose. He glanced at the goal. "Let's see, that'd be . . ." He paced it out, then stared at one of the uprights. "Give me a leg up, Roland?" But Roland wasn't looking at him.

"It needs to be three meters. Same as ours." It was Henri Quatre's voice, from behind them, with an edge in it.

"The new guy says one-third of the width, Henri—"

"The new guy? What's he got to do with this?" Henri turned to Julien, cold eyes flashing. "Where're you from?"

"Paris."

"Thought you'd come show us all how it's done in *Paris*? It's three meters, Gilles. Here's the tape measure." Henri tossed it to him and turned away.

"But—" *That's too high, it should come to about two-and-a-half—*

"You can watch," said Henri, whirling back. "If you shut up."

Watch? "What, you got full teams already? First day of school?"

"Yeah," said Henri flatly. "Since last year."

Julien looked at Gilles and Roland. But they were both looking away.

Dear Vincent, Julien wrote. Wish you were here.

He scratched that out. *Wish I were there. You'd hate it here. You would not believe what happened today.*

Julien sat on the low stone wall and watched the games. Henri brought the ball, real leather, rich brown, and almost new. He wanted to scream at the injustice of it.

He sat in class beside Benjamin, walked home beside Benjamin, stood by the wall with him while Benjamin read his book. Same book as last week. He walked home and did his homework and took his pathetic little volleyball down to the narrow backyard to play against the wall. They were everywhere he turned these days. Walls.

There was nobody. Worse than nobody. At school, they wouldn't look at him; nobody met his eye. At home, Mama and Papa asked him how school was and he wanted to scream but he said fine, looking at their bright eyes that wanted him to be fine, their eyes that in the end were only another wall.

He checked the mail every day. But Vincent didn't write.

He watched the games. It was fascinating. He watched Henri's team beat Gilles's team day after day, but they never mixed up the teams. And Gilles had good players: Antoine was a great forward; Roland was one of the most solid defenders he'd seen. Yet they lost. They lost because Henri had a gift.

Henri was a real captain, a professional. His team worked as a unit, followed his signals—and won. It would never have worked with a different team every time; so they didn't mix them. The whole thing served Henri, and only Henri. And they *let* him. The idiots. The *sheep.*

Gilles won one game and lost four. Then it began to rain.

They had these fall rains back home too; whole pouring days that churned the schoolyard to deep mud to be tracked into the school by dozens of feet, and that drenched the soccer field. At break, they crowded under the *préau* roof, and it rang with the rain and the echoing voices, with the scrape of the bottle caps the *sixièmes* kicked around on the smooth concrete. It rained for days. Julien kicked the volleyball around in his room. He walked to school in the rain, walked back in the rain, stared out the window at the drowned soccer field, and raged.

The rain, the walls, the boys with their stupid boring gossip and their sheeplikeness, Henri with his stupid vendetta. Benjamin with his stupid book. There he was now, huddled under his hood as they trudged home through the rain and the mud, holding a flap of his coat over his *stupid book*. "Haven't you read that before?" Julien snarled.

Benjamin looked at him sullenly from under his hood.

"Like for two whole *weeks*? Don't you have anything *better* to do?" It felt so good to raise his voice. "During break! Does anyone else have their nose stuck in a book during *break*? No!"

"Want to tell me why I should care?"

"Do you just not want to make any friends?"

"With this bunch of farmers with dirt between their ears? Thanks, but no thanks."

Julien shut up. That was exactly what they were like, but coming from Benjamin, it sounded so . . . snobby. He opened the door and stepped into the dim hallway.

A fragile and lovely thread of sound was floating down from upstairs. He stopped. Mama was singing.

Benjamin bumped into him from behind. "What's wrong?"

"Nothing. Shh."

"Julien, get–"

"Shut *up!*"

It was an aria, a bright one, quick golden stairsteps of song. Benjamin stopped as he caught the sound, and in the dim rainlight, his face began to soften as he listened. "Wow," he breathed. "She's *good.*"

"Yeah."

Her singing wove a thread of gold through the dingy air as they kicked off their wet boots on the landing. "Come in!" she called. "I have a special *goûter* for you." She did: three pieces of bread on the kitchen table, a whole third of a bar of chocolate on top of each one. And Mama smiling like sudden sunlight through the rain. Benjamin froze in the doorway.

"Something wrong?" said Mama.

"No," he said thickly. "I'm fine, Ma—Madame Losier."

"There's something for you on the dining-room table, Benjamin. Go see."

Two thick brown envelopes. Benjamin snatched them and ran for the stairs.

"From his parents," Mama said. "Postmarked a week apart. It's a shame how slow the mail is these days."

Supper was merry that night, somehow; Papa smiled, and Mama sang as she brought the bread to the table; even Benjamin's face looked more . . . relaxed. Magali was going on about her new friend at the girls' school: "Her name's Rosa, her parents run the *Café du Centre*, you know, the Santoros . . ." She beamed, and stuffed a whole piece of bread in her mouth.

"Santoro? They're not French, are they?"

"Fe's Fpanif," said Magali. She swallowed. "I mean, she's Spanish. Or was. She says her father'll never go back now that what's-his-name won the war."

"General Franco," said Papa.

"Yeah. Him."

"Your mother's got a new friend too," said Papa. Mama gave him a smile like Julien hadn't seen on her in weeks. "Sylvie Alexandre just asked her to join the sewing circle, so if you ever come home and the place is overrun with women, don't be surprised."

They ate, and Papa began telling stories. About Charlemagne, whose army loved him because he lived in the field with them on campaign and who liked to swim in the hot springs at Aix-la-Chapelle with his knights—sometimes a hundred knights in the water at once. ("I hope they took their armor off!" said Magali.) About Clovis, king of the Franks, whose baptism was the only bath he ever took. And who didn't exactly turn into Saint Francis. Once his soldiers fought over a huge vase taken in the spoils of war, and one of them settled it by splitting the thing from top to bottom with his sword—and Clovis, when he heard, called the offender forward during troop inspection, took his sword, and did, well . . . the exact same thing.

"And the moral of the story is"—Papa finished up with a twinkle in his eye—"don't let anyone kid you about the 'good old days.'"

Even Benjamin laughed.

Julien sat with Benjamin in every class. It was great: a prime, close-up view of exactly how much smarter than him Benjamin was. Benjamin would sit drinking in Ricot's equations, while Julien struggled to keep his eyes open.

"Pierre Rostin, stand *up!*" Julien jerked awake.

Ricot, red faced, was pulling Pierre out of his seat by the ear. "*What* did I just ask you, young man?"

Pierre stood, rubbed his ear, looked slowly around at the class. "Sorry, monsieur. Earwax."

Ricot's mouth shut like a trap. "Who proved," he said slowly and loudly, "that the earth rotates on its axis? And how?"

"Um, Einstein maybe?" Pierre yawned. "Or, uh . . . Napoleon?"

A snicker ran through the class. Ricot's ruler hit the desk. He grabbed Pierre by the ear again and marched him down to the blackboard. "You can stay *right there*, Monsieur Rostin, until somebody smarter than you has answered my question."

Julien was wide awake.

Philippe didn't know; he had to stay standing behind his desk.

So did Dominique, and Antoine, and Léon. Jean-Pierre. Gilles. Jérémie. Lucien. Half the class was on their feet. Roland.

Roland would know. He paused, looking at Ricot.

"I'm sorry, monsieur. I'm not prepared to answer your question."

Ricot sputtered. Julien began to chew his lip; three more guys and he was up. Um. Something about a pendulum . . .

Benjamin raised his hand.

"It was Foucault, *n'est-ce pas?* He hung a pendulum, sixty-seven meters long. He set it swinging, and its axis swiveled slowly over twenty-four hours. And then he proved that it was really swinging in the same plane all along, but the earth was rotating beneath it."

"Ah." Ricot's voice was actually warm. "Well done, young man." He gestured at the class. "The rest of you morons can sit down now."

They sat. Benjamin was smiling. Pierre, Julien saw, was not.

Julien caught up with Roland on the way out of school, crossing the bridge. "You live in town?"

"No. Out that way." Roland waved behind them at the dirt road that went south. "I'm buying bread."

"You lived here long?"

Roland gave him a little smile. "Sure. About as long as that chapel there." It stood on their left by the water, a humble little place; four black stone walls and an arched door, a roof of slates with their edges nicked and broken. It looked like it had grown there, out of the bones of the earth, and would still be there when the square concrete school had fallen to dust.

"I didn't know you were four hundred years old," Julien said. Roland laughed.

"Who told you how old it is?"

"My grandfather." Roland's eyebrows lifted, and Julien named Grandpa by his local name. "*Le père Julien.*"

"He's your grandfather?" Roland gave his head a shake. "Did I know that?"

"Don't ask me!"

After a moment's pause, one corner of Roland's mouth turned up. "You're named after him."

"Mm-hm."

"You should tell people you're from here. If they think you're from Paris, they'll ignore you. That's what we do here. That's what the *estivants* want."

"Yeah? They don't *want* to play soccer?"

Roland stuck his hands in his pockets and kicked at a pinecone on the sidewalk. "Hey listen," he said suddenly, turning to Julien. "Are you good? What position d'you play?"

"Center forward. Yeah," he said simply, "I'm good."

"Just watch for when we're missing a player and jump in, okay? Don't ask. If you're that good, Gilles won't say anything. And Henri's not gonna take his ball home or something in the middle of a game."

"Thanks," Julien said, surprised.

"No problem. We need you. We need *something*."

"Hey . . . did you *really* not know the answer to that question?"

"Foucault?" Roland's quirky smile came back. "Sure I knew. And Jean-Pierre knew. Pierre didn't, that's for sure."

"So why didn't you answer?" said Julien. "Was it some kind of prank?"

Roland gave him a sidelong look. "I don't show up my friends for Cocorico, that's why. So he can call them morons." He snorted. "Nobody likes that. You should tell your friend."

"Hm," Julien grunted. They were at the *boulangerie*; the door opened, and the warm smell of fresh bread wafted out. Roland stuck his hand out to shake goodbye. "Well," said Julien as they shook, "thanks."

He walked on up the street behind Benjamin and his book. *I'm supposed to tell him not to answer questions in class?* He'd laugh. No. If Benjamin felt compelled to make sure nobody liked him, and clearly he did, it was his own problem. Julien couldn't spend his time worrying about him.

He had better things to do. And now he knew how to do them.

Chapter 6

Gone

Nina had never been beautiful. A square, sturdy girl with long, frizzy, wavy hair down her back; the sort of girl who looked right in knee socks and a school skirt. *Right*; not beautiful. Even before what they all called *the accident*. Before the twisted leg.

Now, looking in the mirror in the tiny train bathroom, she was glad of that.

She made a believable boy, she thought. She ran her hands through her short, fuzzy cap of hair. With her chest bound, her square shoulders looked stocky, vaguely muscular. Like a sturdy boy who hadn't lost all his puppy fat, an overgrown twelve-year-old. Gustav's big younger brother. Great.

"Say hi to Niko," she whispered to the mirror. "Hi, Niko."

They were almost there. Villach, by the Italian border. She'd found a map, in the envelope with the tickets, showing the way to the synagogue. Not far from the station. The rabbi's name. *He'll help you. I wrote him. He's helped a lot of people across.*

They would have had to cross illegally, anyway. They had no

visas. They had no right. Their papers wouldn't have helped with the big letters JEW on them. *You'll be safer in Italy. But Nina, if you ever have the chance—if there's a way—get to France.*

Niko heard the hiss of the brakes, felt the train begin to slow. She left the bathroom. Houses were going past the window, streets and alleys, people on bicycles, and behind them the mountains, huge and green. They would cross them. Somehow. The rabbi would know how.

Italiener Strasse, the papers said. Father had marked it on the map.

Italiener Strasse ran south from the station. The air was cold and bright. Father's eiderdown swung behind her, a tight-wrapped bed-roll hanging under her pack. South on Italiener Strasse, left at the traffic circle. Five doors down on the right, the synagogue would be painted white; there would be a sign. They should ask for Rabbi Hirsch and say they were youth volunteers to clean the synagogue. That was the password.

The synagogue was not painted white. It was painted green. Big splashes of sickly colored paint thrown at the door. Windows boarded up, and on the boards things scrawled in black. Pigs. Bloodsuckers. You Have Your Reward.

Niko and Gustav looked at each other. A strange feeling spread through Niko's stomach.

"We have to knock," said Gustav. "Don't we?"

"Of course," said Niko. "Looks like they need us. To clean." Her mouth was completely dry. She was trying to hear the words in her head, the instructions. *Come on, Father. If you can't find the Rabbi—if you can't find the Rabbi—*

He'd never said that. He had never said anything like that.

She raised her hand and knocked. Silence. She knocked again. The silence grew longer, louder, huge; the silence was a pit, and she was looking down it. *Father. Father . . .*

A man was passing by. She had to do it. "Excuse me," she said in the deepest voice she could. "Do you know where is Rabbi Hirsch?"

The man gave her and Gustav a long look. "I do know. And you'd be well advised to stay away from him. Hirsch has been arrested. I presume you two don't have any interest in his—activities."

Niko's head was spinning. She opened her mouth. Gustav had come up behind her, and she heard his laugh, sudden; a nasty laugh like she'd never heard from him. "Nothing like that," he said in a hard voice. "He owed our father money. Guess it's too late now."

"Yes," said the man. "I think it is."

"You were great, Gustav."

"Nina." He didn't sound great. "What are we gonna do?"

"It's Niko. Please, Gustav. You've got to call me Niko."

"What are we gonna do? Did he tell you anything to do? If—y'know?"

No. This is it, Gustav. We're on our own. She swallowed. "Yeah," she said. "He told me some stuff."

"What'd he tell you?"

"We've got to cross on our own."

"How d'we do it?"

"He said there's a fence." He had said that. He'd said, *Hirsch knows where the gaps are.* "There're gaps. Places you can get through. After that, you climb through the mountains. Hills. There's another fence on the other side, and you have to find a way through again. There are lots of ways through. People do it all the time. That's what he said."

"Okay. Okay." His eyes were wide, his lips pressed together, considering. "Are there guards or anything?"

"Yeah. Along the fences. We have to be really, really careful. We have to stay off the road and cross at night."

He nodded slowly. She could see just a spark of light returning to his eyes. "You think we can do it, Nina? Niko, I mean. Niko." He was looking at her, waiting for the word.

"Yes," she said without looking at him. "Yes. We can."

Chapter 7

A Thousand Wings

War was not what Julien had expected it to be. That hot night in September when he'd prayed for God to give him something to do, he'd imagined Paris overrun, German soldiers in the streets, shrapnel bursting through windows . . .

But *nothing was happening.*

It wasn't that he wanted it to happen. It just seemed so strange. He had felt so much *older* for a little while: part of a much larger story, a wartime story. But the troops were still sitting along the Maginot Line, and there was nothing he could do about it one way or the other. So he'd found himself back in his own world, his Julien world, where what mattered was school and soccer. Where the enemy was Henri Quatre, and Julien was waiting for his chance.

He watched Monday's game, poised and ready; nothing. On Tuesday, Lucien fell down and grabbed his ankle—and got up again. He was going to go crazy.

On Wednesday, Antoine was absent. One of Gilles's forwards.

He let them start without him. Roland gave him a glance and a nod. He watched, every muscle tense, till Gilles's team was down two to nothing and fallen back to defend their goal; then it came. Henri jogged off the field to take a leak.

Julien had to get hold of the ball just seconds after he'd got on the field, give no one a chance to throw him out. With Henri gone, Gilles was making one hopeless push toward Henri's goal; Philippe blocked it, and it bounced toward the boundary line.

Now.

Julien ran in and caught the brown ball on the side of his foot, controlled its motion and its spin. It was his. Philippe's surprised face flashed by as Julien dribbled it across to the center—and through the one hole in Henri's defense. "Hey!" someone yelled. He faked neatly around the last defender and fired the ball straight and hard into the lower corner of the goal as Gaston the goalie dived—too late.

The ball shot through the goal and kept on rolling, but Gaston didn't even turn to look. He was staring at Julien.

"Where did *you* come from?"

"*He's* not on our team!"

"Shut *up*, Dominique." That was Gilles's voice, deep with surprised pleasure. "Did you see that *goal*?"

"It doesn't count!" said Pierre, coming up behind them with a red face. "He wasn't even in the game, the goal doesn't count."

"Come on, man. We've got a right to a *remplaçant*. Antoine's gone. Hey!" Gilles called down the field. "Who says it counts?"

Cheers. Julien thought he saw Roland wink.

"We can still beat you, anyway," said Philippe.

More cheers.

Julien glanced at the trees, away to the left. Henri Quatre was coming back, a small figure moving toward them. In the trees' leafy tops, an army of rooks was cawing and fighting, flying up and settling again in a dark cloud. Henri walked faster.

But he was too late. The ball was back in play, and Dominique got it, and he passed it to Julien. Henri had nothing to say. He had to get in there and defend.

Julien's team won.

Dear Vincent, he wrote. *Guess what happened today.*

They played four more games after that, beautiful games. Henri Quatre won two, and Julien's team won two more than they would have without him. He got out on that field and he played, and he scored, and Gilles and Roland slapped him on the back.

Then the rain came again.

It started during breakfast, softly, the first drops sliding down the kitchen window as Julien finished his hot chocolate. When he put his bowl in the sink, it was drumming on the roof, the air outside was filled with it, clouds of mist splashing up from the angled roofs down below. No soccer today. No soccer tomorrow. The rains were back for the long haul.

They walked to school with their hoods up and hung their coats beside the others to drip on the floor. The classrooms that morning had a strange, echoing sound, the sound of an enclosed space; the squeak of wet shoes on the floor and the voices of boys rang through the school. It seemed as if they all felt like Julien—keyed up, on edge, not ready for rain and winter. Not ready to sit quietly at their desks, go home for lunch, and leave the woods and the empty soccer field to soften into deep mud.

But they did. Julien and Benjamin walked up the hill as the water flowed down in muddy little runnels past their feet, and hung their sodden jackets at the top of the stairs, and opened the door.

A huge packing crate sat blocking the entryway, with Paris written on it. Mama stood smiling over it. "From your parents, Benjamin," she said. "Would you like to open it?"

"Um," said Benjamin. "Upstairs. I'd like to open it . . . upstairs, please."

Mama's face fell a little. "Of course, Benjamin. Julien—could you help carry . . . ?"

When they went back to school for the afternoon, Benjamin wore a new wool jacket, gray and expensive-looking, and carried a large new book that he slipped into his coat before stepping out into the rain. Julien caught a glimpse of a submarine on the front.

The new gray wool glowed beside the worn jackets on their pegs on the classroom wall; people were looking. Out of the corner of his eye, Julien saw Benjamin stroking it. Papa glanced at it when he came in halfway through class to call Ricot away for a minute. Ricot left them with instructions to do problems one and two on page seventy-four. They sighed and opened their textbooks.

There were no problems on page seventy-four.

Julien looked around. A buzz of whispers was rising up, a breath of freedom. Pierre was already making spit wads. Even Benjamin had his book open to a huge, color plate of a submarine surfacing. Jean-Pierre at the next desk craned his neck for a look.

Julien was reading about subs in the Great War when it started. A rise in the tone of the whispers; the scraping of desks in the back by the woodstove. Julien turned.

A group was gathering around the coat rack. Where the gray coat had been was an empty peg.

His desk jerked as Benjamin stood.

They were passing the coat from hand to hand back there, murmuring in low voices; admiring it. Jérémie passed it to Gilles, who felt the soft wool, examined the blue and red threads woven through the pattern to give it color—it really was a good coat; it'd probably cost more than Mama ever spent on a piece of clothing in her life.

"Give it back!" Benjamin's face was white, and his eyes blazed. "That's mine. Give it back!"

The coat was passed to Pierre. Pierre grinned. Then he took the coat by the shoulders and stood, shook it twice like a bullfighter's cloth.

"Come and get it," he said.

Benjamin took three steps toward Pierre. The group parted to let him in, and closed around him. Pierre looked even bigger with Benjamin glaring up at him, white fists clenched.

"What do you want from me?"

"Just to see if you want your pretty coat back. Here . . ."

Benjamin reached out for the coat, and Pierre snatched it back.

"Come on," he said in a kind voice. "Here . . ."

Benjamin's jaw clenched, but he did not move. Julien was biting his lip, all his muscles tense. The sound of footsteps came from the hallway.

The reaction was instantaneous. Guys scrambled and dived for their seats. Henri Quatre snatched the jacket out of Pierre's hands and hung it on its peg. Julien and Benjamin slid into their desk a split second before Ricot walked in.

The class got lines to copy: *I attend school to learn, not to play*, one hundred times. Even Benjamin, who didn't hear Ricot's rant. He was too busy searching through his desk, through his *cartable*, through his desk again. He leaned over to Julien and whispered, "Have you seen my book?"

Julien shook his head.

"They *stole* it!"

"Don't let them see they got to you," murmured Julien. "Wait."

He dropped his pen behind his chair and reached down for it, glancing casually back. Pierre still wore that grin. Most of the others were smiling too. At him and Benjamin. Roland was the only one who had the decency to look embarrassed.

He sat up, checked his pen nib for damage, dipped it in the inkwell, and went on copying from the board. Benjamin sat staring straight ahead.

Julien looked out the window. The rain had stopped. Sunlight was pouring down through a break in the clouds, and the peak of Lizieux in the distance glowed.

At the bell, Benjamin was out the gate like a shot, home to his shut door and his books and his crate. Julien took his time. Walking slowly downstairs behind a clamoring group with Henri Quatre in its midst, wondering if Benjamin would still have his book if he hadn't acted like an arrogant you-know-what . . .

Henri was filling in Luc from *quatrième*. "You should have seen his face. It's the first time he's looked at one of us in two months! Man, I've just had it up to here with these stuck-up Parisian snots—"

Julien hung back, trying to look oblivious. Henri gave a disgusted snort and turned back toward him; his heart sank.

"You tell your friend from me: if he doesn't like it here, he's free to go. And you are too."

Julien looked into the icy, arrogant eyes and something snapped. "What do mean, my *friend*?"

Henri, Luc, Gaston, and Pierre stopped at the foot of the stairs, looking at him.

"Maybe the guy you come to school with every day?" said Pierre.

"You mean the guy whose parents pay for him to live in my house?"

Henri's eyebrows rose. "Oh, is that how it is?"

"You have no idea." Deep relief flooded through Julien as he said the words. "Have you ever lived with a guy who thinks he's too good to talk to you?"

Henri Quatre raised one eyebrow this time. He had very sharp eyebrows.

"Don't you people have eyes?" said Julien. "Did *I* come strutting in here with a jacket worth three hundred francs?"

"You think you're a *tanieusard* because you don't have a fancy jacket?"

"You know *le père Julien*? He's my grandfather." Henri gave a hint of a shrug that made Julien want to grab him by the collar and shake him. "My *father* and my *grandfather* were *born* here," he ground out between his teeth, "and you can't even tell the difference between me and someone who was born in *Germany!*"

There was a moment of pure silence. Henri's mouth was open, his face very still. "He's *German?*" he whispered. Julien's heart was beginning to beat faster. *Oh. Oh crap.*

"Well, his parents are," he said hurriedly. "They moved, uh, when he was a kid I think—"

"Oh yeah, that's what we need in Tanieux, some rich little German Jew looking down his nose at us," said Gaston.

"Don't you mean *up* his nose at us?" said Pierre, grinning.

"People should stay where they belong," said Henri Quatre softly, his eyes lit. "Especially *Germans.*"

Julien's stomach was tight. He looked around, half hoping his father would appear, get him out of there. Nothing. "Well. I . . . gotta go."

He tried not to think about it as he walked up the hill; he looked up at the sky where the sun washed through the breaking clouds and tried to think of nothing at all.

Mama had made yogurt for *goûter*; it was cooling on the kitchen windowsill. No one else was there. Julien sat down and laid his head down on the table in his arms. He heard the comforting clink of Mama's serving spoon against the yogurt bowl, the warm sound of her humming under her breath. He heard her push a bowl across the table at him.

"So, Julien. Something happen at school today?"

He looked up slowly. "How do you know?"

"Benjamin looked a bit upset."

"Yeah." He took a deep breath and continued, looking at his bowl. "Some guys at school took his new coat. I mean—they gave it back, they were just looking at it, but . . . Pierre . . ."

"Pierre Rostin? Ginette Rostin's son?"

"I guess. I mean I don't know his mom, but that's his name. So . . . he was kind of teasing him with it. Trying to make him go for it."

"Where was this?"

"In the science room. When, uh, when Monsieur Ricot was gone."

"In front of everybody?"

"Oh yeah."

"What was in front of everybody?" Papa's head poked in the door. This was the problem with being a teacher's son.

"Um–"

"You surely don't imagine I haven't heard . . ."

"Ricot gave us an assignment that didn't exist!"

"So I hear. I also hear you all got lines to copy. So you can tell me everything."

He told him almost everything.

For a few moments no one spoke. The chop of Mama's knife slicing potatoes was loud in the silence.

"Poor Benjamin," Mama said at last. "I think if those boys had seen him when that crate arrived, they wouldn't have treated him like that."

"From what I've seen," Papa said, "Pierre would need to be hit with a hammer before he'd understand that kind of thing."

"Poor Pierre too," Mama added suddenly.

"Pierre?" said Julien. "You feel sorry for him?"

"Would you want to be him?" put in Papa.

"Well, no . . ."

"But mostly as a matter of principle, or virtue on your part . . ." Papa began drily.

"Martin," Mama said gently, "I'm trying to tell Julien why *I* feel sorry for Pierre."

"Oh. Sorry."

Mama stopped working and looked Julien in the eye. "I've been getting to know Ginette Rostin. You know Pierre has a brother in the army, I suppose? André?"

Julien nodded.

"Ginette talks about nothing else. André this, André that, André and his tank on the Maginot Line. The few times she's mentioned Pierre she's called him *that boy*."

Well, poor Pierre then. He looked out the window. The sun was very bright.

Papa picked up a strip of potato peel and twirled it in his fingers, frowning. "I'm sorry my hometown isn't treating you boys too kindly. I wish . . ." He sighed. "Will you do something for me? Your grandfather's about done with that bookshelf for Benjamin. Would you take him down there to look at it, sometime in the next couple days?"

Grandpa was down in his workshop on the ground floor; the little apartment he moved into in the winter. Where he'd promised to sit by the fire and tell Julien stories while the *burle* blew outside. Julien looked out at the wet world and sighed, and added Benjamin to the picture.

"Sure, Papa," he said.

Julien did the dishes after supper because Mama asked him to; when he finally pulled the plug in the sink, he felt so drained he could hardly stand up. He headed for the stairs. "Julien?" said Mama. "Would you tell Benjamin I'd like to ask him something before he goes to bed?"

"Sure, Mama."

He knocked twice on Benjamin's door before he heard a muffled, "Come in." Benjamin was on his knees on the wood floor with his back to Julien, stacking books in the crate.

"Uh—y'know Grandpa's making you a bookshelf for those," Julien offered.

"Maybe you can use it." Benjamin's voice was flat. He put another book in the crate and didn't turn around.

"What do you mean?"

"I'm leaving."

Julien stared at him.

"I'm not staying here. Not if it's going to be like this." His voice cracked wildly on *this*.

"Um," said Julien.

Benjamin swallowed. After a moment, he got out: "D'you need something?"

"Mama wanted to ask you something. Downstairs." He hesitated. "Should I tell her you're—busy?"

Benjamin glanced at the open door, and Julien saw on his face what he had been afraid of: the bright tracks of tears down his cheeks. "Tell her I'll be down in a minute," he said tightly.

"Sure." He turned to go. "Uh—Benjamin?" he said, searching for the right words.

"Mm."

"They want me to leave too. I don't think we should give them that satisfaction."

Benjamin shrugged one shoulder. He picked up another book and put it carefully in the crate. "Good night."

"Good night."

Rooks roosted in the trees by the soccer field, a black army of rooks. Every branch laden with them. Julien was running with Benjamin, passing the soccer ball. Benjamin passed it to the rook-tree. "No!" cried Julien. The cloud of rooks rose, the flap of a thousand wings making a huge, alien whisper. They rose, and fell together toward one place on the ground.

A rookery is a society, said a voice. It sounded like Papa. They punish their criminals. The whole flock pecks the offender. Sometimes to death.

The birds boiled upward and fell, again and again, a cloud turning in on itself in violence, a seething of black wings.

Julien began to run.

He ran toward them, shouting, waving his arms. They flew up, their beaks stone gray, their little black eyes glittering. In the middle lay something flat and brown.

It was the soccer ball, its leather hide pierced by a thousand holes, lying limp on the withered grass. It was bleeding.

Julien screamed. "Benjamin!" Behind him the soccer field was empty to the horizon; the lines and goalposts gone, the school gone. Benjamin was not there. The river ran on in front of the hill. But there was no bridge.

The rooks set up a great cawing behind him. He whirled and went for them, arms flailing, and they flew up away from him in a hiss of wings.

Benjamin lay in the grass, white-faced, bleeding from a thousand small wounds.

Julien shrieked.

"They've killed Benjamin. Help! *Help!*"

A shadow of great wings flying low. "You killed Benjamin?" And Grandpa landed and folded his wings about him; they hung to his feet, black and shimmering.

"No! It wasn't me! I wasn't there! I didn't even see—"

Grandpa looked down at him from his great height, the eyes of a dark eagle. "They were pecking you too."

Julien looked at his hands. There were feathers on them. "Grandpa, no. Don't make me a rook. Bring the bridge back. Please. I have to carry him across—"

The world jerked and tilted. Darkness. A hand was shaking him by the shoulder.

"Julien? Julien? Are you all right?"

He sat bolt upright. It was dark. In the faint moonlight from the window, he could just barely see Magali by his bed.

"Fine. I'm fine."

"You sounded awful! I could hear you from my room."

"Did I say anything? Did you hear me say anything, Magali?"

"You just yelled a couple times. Was it a nightmare?"

"Yeah." He sank back into his bed. "Yeah. Um. Thanks for waking me."

"You sure you're okay?"

"Yeah. Good night."

She left. He lay facedown on his pillow, shaking his head and swallowing. What was wrong with him? He hadn't had a nightmare since he was ten.

He got up and opened the shutters. The clouds were over Tanieux again, and everything was misty down below; he breathed the cold, moist air deep into his lungs, and his head cleared. He looked up, but there were no stars.

"God," he whispered. "What *was* that?"

There was silence, and a cold wind.

He shut the window and turned away. He felt dizzy. He crawled back into bed and slept.

Chapter 8

Night

He could move through the woods without sound. He was the only one who could help them.

They had to trust him because they had no choice. They had a hundred schillings but he said fifty would be enough.

He wanted to help them.

He was from Gailitz, three kilometers north of the border, and he had done this many times. He was tall, with a short brown beard like Father's. When he'd seen them on the road, he said, he'd known they were in need. They should hide the bedroll in one of their packs. Anyone could tell at a glance what they were trying to do. They were lucky it had been him.

He knew where the gaps were.

He moved quietly through the woods, and they followed, Niko's crutches rustling in the leaves. "Maybe I'll have to carry you, kid," said Herr. They called him Herr: Mister. Names weren't safe in this business, he said.

"I'm not tired, Herr," said Niko in her gruff boy's voice.

He gave her a little smile. "You're doing great, *herzerl.*"

The sky above the mountains flamed scarlet and rose with the evening; the peaks were black against it, the mountains huge and dark on either side as they walked west. Herr stopped, and they turned south off the path. Their way was up the mountain.

They walked. The pines were tall and dark. High above, the fiery sky was fading. Herr moved in front of them without sound, then Niko setting her crutches carefully among the pine needles, and Gustav behind her. Her good leg and her arms ached. They had walked for hours. "Wait for me here," Herr whispered, and was gone in the trees ahead. They must be near the gap. Only one on this side, he said; on the Italian side there were three. The sun had set, and the shadows around them were full of tiny sounds: chirrings and rustlings, small things hiding, hoping to live till morning. She shivered.

"Clear," said a quiet voice by her ear. She gasped. "Shhh," said Herr. "We'll need to be very quiet now. That's hard with crutches. I'm going to have to carry you."

He lifted her onto his back, her hands gripping his shoulders, his hands under her knees. Gustav took her crutches. They moved between tall, black shadows. It was full dark. She huddled against Herr's back, trying not to shake. The dull, barely visible gleam of a chain-link fence came at her out of the dark; a swath of blackness running up and down it, a rip. Herr crouched, not letting go of her; cold edges of broken chain-link scraped her arm, and she bit her lip. Then nothing, open air. They were through.

They walked on through the woods, up the mountain, in the night.

No one spoke; no one stopped moving. The night sounds of the forest were around them, a vast world full of tiny, frightened life. The call of an owl overhead. Herr walked, his footsteps firm and quiet, his hands under her knees.

It came on her slowly as they walked through the dark.

It was just a feeling. Just a strange, strange feeling. The way his hands held her under her knees, moving a little. Just a feeling. That something was wrong.

But he didn't know she was a girl. So how—that couldn't be what she was feeling . . . He was helping them. He was—and he didn't know—

He'd called her *herzerl*. She hadn't even noticed. Why hadn't she noticed? Because she was a girl. You didn't call boys that. Not boys her age. And she hadn't said anything, she hadn't—

So did he know? Had that been a test? But if she was wrong—to think such a thing, when he was helping them—he'd be so angry; she'd be so ashamed . . . But her gut twisted inside of her, shouted down her mind. *Something is wrong. Something is wrong.*

Something was wrong.

Her bound chest was against his back. Could he feel it? Feel the difference? She leaned back from him, just a little, in the dark. It strained her back, but she stayed that way. She didn't know how long they'd been walking, how long they would go on. Hours, in the night. Her back hurt. But if she rested herself against him—no. No, he was helping them. Wasn't he? His hands, the way they felt. Strange. Wrong. As if they weren't there just to hold her up. As if they were there to *feel*.

And they were alone with him. In the woods. In no-man's-land.

She felt sick.

They walked through the dark, and she began to cry, soundlessly, knowing. Every step; every minute; a year of fear and sickness, at him, at her own stupidity, her helplessness, the dark. *Yes we can*, she'd said. *Oh Father, no. No.* They were going downward. How long had they been going down? What was going to happen? *Father.*

Herr stopped. The hands lowered her to the ground. She stood, shaking. They were in an open place. There was faint moonlight. Gustav handed her the crutches.

"We're near the second fence," Herr murmured. "The hole in

this one is smaller. I'll go check if it's clear, and then I'll take you through one at a time. The other must stay quiet and not follow. This crossing is very dangerous." In the faint light, he gave her a little smile that chilled her.

And then quietly, in the dark, he was gone. He was gone, and she knew what he meant to do. They had no time to lose.

"Gustav," she whispered. "We have to get away from him. Now."

"What?"

"Gustav. He knows. He's . . . he's going to hurt me." Gustav was staring at her, the moonlight glinting in his eyes. He didn't move. "We have to hide."

"Niko, did he . . . do anything?"

"Not– Gustav, you have to trust me, Gustav, I *know it!*"

"Nina–" Herr might be here, he might be right behind them, silent in the dark. He might have heard that. *Nina.* Silence and darkness, all around. Tiny rustlings underfoot, and overhead the owl's quiet wings. She set her crutches down to take a step. The rustle was loud and clear.

She ran.

Swung her crutches out and ran, crashing through the bushes, branches slashing her face, running, running because she wasn't going to just stand there and let him catch her, she wasn't, she'd rather die–footsteps behind her, *oh tell me it's Gustav, Gustav–* something caught her crutch and she went down, her arm hitting a heavy branch, her cheek scraping bark, painfully–and she was on the ground, in the deep dark under a pine, and Gustav threw himself down beside her. They froze.

Silence. Darkness. He was coming for them, so quietly they could not hear him. He was coming for them with a knife. Then they did hear him, quiet footfalls, branches rustling and cracking where he put out his hands. Groping in the dark. He stepped right past them. He couldn't see them. They didn't breathe. He moved in the dark, searching, for hours. Years.

Then he stopped. He stopped silent, somewhere down behind them, and spoke.

"You little brat," he said. "They'll catch you, you know. Thought you could fool Herr, did you baby? But they'll catch you. Maybe they'll have a little fun with you, instead of me. Yeah. Yeah. A little fun." Gustav gripped her hand so hard it hurt.

Then soft footsteps. Going. Going back the way they'd come. Then silence.

Silence. And silence. And waiting, holding Gustav's hand, *don't move Gustav, he's coming back down, he's trying to lure us out, don't move.* It was dark. Fear was everywhere. Herr was everywhere, in the dark. She could still feel his hands. Hours. Years. Gustav stood. Branches rustling around him.

Silence. All around them.

Now for the fence. *Hear, O Israel. Hear—oh hear—*

And they were off together, crashing through the trees, down the mountain, to the border—where they would catch them, they would catch them, because how could two teenagers get through a border alone? Guards in front of them and a criminal behind? Three holes, he'd said. Three holes on the Italian side.

The chain-link loomed at them out of the dark. Tight-woven and intact. Niko turned left along it, away from the place Herr had checked; and they went along the fence in the dark as quietly as they could. Whole, and tight, and dully gleaming. Except there—there at the bottom—a scribble of darkness jutting up into the grid. A tree trying to grow up under it, buckling the chain-link slowly upward. A little space of darkness. She went down on her belly and slid. Her jacket caught, she heard a rip, she pushed at the earth with her good leg, and she was through. Gustav slid her crutches under, then the pack, then he was under and through and she had her crutches and they were gone. Gone down the mountain faster than she had ever gone before, breaking branches, pine needles whipping at her face, the night air burning in her lungs. Far up ahead through the trees was a light—a house, no border-guard post, but a farmhouse and the sharp scent of wood smoke from the chimney and a lighted window. She stopped. Her knees started to buckle. Gustav took her hand.

They were through. She had done what her father had told her to do. She had gotten herself and her brother out of Austria.

She knelt and vomited into the bushes.

Chapter 9

Where We Come From

Julien groaned and rolled over. It was Thursday morning—his one day off from school besides Sunday. He wanted to go back to sleep. But . . .

But at breakfast, Benjamin would tell Mama that he wanted to leave, and everything would blow sky-high, and Benjamin would have already written his parents to come get him, and . . .

And they would. And no one would ever find out what he'd told Henri. And he'd go around telling the *troisième* class how glad he was that that rich Parisian snot was gone, and he'd play soccer and tell them his father was born here, and . . .

The space inside his head was full of darkness, cold and heavy. He shoved his face into his pillow and slept.

The kitchen was empty when he came down, two clean plates still on the table with the bread and jam. Who else had overslept? *Mama?* Even the milk was still out.

He tore a piece off the baguette and laid his notebook on the table. He had an essay due tomorrow. A question from *Les Misérables*: Was Javert right about human nature, that people were either good or bad? He chewed his bread, thinking.

Javert seemed to think people couldn't change, and that didn't sound right at all. It was called repenting, it was all over the Bible. But he wasn't supposed to use the Bible in a public school essay, even if the principal was in his church, and none of his own arguments sounded any good. *Can people* really *change?* he wondered, scratching out his third sentence. Imagine Benjamin changing, or Henri.

Or Julien.

He felt light-headed. He left the essay on the table and walked out into the dark stairwell, hands in his pockets, and sat on the cold stone stairs. He could hear Monsieur Bouchard, Grandpa's reclusive tenant he'd never seen, singing snatches of something off-key; and from the other apartment, Grandpa's, the soft *tap, tap* of a hammer. He went on down.

He slipped into the apartment and closed the door softly behind him, and Grandpa smiled at him without looking up from his work. Julien sat and watched his grandfather hammer the nails in with his broad, careful hands, and felt the silence, and the peace in Grandpa's breathing, and listened to the rain.

Finally Grandpa put down his hammer and smiled at him, and Julien opened his mouth and began to speak. And told him everything.

Almost everything.

"And Grandpa–last night he was packing. He says he's leaving. He says if it's gonna be like this he can't stay. All they did was tease him!"

Grandpa studied the shelf he had just nailed, tired lines in his forehead, a web of wrinkles around his eyes. "What did he think they were doing?"

"He thought they were a pack of wolves about to have him for breakfast," said Julien bitterly.

"And what do you think they thought?"

"They know he thinks they're stupid hicks and he's too good to talk to them."

"Do they treat you like they treat him, at all?"

"Sort of. Not that stuff, but . . ." He looked away, at the blank white wall. "We're in the same category." The *rich Parisian snots* category.

"Julien, is something bothering you? Do you feel like you should have done something yesterday?" Julien didn't look at him. He didn't dare. "Maybe you should. But it's hard. It's very hard in a situation like that to stand up to the crowd. Maybe you'll learn. I hope so. But don't beat yourself up."

Julien nodded, looking at his feet.

"And listen. I didn't know Benjamin said he was leaving, but I know that he and your mother had a talk last night. A good talk, apparently. Till fairly late. So please don't worry."

He swallowed. "Well. That's good."

"Will you do something for me, Julien? It's a simple thing, but I'd appreciate it."

Julien looked up. "Bring Benjamin down? Papa asked me."

"No, although that would be wonderful. But there's something else. I don't know if you pray every day, but there's something I'd like you to pray for me. Just this. Ask God to show you what he wants you to do. If you'll do that for me—let's make it a deal. You pray that; I pray that the boys at school see the light. How does that sound?"

Julien swallowed again. "Pretty good," he said.

His name was Emmanuel, Grandpa said, but he was called Manu. He lived in the sixteenth century. He had no last name because he was a servant born in the service of a noble family near Le Puy. He was raised with Philippe, the lord's younger son, raised to be his loyal servant for life.

Julien and Magali and Benjamin sat around Grandpa's table, warming their hands around mugs of mint or blackberry tea. Grandpa's eyes had a quiet glow like the flickering light from his fireplace, like the candle in the center of the table.

Manu and Philippe were the same age, he said. They swam in the creek together, tussled with each other, threw cherry pits at the girls. They learned to ride together and raced their horses; they went hunting together, Manu carrying Philippe's spear. They even—though it was supposed to be forbidden—studied together.

Philippe taught Manu to read, Grandpa said, and this, in the end, is why Manu would have died for him. For Philippe, books were interesting; for Manu, they were the world. Philippe learned more from Manu's excited accounts of his textbooks than from reading them. It was only natural that, when Philippe was to be sent away to learn a profession as a younger son should, he asked for Manu to be sent with him. And—hesitating between his different options—asked Manu which he thought was best.

"Medicine," said Manu, his eyes big with delight.

They went to Montpellier to study medicine.

Montpellier was in ferment in those days, Grandpa said. Boiling with new ideas. Not only the latest theories in natural philosophy and medicine, but the strange new ideas of the Reformation, which had seemed so distant back at their château—and here were discussed in the streets. Dangerous, enticing ideas, like reading the Bible for yourself in your own language. They met a man who could get them a copy. Manu couldn't resist.

They read medicine. They read the Bible. Philippe would come home and tell Manu everything he had heard in class, and Manu would tell him everything he had read. They stayed up, talking about the Bible all hours of the night; they talked about it with other students, with men at taverns, with anybody. The radical new ideas—that God forgave simply, by grace, that you could know God for yourself—were one by one confirmed by what they read. They became Protestant.

Then they got the message from home. Sickness at the château. Come quickly.

News traveled slowly in those days, Grandpa said. When that message reached Philippe, his father and brother were already dead. He reached home to find himself lord of all his family's lands.

Philippe was overwhelmed. Grieving, unprepared for the work of ruling, he leaned on Manu in those first days; but one thing gave him joy in his new life, one thing he was sure he wanted. As a lord, he could set up his own Protestant church. He did it right away.

It was his undoing.

Protestantism wasn't illegal, exactly, Grandpa said. Protestants just didn't legally exist. Church and state were the same thing; cardinals and bishops more powerful than lords. It was like renouncing your citizenship. The bishop seated at Le Puy summoned Philippe and told him he had the power to give all his lands to the neighboring duke if Philippe didn't recant.

Philippe went home in turmoil and talked to Manu. To Manu, raised on an ideal of boundless loyalty to his lord—a lord he knew and loved—there was no question. The God he had once feared was now just such a lord and friend as Philippe had always been, but a thousand times more. He would not have turned his back on Philippe to save his life. How could either of them turn their backs on Jesus?

Philippe was stripped of his title and all his lands. He left his family's château, and Manu left with him. They did not look back.

They traveled and lived on what they had learned: going from town to town offering their medical skills to lord and commoner for a reasonable fee—or, if need be, for free. And for free, also, they would read their French Bible aloud to anyone who wanted to hear it and share their enthusiasm for knowing their Lord as a friend.

One day, they saved the life of a lord's only son, and in gratitude, he gave them land. Nothing much, a few hills up on a cold plateau by a small river. A river called the Tanne.

Grandpa smiled at their look of enlightenment. They built two things there, he said. First a chapel. Their work of praise to God, built with their own hands out of the black stones to be found by the river. Then a school. Manu was the teacher; and as the place grew into a settlement, he welcomed the sons of lords and peasants alike to share his passion for learning. Soon they could worship in their chapel without fear; the Edict of Nantes had been signed, and their faith was finally legal. The edict came from a new king who had once been Protestant and had not forgotten: the former Henri of Navarre, now Henri Quatre, king of France.

Henri Quatre. Julien shook his head.

It was the beginning, Grandpa said, and it laid the foundation for what was to come. When one hundred years later the edict was revoked, Tanieux was a town where Protestants and Catholics lived together in mutual respect; where people learned, and thought for themselves, and weren't swayed by every political wind from Paris. And the refugees came, fleeing from the persecution, and they were accepted here. "And that," said Grandpa, "was when we came. The Losiers. We were refugees. Half the families in this town were refugees."

There was silence. The light from the fire and candle turned the white walls golden, turned the pine table a deeper gold still. Julien was thinking, *We*. Who were they, these medieval refugees? Benjamin was running a finger around the edge of his cup, slowly. Finally he opened his mouth. "But," he said, looking away, "that was then."

Grandpa turned his quiet eyes on him. "Do you think," he said, "that they have forgotten?"

"Yes." Benjamin dropped the word like a stone.

The shadows deepened in Grandpa's face. He spoke slowly. "I know. It looks like they never knew. But you have to understand what memory is, in these hills. We put our roots down deep here. And the earth sustains us, down deep in the dark. But the earth grows crusted and hard with the years and won't let in the rain." He fell silent, his hands on the table gnarled and still. The wind beat the rain against the window.

He looked up, a light in his eyes.

"But God is a good farmer," he said. "Do you understand that, children?" His laugh rang out, sudden as thunder. "God is a good farmer, and he loves his land. And he plows it." He lifted his eyes to the window, to the rain-curtained hills. "He is going to plow Tanieux. I think," he added with a strange smile at Benjamin, "he's begun already. They haven't forgotten, you know. The memory is buried deep, down in the dark where the earth is rich—and God's blade will turn it up." His smile dug a hundred tiny furrows round his eyes. "Yes. You wait and see."

Julien followed Benjamin up the dark stairway in silence. They could hear the rain against the windows in the gusting wind. At the top of the stairs, Benjamin turned.

"Julien," he said.

Julien stopped with one foot on the stair in front of him. He could hardly see Benjamin's face.

"Have I been"—Benjamin hesitated—"a jerk? Sometimes, I mean?"

"Um." Julien thought Benjamin couldn't see his face either. He hoped not.

"I mean I hated it here at first. I thought they . . . well. I never thought there was anything worth caring about here, and your grandfather . . . I don't know, I just wish . . ." His voice trailed off. Julien had no idea what he was trying to say.

"I wanted you to know, anyway," said Benjamin, "I'm staying."

"Staying?" Julien repeated stupidly. But Henri. Henri hates you. "I . . . good. Um. I'm sorry. That I haven't been much help."

Benjamin gave a quiet snort. "Well, I haven't either, so I guess we're even." He stood there for a moment, a step above Julien, hunching his shoulders awkwardly, then stuck out his hand. They shook. The rain lashed against the window.

"And–" Benjamin started. He paused a long moment, then said abruptly, "You should be grateful. For your family."

With that, he turned and disappeared into his room.

"I'm going to report they stole the book," said Benjamin. They were walking to school through the mud, their shoes squelching.

"Are you sure you wanna do that?" *Bad move.*

"I want it back, Julien."

"What if you waited a little. Just in case."

"In case what? In case they come to me and apologize? Why don't I just apologize to them? I'm sorry I'm from Paris, I'm sorry I'm Jewish, I'm sorry I'm smart. Look, when I was a kid, one day at school they made fun of my yarmulke. And when I came home and told my father, he said it was time to stop wearing it. The next week, he quit wearing his. I'm not doing that anymore, Julien. I'm just not."

Julien looked at him. He wasn't wearing the skullcap now. Benjamin looked him in the eye.

"Okay," said Julien, "I can see that. Listen, how about I talk to Papa? I can do it at lunch."

"Shoulda thought of *that* last night," said Benjamin. "Sure. Fine."

They stood by the wall together that morning in the watery sunshine, saying nothing, their faces turned vaguely toward each other in silent companionship. It was the way Julien and Vincent had often stood together in their own schoolyard, at odd moments of recess with nothing to do. Just standing together.

The bell rang. The class filed into the classroom. And there it was.

On Benjamin's side of the desk. Neatly placed and gleaming in the pale light from the window sat a wide, blue and white book entitled *Submarines*. Not a scratch on its perfect cover. It sat by the inkwell innocently, as if it had been there from the beginning.

Benjamin slid into his seat without taking his eyes off the book. He slipped it off the desk onto his lap. As Monsieur Matthias began to speak, Benjamin's fingers were running gently over the pages, as if they might bruise; leafing quietly through the diagrams, the color plates; all clean, untouched. Inside the cover was a scrap of paper. Julien leaned over to look.

Sorry, it said in messy block capitals. My friends don't know when to stop. Good book. He glanced back. Roland glanced at him and then away. Julien grinned.

Benjamin stared at the note for much longer than it took to read it. He pulled it out of the book, folded it neatly in fourths, and put it in his pocket.

"I'll collect your essays now," said Monsieur Matthias.

They went home for lunch together, walking in step in the sunshine, Benjamin telling Julien about the book. Diagrams of every sub, from the German U-boats to the latest American ones, every part labeled, and the combat strategy—torpedoes, depth charges, evasive maneuvers. Now *that* sounded cool. They spread it out on the table after lunch and read that chapter until the soccer game.

The teams played a hard-fought game in bare feet, in a sea of mud. They played like they knew snow was coming and this game might be their last. They tied. Julien scored two goals. When they lined up at the pump to wash the mud off their feet, the rest of the boys coming in for class crowded around them, as excited as if they'd just run the annual footrace from Saint-Agrève to Lamastre, excited as if they'd all won. Julien laughed along with the others and tromped up the stairs in bare feet, carrying his shoes. Life was good.

As they went out the gate that afternoon, he heard Benjamin's voice beside him "Hey, Roland."

Roland stopped by the gatepost, looking at them.

"D'you like submarines?"

"Um, yeah," said Roland slowly.

"I've got this great book about them, if you wanna borrow it."

Roland's eyebrows shot up. He hesitated. "I couldn't do that. It's brand-new." Benjamin blinked, and Roland filled him in with a flat voice: "My parents won't let me borrow stuff I can't replace."

Benjamin's head tilted to one side. "Um. How about homeroom . . . or during break?" Yeah, Roland who pretended not to know who Foucault was, sitting in homeroom with a bona fide *boche*.

"My brother Louis, he loves this stuff. How about after lunch?"

"Sure. I'll give it to you after history then?"

"Um, yeah . . . or you know, we could look at it together. If you've got time."

Benjamin's eyes lit. Julien blinked. The mud-puddled schoolyard and the hills and pale sky had all taken on a slight spin.

"Sure. Yeah. That'd be great." Benjamin was beaming.

Roland shook hands solemnly with both of them. Then he turned and set off down the farm track, between puddles full of sky, toward home.

"You should come next time, Julien. They said so. Hey, you're not gonna believe this. You know his family's in that, uh, unusual religious group? That 'fellowship' thing?"

"They are?" The Fellowship was weird but harmless, was what he'd heard. No pastor or leader of any kind, no church building, no short hair or makeup on women, things like that, and all about preparing for Jesus to come back in twenty or thirty years.

"So . . . he introduces me to his little brother Louis, and the kid goes, 'Oh. You're the Jewish guy. Right? Is it true?' And I say yes, and he grabs my hand and shakes it all over again and says he's always wanted to meet *one of the Chosen People!*" Benjamin was shouting under his breath. "I have *never* gotten that from a Christian before!"

"Wow," said Julien, blinking. "Well . . . cool."

Louis was a black-haired, bright-eyed, wisecracking kid; he only shook Julien's hand once, but Julien liked him immediately. The four of them stood by the wall, Roland wearing his quirky smile, Louis wearing Vincent's own grin, trading jokes and friendly insults with his brother. Benjamin sat down on the wall and spread the book out on his knees, and their eyes lit up; and Julien's lit with them.

Julien prayed every morning as his grandfather had asked him—his knees on the hardwood floor by his bed—asking God what to do. After a few mornings of asking and getting flat nothing—no words thundered from the sky, no quiet whisper in his soul—he started to feel stupid. It sounded especially dumb as a question: "Lord, what do you want me to do?" Then kneeling there, listening to the silence. "Lord, please tell me what you want me to do" felt more open-ended, like a letter or a telegram that God could answer at his leisure—less like asking someone a question to their face and being ignored. He knew they'd say God was in the room with him and all that, but he just couldn't see it. Really, it felt more like writing to someone in Russia or America; a letter to a faraway, incomprehensible place, a flimsy little message that, for all he knew, might end up at the bottom of the sea.

He prayed about other things too.

It had made the rounds pretty quickly that Benjamin was a *boche*. Probably the only one who didn't know was Benjamin himself. Nobody talked to him.

Except Roland and Louis. And they'd never tell him.

Julien prayed to God to erase it, to make it never have happened; he prayed much more foolish prayers than Grandpa's question, but he didn't care. God could do anything. Just make it go away. And maybe God was listening. It was good to be with the guys, sitting on the wall after lunch together, laughing out loud. It was something he'd never expected.

Julien was sitting at the table with his homework when Papa came home from a meeting about the new school, wiped his shoes on the mat with a jerk, and banged his briefcase on the floor.

"Martin?" said Mama. "Is everything all right?"

Papa took a deep, trembling breath. "No. No, it's not all right." He sank down onto the couch and ran his hands through his hair. "I cannot believe that man."

"What happened?"

"I'll tell you what happened. We were having a bit of debate on wartime and Alex's vision for this as a sort of international school, and then Victor Bernard—" He drew in his breath. "Victor Bernard informed the assembly that a family in town is boarding a young man from *Germany*. And asked us all whether, *times being what they are*, it might not be *safer* to look to our own."

Julien swallowed. "Victor Bernard? Henri Bernard's father?"

"Yes," said Papa absently.

"He thinks *Benjamin* is a threat?"

"I don't understand it, Maria. I don't."

"Maybe he was under the impression it was a young *man*—in his twenties or so?"

"That's what I thought. But he never batted an eye when Alex explained the truth. Oh, Alex gave a magnificent defense, Maria. And then just when he was really getting into it, someone in the back raises his hand and says that if the school's going to take German students, maybe people should just be told who they are. It sort of knocked the wind out of his sails." Papa snorted. Mama wore a look of distaste.

"I think," she said slowly, "that we've been insulted."

"Well, yes, Maria. We have."

There was a moment of silence. Papa's mouth quirked. "The funny thing is, that other guy didn't mean any harm. You could tell. He thought he was proposing a compromise. Alex was just floored." Papa shook his head. "That's the one thing he doesn't understand, really. Stupidity."

"Speaking of stupidity, I wonder how Bernard got the impression Benjamin is actually German?"

"Well, technically—"

"Technically he spent the first five years of his life there. He doesn't even *speak* German. They didn't—take the man's suggestion, did they?"

Papa sighed, and looked into the fire. "No. They didn't. Someone changed the subject, and everyone was happy to move on. Nobody's interested in Bernard's obsessions. But when we got around to talking to old *père* Gautier about renting that old children's home he owns by the Tanne, *he* said not if we were going to put Germans in it. You should've seen Alex. But it's his building, Maria. Nobody can force him. I saw Monsieur Raissac talking to him after the meeting, and Gautier was just shaking his head *no, no, no.*" He sighed again. "That was going to be our largest dorm, Maria. We can't do what we've got planned anymore—we'll have to cut the numbers and start with only *sixième* and *cinquième*, and even then . . ."

"There won't be enough work for you—"

"We'll figure it out, Maria. Astier might keep me on."

Mama shook her head, her brow creased with worry.

"That man . . . to go and ferret out that information on Benjamin . . . I will never understand."

No, thought Julien, staring down at his book, his heart beating fast. *No, you never will.*

Julien lay in his bed, the dark pressing hard against his open eyes, running the words through his mind for the hundredth time. *There won't be enough work for you. We'll figure it out, Maria.*

What have I done?

His father's job. He'd messed up his father's job.

And Pastor Alex's plans; and the next school year for himself and Benjamin, they were supposed to be switching schools next September; and . . . and his father's dreams, the light in his eyes when he talked about it . . . he saw him sitting by the fire, the lines of worry in his forehead. He saw the shining tracks of the tears down Benjamin's face. *But all I did was say something true! They were sneering at me!*

"God, I'm sorry, I'm so sorry," prayed Julien, hands pressed against his face. But underneath were deeper, quieter words pounding in time to his heart: *No one. Must ever. Know.*

Chapter 10

Broken

Herr still had her pack. He'd been carrying it when they ran.

All their money and half their food. One of their blankets; but they had the eiderdown. All her clothes but what she had been wearing.

The first three days were terrible, walking and hiding and walking again under pine trees tall and black as fear, looking behind at every sound, not daring to stay on the road. They slept on the ground in the woods; or Gustav slept. Niko lay looking into the dark, trying not to think. Not to remember what Uncle Yakov had said. *Nina, he's delirious with fever. It's madness to send two children out into the world alone. Nina, listen to me: there is no safe place for Jews on this earth, nor for women. Everywhere there are evil men.*

Everywhere there are evil men.

I know about evil men, she'd thought. *Here in Vienna.* The Nazis marching in the streets, the men roaring the latest drinking song from the bars, the one with the chorus of "We are hunting Jews." The boys from Gustav's school who'd crippled her.

Friedrich had been with them; tall, blond Friedrich, the boy she'd dreamed over for a year when she was fourteen—till he'd turned up in a Hitler Youth uniform, and the dreams had gone. Five or six of them chasing her up the alley—she never knew who threw the rock—but in her mind it was Friedrich laughing his loud, manly laugh as she fell, heavily and wrong, something breaking painfully in her left knee. "You got her!" someone had called, and then feet pounding around her and the pain in her knee exploding into white fire as one of them kicked it hard . . . and the scream she had heard, not even knowing it was herself, and the voices. "No one'll care, she's just a Jew." "I think it's broken." "Maybe we should go . . ."

She remembered the market basket she'd been carrying, tipped on its side, the eggs spilled and broken, their gold yolks bright against the paving stones. Broken. She remembered the walk home.

So she'd known about evil men. *But not everything*, whispered the shadows. *Not even close.*

She stared into the dark, seeing the rabbi in prison or dead; seeing Father still and cold in his bed; seeing Herr roaming the woods in the dark. *Did you know this, Father? About the world you sent me out into? Did you know about the evil men?*

Now she knew. She knew, and she would not forget, though she lay awake at night trying. Back to back with Gustav, wrapped tight in Father's eiderdown, staring into the dark, listening for footsteps. Hearing only Gustav's breathing and the tiny noises of the forest all around her; the small sounds of the hunted, filling the night.

They walked on the road. It was cold up here in the mountains. Herr had her gloves; Gustav gave her his and put his hands in his pockets. They ran out of food and went to bed hungry, and still Niko did not sleep. The next day, she could hardly walk for weakness, but she did; they came to a farmhouse, and Niko hid shivering in the woods while Gustav went in to ask for work and food. He was gone a long time and came back sweaty and grinning, with a bag of bread and cheese and a story about learning to split wood. She ate, and the shivering left her.

They slept in a barn the first night that it rained; they walked on, the food ran out, Gustav stopped and worked again. He told people he was looking for his father, who had left his mother when he was young, and lived in Italy. In what town, people asked. Oh, he didn't know the name, some city not far from the border, on this road. You must mean Trento. Just keep going, down out of the mountains, you'll find it. They say there's work there too.

They made for Trento.

It was cold, and getting colder. Gustav wore socks on his hands. He wouldn't take his gloves back from her. Her arms ached from walking all day on the crutches; ached and then hardened. But it was so cold. At night they huddled, back to back, wrapped in the eiderdown, shivering. When they found a barn to sleep in, it was warmer, but Niko started full awake at every sound. She got up each morning and kept walking, but her head felt hollow and full of wind, and her heart shivered in her chest, and fear and hunger fought in her belly every time Gustav stopped to ask for work. And everywhere there were evil men.

They were filthy, their clothes were filthy, the white stars on the eiderdown were black as dirt. The streams they found were icy; if they washed, they would never get warm again. They had no fire; they didn't dare. They had no matches. Father hadn't said to pack matches. She didn't know what he'd had planned for them with the rabbi; but it wasn't this.

It rained. Icy, pouring rain, and no houses or barns, and nothing to do but walk, their wet clothes clinging to their skin. Gustav's pack was soaked; the eiderdown wet and heavy, the bread sodden and falling apart. It was so cold; and nowhere to stop and get warm and dry again, no help, no one they could trust. She had never imagined anything like this. She wanted to sink down beside the road, to give up, but she kept going. The rain stopped before nightfall, and they lay in the wet woods under the soaking eiderdown, and Niko knew in her heart that they could not go on much longer. They ate their soggy bread and said nothing. She would not let him see her cry.

Chapter 11

Stupidity

Winter came in quickly, without preliminaries, like an uninvited guest who means to stay; like an invader.

The school went on winter rules, every class spending break in their homeroom. Ricot let them put the desks in a half circle near the woodstove, and the guys arranged themselves on them, sitting on the tops of desks, the backs of chairs, in a perfect echo of Henri's court under the oak tree. Roland had his place by Jean-Pierre at the edge of it. Benjamin and Julien stayed at their desk.

At home in the mornings, Julien still prayed. He prayed that the school would get the old Gautier place, after all, that it would be like nothing had ever happened, that God would please, please help. He didn't know if anyone was listening.

It snowed, and Tanieux finally looked the way he remembered it: a winter town of soft white curves and blue shadows, the tiny warm glow of windows down along the white streets. Magali and her friend Rosa ambushed Julien and Benjamin on the way to school with snowballs, and they gave back as good as they got. The schoolyard rang with shouts when they got there, snowballs flying; Julien fell on the deep snow by the wall and started packing snowballs. He got Léon Barre in the ear, and Léon's friend Antoine got him back, and then he got Pierre in the neck; that was sweet. He filed into class with the others and listened to Henri and Philippe and Pierre behind him planning a battle, a real one; a whole-class snowball fight fought by the rules of *ballon prisonnier.* It was brilliant. He had to give them credit. It was going to be perfect.

And he was going to be there.

The sun was bright and the sky deep blue, and the wind had blown the snow into knee-deep drifts and long sparkling curves in the sun. The trees were a black-and-white tracery, the river clear and edged with ice, and in the schoolyard Henri Quatre and Pierre were picking teams.

The lines were laid out: two team zones facing each other across a narrow no-man's-land, and behind each team's zone, its prison, bounded by a hand-high wall of snow. If you got hit, you were taken. If you managed to catch a snowball someone had dodged, you could remake it and throw it at the enemy, and if you hit one of them you went free. The military implications were beautiful. Julien took one look at those prison walls and instantly craved the same thing as every boy in that schoolyard: to be the brave French soldier, captured but not cowed, resisting, breaking through the lines of the cowardly *boches.*

Gilles for Henri's team, Philippe for Pierre . . .

"Hey we're the French, okay, and you're the *boches!*"

"*You're* the *boches!*"

"Julien," said Pierre.

He was in Pierre's camp in a flash, bending down to pack a snowball; it crunched delightfully, perfect snow. He was shaping another when he heard Benjamin's voice.

"Um . . . can I join?"

Julien straightened but did not turn; he stood motionless as Pierre shouted, "Hey, we're the French Army, we can't take *boches*. Go ask them over there!" And laughed.

"*You're* the *boches!*" hollered someone from the other team.

Julien turned then and saw Benjamin's face.

Benjamin turned away and walked silently across the field. Something stuck and burned in Julien's throat. He looked across at the no-man's-land, at the prison camp, all the lines and colors of high adventure drawing themselves in those packed snow walls. He wanted it. He wanted that daring escape, that courage under fire. The battle was gearing up, his team assuring each other confidently that they were the French Army, that the line would hold. He was a part of this. No one had thrown *him* out. But as he bent for a snowball to hurl at the enemy, before his eyes was Benjamin's face collapsing like a bombed house. The windows shattered, the walls falling inward: a direct hit.

Julien looked at the wall. Benjamin stood in deep snow, his head down, a small gray figure against the white. Snowballs flew; around him boys were calling, their voices thin and distant as the cries of rooks. He dropped his snowball and walked off the field.

The snow muffled his steps as he approached the wall. "Hey."

Benjamin's head came up fast, and Julien caught the gleam of tears in his eyes before he looked away, blinking hard. "Yeah?" he said roughly. "Why aren't you out there?"

"Because that was wrong."

Benjamin looked at him. The tears in his eyes wavered and spilled. "There's no place for us," he said. "In Germany they hated us because we were Jews. They broke all the windows of our shop. That's one of my first memories. I was four. That's when we left. Last year they beat my uncle David and broke his hands so bad he can't work anymore." He swallowed. He took off his glasses and wiped a sleeve across his eyes.

"Oh," said Julien. "Oh." No other words came.

"And we came to Paris, and they still hated Jews. They talked about us behind our backs. And Papa wouldn't let me wear my yarmulke, and he stopped wearing his, and we stopped going to synagogue—we kept changing so they wouldn't hate us, and now they hate us because we're *German*." He almost choked on the word.

And at that precise moment a snowball flew past Julien's left ear, and hit Benjamin directly across his weeping eyes.

It was packed hard, and shattered against his face. He fell back against the wall, dropping his glasses, clawing blindly at his eyes; then he was blinking frantically, compulsively, his face crumpled in pain.

Julien had seen the motion out of the corner of his eye; over there, on what had been his team. It was Pierre.

The field blurred. He saw nothing; only Pierre. Laughing.

He strode across the field and up to Pierre, drew his arm back, and punched him as hard as he could right in his stupid, laughing face.

It felt glorious.

Pierre stumbled back with a look of pure shock; then his eyes narrowed, and all Julien caught was a glimpse of his thick-jawed face before pain hit him in the left eye, and he fell. The snow was cold on the back of his head, and there were shards of red light around his eye, and oh it hurt. He rolled out of Pierre's reach as Pierre came down with another blow.

"Fight!" "Over here! Fight!"

They were up again, eyes fixed on each other, circling warily. There was no one, only the two of them inside the tight, pulsing circle of their rage. Julien's blood pounded in his ears in rhythm with the pain in his eye and the dimly heard chant: "Fight! Fight! Fight!" Then Pierre swung.

Julien dodged, and Pierre overshot his aim. Julien grabbed him by the sleeve and tried to follow the motion, trip him at the ankles and send him down. It was like pulling on a boulder. For a moment they were locked, struggling; Julien let go. Pierre's lip lifted. Julien faked with his left and then threw his right fist with all the force of his body behind it, right at that sneering mouth.

He connected, felt the hard edge of Pierre's teeth against his knuckles and the soft lip caught between; when he drew back his fist, he saw blood on Pierre's face, blood down his chin. A fierce joy rose in him, and as Pierre blinked, Julien pulled back and slammed a fist into his face again.

A hand grabbed the back of his collar, hard. Behind Pierre, suddenly, was the muscular form of Monsieur Astier. Astier had Pierre by the shoulders, struggling. Julien struggled too for a moment; then the teacher behind him spoke.

"Julien, control yourself," said his father's stern voice. "*Now.*"

Pierre was marched through the watching crowd and into the school by Monsieur Astier; Julien followed, walking in front of his father. That way he didn't have to look him in the face. *It wasn't what it looked like, Papa.*

But Papa didn't ask. He put his hands on Julien's shoulders as they entered the building and let them rest there till they reached Astier's office; then Julien felt them lift and let go. He heard, before his father turned away, his voice with an edge of weariness.

"Georges," he said. "Will you handle this one?"

"A *snowball?*" Astier sounded incredulous.

To hear Pierre tell it, Julien had just walked up and punched him, God knew why. Julien told what he could of the truth. How could he explain Benjamin's face, or the broken bloody hands that had flashed so vividly into his mind? Astier's eyebrows rose very slightly at the word *boche* connected with Benjamin, and he gave a tiny nod.

Pierre swore wide-eyed on his mother's grave that the snowball had been an accident.

"That's impossible, monsieur! We were by the wall, and he got him right between the eyes!"

"You were on the other side! I was aiming at the other team, *non mais m—*" Pierre bit off the end of the swear word with a glance at Monsieur Astier.

Julien turned on him. "You liar," he said. "You've had it in for us since the day we got here, you and Henri. You think I don't know who stole Benjamin's book?"

"Slow down," Monsieur Astier's deep voice cut in. "First," he glared at them, "do *not* start this fight again in my office if you know what's good for you. And second, if there has been a theft at my school, I'd like to know why I wasn't informed." He turned a sharp eye on Julien, who swallowed.

"It was returned, monsieur. Someone left it on his desk."

Astier nodded heavily. "And are you certain that Monsieur Rostin here stole it?"

Julien hesitated. "No," he said finally, and hung his head. "I didn't see."

Astier sighed. "Well." He gave them a hard stare. "I'm going to have to find a detention room for each of you for the rest of the school day. During which time, I want each of you to do some thinking."

He turned first to Julien. "Monsieur Losier, *you* will think on this. You have attributed to Monsieur Rostin a cowardly and premeditated cruelty which I personally doubt his capacity for." Pierre looked up. "Though today's callous stupidity, I don't find surprising at all," Astier added drily. "You have also for some reason decided without direct evidence that he is a thief. Think about how you would feel were such assumptions made about you.

"And Monsieur Rostin." He turned to Pierre, who shrank back a little at the stony gaze. "Here is what I want *you* to consider." His voice grew even heavier.

"At our school, we do not tolerate insults that relate to a person's race or nationality." His eyes flashed. "Not even if that person's nation is at war with us. I am going to notify the teachers to be on their guard, and if I ever hear of such a word applied to young Monsieur Keller or anyone else—" He broke off, taking a deep angry breath. "If I hear of *any* student being treated differently from others on the basis of race, nationality, or religion, in *any* way, believe me: the offender will be punished."

He puffed out the rest of his breath and looked at the thoroughly cowed Pierre. "I am sorry," he said. "That is not exactly what I want you to meditate on. You were in church last Sunday. If you were listening, you may recall that God instructed the Israelites settling into the Promised Land to be kind to the foreigners among them, remembering that they, too, were once strangers in a strange land. You will think," he said, "about the meaning of that command."

Julien sat at a dusty desk in the storage room Astier had stuck him in, a cluttered place with one pane of window golden from the high sun. There was blood on his knuckles, and he didn't know whose; his eye hurt, his head hurt with the pressure of trying not to weep. *What else could I have done?* The tears grew in his eyes and escaped. He laid his head down.

He cried a long time, silently; then lay, not moving, his cheek on his wet sweater sleeve. Feeling empty. Washed. The window was bright above him. It was still there when he closed his eyes, a shadow of light.

He woke when the bell rang for break. The sun was lower and streaming in, turning the dusty air golden, full of drifting motes. He watched them, their slow unhurried play.

"God," Julien whispered.

God, why did he keep screwing up?

It wasn't right; it wasn't fair; it was so confusing. The way you could mess up everything with a word, without meaning to, one little word, and when you tried to fix it, that was wrong too. And the way you thought it was turned out not to be the way it was at all. His face . . . how was he supposed to know, he didn't know, God.

They broke his uncle's hands. Did they really? In the twentieth century? "I didn't know, God, I swear. I didn't know *boche* would make him look like that. Oh, God. I'm . . . sorry . . ."

"That's the one thing Alex doesn't understand, really," Papa had said. "Stupidity."

Oh God. Do you *understand stupidity?*

He really hadn't known, but did that make it any better? Had Pierre known? *Oh God, forgive me. Please.*

Forgive me.

He sat with his head in his hands. The dust drifted in the light, dancing in slow patterns, unknown and unknowable, golden and silent as God. He watched it dance, sitting motionless; he watched, and thought nothing as the bar of sunlight narrowed and bent toward him, infinitely slow, in the gathering of the early winter night.

When the bell rang, he did not move. He was so tired. His mind was so . . . still. He hardly lifted his head at the sound of the door opening.

"Hey." It was Pierre's voice.

Julien looked up.

"You okay?"

He started to nod, but it hurt. "Yeah." The crack in Pierre's swollen lip was reddish brown with dried blood.

"You were pretty good," Pierre said. "For a Parisian."

Julien let out a laugh. That hurt too. "So were you." There was a pause. "How bad do I look?"

Pierre grinned. "Awful. That's the biggest shiner I've ever seen."

"Great."

"Hey, uh . . ." Pierre looked out the window. "Thanks for not saying I stole that book."

"Sure. I mean it was true. I didn't see who did it."

Pierre huffed. "Not me. I was playing with the coat, remember?"

"Yeah. I remember."

"Hm. Well." Pierre looked away, then at him again. "Hey," he said. "I really wasn't aiming for him, okay?" He was looking straight at Julien, his light green eyes serious. Julien had never seen that look on him. After a moment, Julien nodded and held out his hand.

They shook. Julien stood. "Something I should tell you, though." How should he put it? Some way that would make Benjamin look good. "I think it would be good not to call Benjamin a German." Pierre was giving him a puzzled frown. "It's not about being called *boche*, it's—he hates Germany. They did some really awful things to his family. Because they're Jewish. I didn't know that . . . before."

"Oh," said Pierre.

Benjamin was waiting for him on the bridge. "How's your eye?"

"I guess I'll have to put something on it." It hurt bad. Benjamin was giving him a rueful smile; last time he'd seen him, he suddenly remembered, he'd been blinking compulsively in pain. "How're *your* eyes?"

"They're all right. They felt better after five minutes," Benjamin said. "That was weird. I just couldn't stop blinking. I knew you guys were fighting, but I couldn't even see what was going on." He paused for a moment. "Uh—who won?"

Julien snorted. "I have no idea," he said.

As they climbed the steps they heard voices upstairs. Julien thought nothing of it. Not till he'd stepped full in the door did he realize.

The entire sewing circle was in the living room. Including Madame Rostin.

He made to close the door again, quickly, and slip on up the stairwell. Mama had seen him.

"Boys, your *goûter* is in—*mamma mia,* Julien! What happened to your eye?"

"I'm fine—" Julien started, but at the same moment Benjamin said, "Pierre—"

Julien motioned wildly at him; too late. Madame Rostin was rising from her seat, all the ominous gray-clad bulk of her, looking like she was about to blacken his other eye.

"Did my Pierre," she said slowly and savagely, "do that to you?"

"Um. Ye-e-es . . ."

"That. *Boy.*" She snatched her coat from her chair back and slung it over her arm. "He will regret this."

"But . . . but . . ." Julien stammered as she pushed past him. "It wasn't like that. It was a misunderstanding—he didn't even start it! I hit him too! Hard!"

"Good!" she snapped over her shoulder. And was gone.

He heard her clatter down the stone stairs like a carthorse on cobblestones. He heard Magali greet her at the bottom, and *her* shoes coming up, and the babble of voices from the living room—he stepped out the door and closed it, pushed the heels of his hands against his temples. If only they would all go *away* . . .

"Wow," said Magali. "*She's*—" She saw Julien, and her jaw dropped. "Pierre! Pierre! He did it! Right? And you messed him up too. C'mon, tell me you did."

Julien slumped against the wall and nodded.

"All *right!*"

"*Shut up,*" Julien growled. "Did you see her? Did you? She's gonna go home and make me an enemy for *life.*"

"*Pierre?* What do *you* care?" He bared his teeth at her, and she recoiled. "Okay, okay, sorry . . ."

Mama put her head out the door. "Is Madame Rostin gone? She left her purse."

"I'll take it, Mama," Magali said quickly, and took the big black purse. "I can catch her." Benjamin turned without a word and followed her down the stairs.

"Julien. Come in here to the kitchen, and I'll make you something. The sewing circle's over. Come." The scrapes of chairs and shoes on the floor were jabs of pain in his skull.

"My head, Mama. It hurts."

"Come."

She felt his skull all over for what hurt most. She put a steaming bowl of tea in front of him, and he made a face at the bitter smell. "It's willow. *La mère Cagni* in Bassano used to swear by it. It works."

The sound of footsteps at the top of the stairway; heavy steps; Papa. Oh no.

Papa walked in and said nothing, just looked at him and sat down. "Do we all have to drink that vile-smelling brew?" he asked plaintively.

Mama laughed. "Tea or coffee?" she asked.

Papa sighed. "Coffee's up to forty francs a kilo." Mama nodded. There was silence while she poured him *verveine* tea.

"Well," said Papa. Julien looked down, studying the patterns of steam in his bowl. "So. You tried a little 'Vengeance is mine, I will repay . . .'"

If Julien remembered rightly, the end of the quote was: "saith the Lord."

"I–"

"You punched that young man in the teeth with quite visible pleasure," Papa continued in a dry tone. "It was not the sort of look I expected to see on my son's face."

Julien winced. Even that hurt. The pain was descending from his head into his neck; he imagined shards of glass working their way down. He shut his eyes.

He heard Mama, her voice sounding far away: "Martin, don't you think this can wait till he's recovered a little?" He heard his father's sigh. "As always, Maria, you are right."

He felt Mama's hand on his shoulder. "I'm putting you to bed."

It was dark, and his head felt full of wet cotton. The towel Mama had packed with snow for his eye was on the floor, and his pillow was wet and cold. He sat up gingerly. His head did feel better.

There was a knock. "Julien?" said Magali's muffled voice. "Want supper?"

"Um. Sure."

She came in with a tray. "It's still warm. Kind of. How d'you feel?" She flicked the light on, and he shut his eyes against the stabbing glare.

"How do I look?"

"You oughta be in a beauty contest." She grinned.

It was leek and potato soup, and he was surprisingly hungry. He ate carefully, Magali watching him. "Boy, Julien, I wish you'd been there. It was priceless."

"Been where?"

"We caught up with her right outside the train station, and boy did she look mad. So I gave her back the purse, and then *Benjamin* starts talking faster than *me*." Her eyes were wide. "She couldn't get a word in edgewise!"

"*What!*"

"All about how it was an accident and you and Pierre had worked it out and you'd both gotten punished already, and just as I'm opening my mouth to back him up, Pierre walks around the corner and almost barges into us. That's when things got hot."

"Hot?"

"He was seriously swaggering. Him and those older guys he goes around with, and this big fat smirk on his face you just wanted to wipe off. I think that's why she hit him—"

"She *hit him?*"

"With the purse! On the ear!"

"Oh no. Oh no."

"It was *hilarious*, Julien! I almost died laughing!"

"I'm happy for you," he growled.

"I'm sorry, okay? But honestly, that guy, I don't know why you care—he's an oaf in training, that's what Rosa says. He comes to the café with those older jerks, and they act like they own the place.

Listen, you should've heard Benjamin at supper, he can't stop talking about you. He thinks you're the best thing since baguettes."

Papa stuck his head in the door. "How's the wounded soldier?"

"Um. Not too bad."

Magali threw him a wink from behind their father and slipped out. Papa sat down on the bed. There was silence for a long moment. Julien looked down at his soup.

"I'm sorry, Papa. I really am."

"I know," said Papa quietly. "Listen, Julien. Tomorrow, we'll have a talk about what happens when you start solving problems with violence, okay? But for now . . . well . . . you know," he said, looking at Julien seriously, "it was true what I said about the look on your face. It shocked me."

Julien look at his soup, at his bed, at his hand.

"No. Listen, Julien. I didn't know then why you were doing it. Now I do." Julien looked up. "Son, I want you to understand: you made the wrong choice in fighting him. But you made another choice today that was very right. You could have stood aside when they called him *boche* and pretended nothing happened. Very easily. You didn't do that. For that, Julien, I'm proud of you."

Julien looked up into his father's eyes. He felt a warmth spread through his chest.

"Hey Papa. Is it . . . okay if I stay home from church tomorrow?"

Papa grinned. "Julien, you want to hide that thing, you'll have to stay in from now till Christmas. Hold your head up! At least you've got something to show for all that!"

Julien grinned too.

Chapter 12

Everywhere

In Trento there was a house; and the house had a door.

It stood in a deserted place between railroad tracks and an old factory with broken windows and weeds growing up from the foundation. Most of the roof was caved in, but the kitchen was whole and had a chimney and a door. The kitchen was where they lived.

At first, Niko slept like the dead. Gustav came and went; Niko woke long enough to wedge the door securely shut behind him and slept again. Gustav brought matches from somewhere and made a fire with bits of broken boards; Niko hung their wet clothes on a string in front of the chimney and slept again. Gustav brought food in greasy brown paper: cold pizza he'd been given at a restaurant's back door. Niko ate, and slept.

And they lived. Through the long day, Niko lay on her father's eiderdown, looking into the fire, putting on more sticks and boards when it sank down; and at evening, Gustav came with food and stories. Showing her the routine he used at the back doors of restaurants, big puppy-dog eyes and a hand on his stomach, and "Food?

Food for empty belly?" It made them laugh, he said. Italians liked a laugh, even when you were begging. He liked Italians, he said. A camp of Gypsies had settled out that way, he said, in the field across the drainage ditch. He said he liked them too.

Then they would bed down by the fire, but now Niko could not sleep. She lay awake long hours in the dark, by the dim light of the fire, wondering. Wondering what Father knew.

Everywhere there are evil men. It was why she stayed in this house and did not go out with Gustav. *Everywhere. Was Uncle Yakov right, then?* she asked Father. She asked God. *What is this world you made?* Father had told her stories of corpses piled up in ditches, just for being Jewish. He hadn't said what happened to the women. But she could guess. *God. Why? Why do you let them?* She couldn't do it, she couldn't lie here all day and all night with only her and the questions in her head, and a God who did not answer—she couldn't do it. But outside, she heard voices sometimes; men's voices, laughing. Outside, for her, there was nothing but fear.

Then came the pain in her throat, and outside, the snow. Niko lay under the eiderdown, shivering, no matter how high the fire was, and sweating. Two, three, four days, and the fever did not go. Gustav felt her forehead, his eyes dark. "I don't know what to do, Niko. I need to get help."

"Gustav, no. You can't tell anyone I'm here. Gustav, promise. Gustav, you have to promise!"

He promised.

She lay staring at the fire, wandering a dark wilderness in her mind. She was in the woods on the border with Uncle Yakov—he was saying run, run, the Cossacks are coming. Father was up ahead, maybe she could catch him and Mother—Mother who ran so fast that she'd never seen her. She called out to them—wait, wait, you forgot Gustav . . . Don't worry, Father called. Gustav can look after himself. He knows their language. They like a laugh. And he was gone, ahead of her in the dark woods, over the border, and she couldn't find the gap. Father, Father come back, Gustav wants you to come back! And then Gustav was there, and a fire, he had made a fire in the woods, but the Cossacks would see it, and he was saying something, he was shouting. "No, Nina, no. I won't let you. I won't let you die!"

And then he was gone.

Chapter 13
Weapons

It happened exactly like Julien had expected.

He heard the news Monday in math class from Gaston, who was telling Dominique behind him. Apparently he, Julien, was a snitch of the lowest kind who had gone straight to Pierre's mother with a pack of lies about the fight. He heard Dominique respond to this information with a soft, shocked, "He *did*?"

Benjamin turned, but Julien elbowed him. *Eyes front. You can only make it worse.*

Pierre's eyes were cold and hard as the crusted snow, as cold and hard as Henri's. That moment they had looked each other in the eye and shaken hands was gone now. Never happened. Julien sat beside Benjamin, staring out the window. He was going to sit this one out.

Two weeks till Christmas break.

The road to school was gray frozen slush; the bridge over the Tanne coated with ice. He walked down it in the early morning dark, the stars overhead, and he walked back up in the dim blue evening, thinking of home and warmth and firelight. Mama would have the fire roaring, the light dancing golden-warm on the walls; he would hang his wet socks up to dry and stretch his feet out near the blaze, and the chill would melt off till he was warm all through.

Benjamin asked if he'd like to do homework together. They sat at the table, mugs of mint tea by their books, the firelight from the living room turning their notebook pages a pale honey-gold, and Benjamin showed him how to work those equations Monsieur Vanier had them on just now. They worked together every night, and Benjamin shook his head and grinned at Julien's complaints about how the teachers piled it on.

"What else is there to do?" he asked wonderingly.

"Soccer," said Julien, rolling his eyes, then looked out the window at the blowing snow and sighed.

Benjamin left a week early, before Christmas break, to see his family in Paris. There was a light in his eyes as Julien shook his hand goodbye at the station, in the howling *burle*. Julien walked to school alone, his head down against the wind.

Back in the science room, he looked over at the circle of the class and wondered if he should try them now, with Benjamin gone, but he wasn't so sure anymore. To have the *troisième* class tolerate him, was that what he wanted? He took a seat on a desk among them, closer to the fire, and no one stopped him. But he saw no friendship in their faces.

Suddenly he hated doing his homework alone.

The air was bright and bitter cold as Julien walked out the school gate, and his boots kicked the powdery snow into glittering clouds in the sun. He was free.

At home, there was the roaring fire, and hot chocolate, and preparations for Christmas. It was going to be a simple one this year. Prices were up, Papa said, and there was a freeze on raises for all government employees—and he was teaching at the public school next year instead of the new one. Except for two unpaid courses he'd volunteered for, for love of Pastor Alex. More work, less money. Thanks to Julien.

There was nothing Julien could do except pitch in and not complain and try to think of a good Christmas present with no money. Which was what he intended to do. For Papa and for Mama.

One night, he came down to the kitchen for a cup of milk to help him sleep, and she was there. Candlelight wavering on the walls, and Mama with her little Bible in front of her, eyes closed, moving her lips in a faltering whisper, in Italian. He froze in the doorway, staring. Tears were streaming down her face. He turned and fled in silence.

He lay awake a long time, gazing into the dark.

He wanted to learn to carve.

Grandpa was carving Magali a deer. It was beautiful. It was beautiful just watching the skill in his hands, taking off a shaving here and there, bringing a shape out of formless wood. There'd been a porcelain statue Mama had wanted in a Paris shop—cupped hands cradling a baby that barely filled their palms. God's hands or something. Papa'd wanted to buy it for her, but it was too much. Julien would make it out of wood. For them both.

"That's a pretty advanced project, *mon grand*," Grandpa told him. But he gave him wood and his second-best knife, and they sat by the fire together peeling golden shavings of wood onto the floor. For a couple of days. But Grandpa was right.

Grandpa taught him wood-burning, and brought him and Magali in on his project: two wooden Bible covers for Papa's big black Bible and Mama's little Italian one. Magali did the sewing in strong canvas, Grandpa cut and planed the thin oak boards for the front and back, and Julien sanded and finished and polished them until they glowed.

There was firelight and wood and snow; they went out to cut pine boughs and holly for the house and came home to hot mugs of tea and Grandpa's stories after supper by the fire. A letter came from Vincent. He missed Julien; their soccer games just weren't the same; he had Madame Larron for social studies, wasn't it awful? He'd wanted to send him a present, but he couldn't, so he'd lit a penny candle in the church and prayed Julien would get a soccer ball. How was he, anyway?

He was all right.

On Christmas day, they cut a pine tree in the woods; they brought it in and tied candles to its branches. They helped Mama stuff the chicken with chestnuts Grandpa had gathered and told her it was better than turkey. They sat round the fire and read the Christmas story, with all the candles lit, and Julien got a new coat, and from Grandpa a carving of a wolf, its head thrown back howling: beautiful. And Magali liked her wood-burned tree picture, and the Bible covers glowed in the candlelight with the high shine he had put on them, and Mama and Papa glowed too. And Mama cried.

"So, Julien," said Grandpa. "You still want to learn to carve?"

"Yes." Next year he'd make them the hands.

So Grandpa started him on his first project: a simple, stylized, round-crowned tree.

Soon it was the only good thing left in his life.

Benjamin came home and looked at his plate during meals and hid in his room. He gave Julien an illustrated history of soccer and offered a pale smile and a thank-you for the wood-burned Bible verse Julien had made him: *The Lord is my rock and my fortress, my deliverer, in whom I take refuge.* The Jews *wrote* the Psalms, Grandpa had insisted; but that didn't make them Benjamin's thing. He'd been right. He backed out of the room, away from Benjamin's pale, unseeing face.

They were frozen in time, all of them; frozen at the worst possible time. At school, nothing had changed, just hardened into a permanent shape like the footprints in the schoolyard that had been there since fall, frozen solid in the mud. Puddles lay in them, gray, flat, lifeless ice reflecting nothing of the sky. The circle of the class was as it had been: Henri Quatre hard and proud at its center; Pierre throwing dirty looks; the rest not seeing Julien, even Roland. Roland, who had almost been his friend. He had no friends now. He sat at his desk beside a pale, silent Benjamin, studying motionless images of soccer, and did not look up.

But he carved.

Every morning on the way to school, a picture of the day was in Julien's mind, a picture of the week, like the one on his class-schedule sheet, but in color. The school hours were a flat, gray collage: the dirty snow and the hard, gray puddles, the bare concrete walls and the cold faces. Everything frozen, everything numb. The evenings and Thursdays and Sundays burst into light, golden and brown, the firelight and faces around the table, Grandpa's eyes and all the wood tones of his workshop, the golden shavings peeling off under his knife. This was not frozen; this blocky, solid piece of wood—this he could change. After the tree, he carved a fish with carefully etched scales and a lifelike bend in its tail. Grandpa said he had the touch and started him on a dolphin.

Halfway through the third week of January, the schedule-picture in his mind was blown into a blinding whiteout, all the lines erased: blizzard. He looked out the window at the sheer aching white and praised the Lord.

Down in the workshop, it didn't hurt.

Grandpa worked with him on the dolphin, trying to shape the flippers without cutting them off. It was a lot harder than a fish; fish were *flat* on the sides.

On Saturday, a clear blue sky; Julien and Benjamin waded to school through knee-deep snow to find a third of the school absent. Out on the farm track, it was thigh deep or more; those farm kids knew impassable when they saw it.

Then Jean-Pierre Reynaud, the doctor's son, fainted in Papa's history class, and Papa sent Julien for the doctor. It was while he was skirting close to the buildings along the *place du centre*, trying to stay out of the *burle*, that he saw disaster looking him in the face.

Pierre. In the Santoros's cafe.

Julien stood riveted by the scene: Pierre lifting his cup, head tilted, a loose grin on his lips, his older friends laughing. But he was clowning, not drunk. Because before Julien could move, Pierre was giving him the death stare.

I didn't do it, Pierre. I'm not going to do it. Right in the Café du Centre *during school hours, you moron! I'm not gonna say a word.*

And much good it'll do me.

"Love your enemies," boomed Pastor Alex.

Julien shifted on the hard, wooden pew. "'Love your enemies, pray for those who persecute you, so that you may be sons of your Father in heaven.' *Why* does Jesus instruct us to love our enemies? *So that we may be sons of our Father in heaven.*"

Julien found himself listening. More often than he expected, when that voice rang through the stone church, he found himself listening. Our Father in heaven, Pastor Alex said, as if he were talking about his own father, as if there was nothing better in the world. The Father who made the hills and the rivers and the sea, who sent rain on the crops of the just and the unjust, whose mercy fell on all—and where would we be without that mercy? How, the pastor asked, could we turn down a chance to be sons of that Father? And Julien, listening, could hear it in his voice—the note of terror, sorrow, loss at the very thought.

Then Pastor Alex shifted. He spoke of the training of soldiers, how it cut against the grain of human nature to look another human being in the face and shoot him dead. The heart balks, said Pastor Alex; the hand hesitates. He gave stories, statistics. Those who train soldiers, he said, know that somehow they must take away the enemy's face for their men, train them to think *sale boche* and not *human being.* So if even ordinary regard for a fellow man is an obstacle to war, what of love? Can you love a man and look into his face and shoot him?

"Friends," said Pastor Alex, "you cannot."

Julien looked up to where the stone vault of the church curved into shadow, and remembered the night this strange war started, and his prayer: *I just want to do something.* He didn't know. He bent his head.

Then Pastor Alex spoke of evil.

He spoke of the Nazis and the things they did. He spoke of Kristallnacht, and Julien clenched his teeth. He asked if we must sit passively by while evil overcomes good. Julien lifted his head.

Pastor Alex leaned forward. Jesus didn't say, "Don't kill your enemies." Would Jesus simply command us *not to act* in the face of evil, he who won the greatest victory, who conquered sin and death? No, friends, no. What did Jesus tell us to *do* to our enemies?

Love them.

"Jesus," said Pastor Alex, and his voice almost shook. "Jesus, the only begotten Son of the Father, offers us this chance to be his brothers and his sisters and to fight as he fought; he gives us his weapons, the Father's weapons, the weapons of the Spirit." He sounded reverent, almost in awe. "The weapons of love," he said. "Fearless love."

Julien sat straighter. Fearless love. Even if he was never a soldier. Was that what Pastor Alex was saying? He could still fight.

"Why, Julien? I didn't think you were that dumb!" Roland looked disappointed in him.

"I didn't do a thing. If you're gonna believe everything Pierre—"

"Look, I didn't believe it about his mom—"

"Roland, if you'd been in the *Café du Centre* in the middle of the morning when everyone's walking by, who would you figure told on you? Huh?"

Roland looked at him and sighed. "Yeah. Okay. But watch your step a little, okay? He's got it in for you."

Julien walked into the classroom after lunch, and on his desk lay a note in block letters that disguised their origin not at all: Go back to Paris tattletale. And take your *boche* friend with you. Your kind isn't welcome here.

If only Pierre knew how much he wanted to. And his *boche* friend too.

Boche again. He could take this note to the principal right now and bust Pierre—he'd given it to him in writing, the moron. To think he'd shaken hands with him—almost liked him. Now they were enemies again

He froze, the note still in his hand. *Enemies.*

No. The grandeur of that sermon, the rush of rightness he had felt, and for *this*? This *stupidity*? He had sat in Grandpa's workshop thinking and thinking, digging his knife into the side of his dolphin, trying to carve flippers. Weapons of love. *What* weapons? How did this even work? For all his fine words, Pastor Alex had in the end left Julien with nothing but *don't fight him*. Fine. He wouldn't fight him. He wouldn't *lower* himself to fight a moron like that. Why should he?

You're Going to find out what not welcome means.

As Julien walked out the school gate with the new note crushed in his hand, a blow from behind sent him sprawling into a dirty snowbank. He leapt up and whirled, ready to grab Pierre by the collar. No Pierre. Nobody. Guys walking past like nothing had happened.

His cheek stung where the crusted ice had scraped it. He stood with his fists clenched uselessly, looking at the stream of faces. They had *all* seen. And Pierre wasn't there. How many *friends* did the guy have? Was it the whole school now?

That evening, he knelt beside his bed, rubbing his face with his hands. He couldn't fight Pierre. Last time had been horrible, and this time would be worse. That was Pierre's plan, probably: make Julien start it, make Julien take the blame.

All right. He'd do it then.

Pastor Alex had said to look to Jesus to learn the weapons of love. He meant, Julien supposed, read the whole story and see how Jesus acted; but he didn't have time. He looked up what Pastor Alex had read to them from Matthew 5; "love your enemies" wasn't much use, but the next bit—"pray for those who persecute you"—he could start on that right now.

Lord, please bless Pierre and make him willing to be my friend again. Please make Pierre understand that I never even told on him once.

It was embarrassing, praying those things; it felt weak. Did it sound to God like he was afraid to fight Pierre again, afraid of getting in trouble? Afraid of Pierre and Henri, how everyone was on their side, how they could make those gray school hours even darker? God knows the heart, Papa had always told him; but that was no comfort at all. God might know better than him; all of those things might be true, and he only a coward. Fearless love, Pastor Alex had said.

I'm not scared of him. I think.

Sunday, Julien was forced to sit beside Pierre, sandwiched in the pew between their families, as Pastor Alex preached on the Good Samaritan. They looked straight ahead as Pastor Alex told them we all have people we'd prefer not to be in the same room with. After the service, they sat awkwardly as their fathers shook hands over them; finally they stood, and Julien put out his hand, and Pierre shook it, looking away.

On the walk home, Magali went on about some new teacher at the girls' school as Julien thought about the sermon, tried to picture Pierre lying beat up in one of the alleys of Tanieux. *Great, now I know what to do if he gets mugged by a gang of mad farmers. That's a real help.*

"Her name's Miss Fitzgerald, she's from England, and everyone's calling her *la Meess*. And she knows *Greek*, and there's this new girl Lucy who's her niece—her father's a reporter and she's lived *everywhere*. He's in the United States reporting on why the Yanks won't fight the Nazis. But she can't go. I'm glad. And she's in my class!"

"I really don't think she's from England, Lili," Papa put in.

"Oh, yeah—I don't get it, Papa. They *speak* English, and *la Meess* says the part they're from is *part* of England, but when I called Lucy English, her eyes got all big, and she yelled, '*Ire*land! We're from *Ire*land!'"

"Ah," said Papa. "History." He smiled at Lili. "What did you think of the sermon?"

Magali gave him a sideways look. "Ever wonder why there's no women in these stories?"

Papa's eyebrows went up. "Should the Samaritan be a woman? Or the wounded man?"

"The robbers," muttered Julien, and Magali made a face at him. "Not the wounded man," he said. "It'd change everything. *Anyone* would help a wounded woman. If you don't—that's just wrong."

"But with a guy it's okay?"

Not . . . *okay*. But for him to help Pierre, it would take . . . something. He'd do it though. "It's just different."

"Oh, yeah. Girls are *different*."

Julien ignored her and walked on, picturing Pierre by the roadside, bleeding.

Julien kept praying.

He spent his school hours watching the clock; he came home to the golden-brown workshop and carved. He carved out one good flipper on the side of his dolphin and began to smooth the wood below it into a tail.

Nothing happened Friday, or Saturday. Sunday, in Grandpa's workshop, he took a long stroke of the knife along the dolphin's side and gouged the flipper half off. He sat staring at it for a moment, then threw it hard against the wall. The flipper broke off with an audible *crack*.

"I'm sorry," said Grandpa. "The dolphin was my mistake. I didn't realize how difficult those flippers would be."

Julien threw the dolphin away.

Roland stood by the school door, beckoning, eyes wide and urgent. Julien followed.

"I don't know who did it, Julien, I swear. But no one was gonna tell you. It's not right."

His books and papers were strewn across the floor. On his desk, the inkwell was overturned—onto today's homework for Ricot.

"I wasn't there, Julien, I swear." Julien wanted to hit him. "I'll get us rags from the broom closet. Quick."

Julien stood staring at the deep black stain as Roland raced out the door. He was back in a moment with a wad of rags; Julien mopped at the ink, thick black stuff that soaked in and would never come out; he was powerfully reminded of a Sunday school lesson long ago about sin. *Exactly. But not my sin.*

They rinsed the rags in the bathroom, and the ink turned the soapsuds gray and the water blue; they stuffed them under the sink for the janitor to find. They put the papers in the desk; the ink black homework in the trash. The bell rang.

"I'm sorry, monsieur," said Julien when Ricot collected the homework. "I did it, but I'm not sure what happened to it." He thought he heard a snicker from the back of the class.

"Well, *that* takes the prize for lamest excuse of the year," said Monsieur Ricot caustically. "Have it for me on Friday copied five times over." Another snicker.

Julien didn't hear a word of the lesson over the blood pounding in his ears. He spent the whole hour composing his note to Pierre on a half sheet of paper with Pierre's muddy footprint on it. This was the guy he had *prayed* for this morning. It was ridiculous. And it was over.

You are so stupid, the note read, *you don't need anyone to tell on you. I never did, not even the first time, and if you want me to prove it by smashing your stupid face in, I will. Friday after class. You choose the place.*

When the bell rang, he walked back to where Pierre was sitting and slammed the note on the desk in front of him.

"Let me know," he said and walked back to his seat.

It was Roland who let him know. After the last bell, at the gate, he handed Julien a slip of paper: *Take the road out of town till you get round the bend. I'll be there.*

"Thanks."

Roland grunted.

There was a spring in Benjamin's step as they walked home through the deepening blue evening. Julien looked at the lit windows of houses and thought of blood on the snow. Benjamin turned to him with an eager look, and Julien scowled.

"Are you okay, Julien?"

"*Yes*," he snarled. Benjamin recoiled.

"Fine," said Benjamin. "Don't tell me. It's not like I couldn't see your note. *I'm* behind you a hundred percent. If you were wondering."

Julien looked away. "Don't tell my father, okay?"

"Don't worry. I won't. Anyway, he deserves it."

"Yeah." Julien looked at the warm-lighted windows and the darkening sky. "He does."

Chapter 14

Wake

Niko came back to herself slowly, floating up through the darkness of her mind, floating like thistledown on water. Was she dead? She couldn't move. She was in a bed, under heavy covers.

She was at home in her bed with the yellow bedspread; she would open her eyes in a moment and see her mother's painting on the wall, the little house between the trees, the yellow flowers. Soon Father would call her: Nina, Nina, it's your turn to make breakfast, *herzerl*, get up . . .

No. She wasn't Nina; she was Niko. She had no father, no mother; everyone was gone, even Heide, even stupid, stupid Friedrich; everyone she'd loved right or wrong except for Gustav was gone. They were homeless, they had no papers, they were nothing.

Why was she in a bed?

Her eyes flew open, and she sat up in bed. Gustav, where was Gustav—a room she had never seen before . . . a narrow, crowded room, white walls and a low curved ceiling, bric-a-brac everywhere. A long rope strung from wall to wall with clothes hanging on it, dark clothes, red shawls—she had seen women wearing those, bright-eyed, dark-haired women, their hands quick as birds, speaking some guttural language. And Gustav! He'd been with them; he was here! She remembered them . . . forcing her mouth open, pouring bitter-tasting liquid down her throat . . . and soup, she remembered soup. And music, from outside—the light of a fire, and a woman's voice singing a high, quavering song, and drums. Gypsy drums. Gypsies.

No, he had said, *I won't let you die.* And then he had told them where she was.

Chapter 15

The Powers of the World

Tomorrow after lunch. This would all be decided.

But today they were hauling firewood from the farm. Papa had rented a horse and cart from the butcher. They set out a full hour before dawn.

The clouds hung low over the hills; the *genêts* waved in the wind, wild dark fingers pointing at the pale sky. The horse's hooves scraped on the ice. Julien huddled into his coat, remembering blood on the snow and the flash of pain when Pierre had hit him. What was he thinking? Pierre was huge. Julien wouldn't have the advantage of surprise this time. This time Papa wouldn't crack jokes or say he was proud of him. The *burle* blew bitter in his face.

Light shone in the east when they reached the farm, and everything moved into high gear. "Going to snow before evening," Grandpa said. "Let's get this done." They loaded the cart so full it creaked and started home, Papa and Grandpa on either side of the horse, Julien and Benjamin on either side of the cart, all watching, ready to grab hold and push if anything slipped on the steep road.

Then home, and tipping the cart into the backyard—"We can stack it tomorrow," said Papa, "let's move"—and Mama handing them sandwiches through a door that opened onto warm, firelit heaven and closed again. Magali came with them, rested and disgustingly cheerful. Julien's face was starting to hurt, and his bones to ache, from the cold. Magali stood up suddenly, jolting the cart. "Hey!" She threw her head back and shouted to the looming sky. "We're not scared of you!" She swayed with the motion of the cart, her hair wild in the wind. "Hey, Old Man Winter," she cried merrily, "we're not scared of you! Whoo-*hoo!*"

Julien hunched miserably in the bottom of the cart, too tired to even say shut up. Maybe it would snow tonight. It would all be off. He'd carve. He'd start a cat, a dog, a wolf. Please.

It was already snowing when they started the second trip home.

His arms ached in earnest, and the sky was dark as evening and heavy, starting to drop its load onto the earth. The air was thick with snow; the wind flung it in their faces, and it stung.

Julien pulled his scarf and hood over his face till only his eyes showed. In the blinding white, he could just see the dim forms of Benjamin and Grandpa and the straining horse, and Papa and Magali on either side of the cart. His shoulders hurt. It was so cold.

Julien's world had shrunk to a small, white sphere: two meters in every direction, no more. The hills were gone, the sky pressed down like a white blanket. He forced his feet forward through the snow; flakes stung his eyes, and he lowered his head against the wind, his mind losing itself in an endless round. The pain in his shoulders. The weight of his boots. Fire, hot chocolate, hot soup on the table. How deep the snow would be tomorrow. How he could fight Pierre when he ached like this. How Pierre could take him anyway.

When he looked up, he was alone.

There was nothing. Just pure, aching white, like blindness. He looked down and saw cart tracks and footprints.

He began to run, stumblingly, in the ankle-deep snow.

He ran looking at the tracks; he lurched to his knees, got up, and ran again. He looked up, staring hard through the snow, and saw nothing; he ran. They were gone. There was nothing, just white, and a crisscross of flakes against it blown by the wind. He looked up a third time into blank, agonizing white. Then fear welled up in him like a terrible spring, and his voice came out in a yell.

He called for Papa and Grandpa. The wind stole his breath; his voice was distant and muffled in that air filled fathoms-deep with snow. He called again from the depths of his lungs; he could feel his heart pounding. He listened.

Silence. Only silence and the wind.

He stood for a moment, seeing it all: night falling, the snow still coming down, the cold seeping into his body like a dark tide. Papa and Grandpa and Benjamin out in the snow with flashlights, searching, the fear in Papa's eyes. A groan shuddered from deep in his stomach. The wind fought him as he ran again, wildly, his mind a welter of darkness and the word *No. No, please God, no.*

His panic-darkened mind cleared for a moment, an instant at the edge of time. The same instant he felt a sharp snap of pain in his ankle, a jolt that rushed up his leg; felt himself falling. The snow coming up to meet him. As the fluffy coldness touched his cheek, and his eyes and mouth were lost in white, the one clear thought came to him that had been trying to beat its way into his mind.

He had veered away from the cart tracks.

He lifted his face from the snow, straightened, began to get up. He cried out from the pain.

His left ankle was broken. He could see in his mind's eye, when he moved it, how the sharp shards of the bone were sticking out through his flesh. So vivid was the image that, crumpled there in the snow, he felt down to his ankle with his hand, knowing his touch would confirm it.

No sharp edges of bone. No blood. His ankle was whole and firm. He breathed.

Then, because he had to, he got his right foot under him and stood. He touched his left foot to the ground, a tiny touch, enough for one limping step. He gasped with the pain.

But he had to.

A deeper terror had entered him. His mind was clear now, horribly clear. This was not a story he could tell himself about courage in the face of the storm. This was death if he was not found.

He must have veered off toward the edge of the woods. To the left, he thought, from the slope of the hill. So go right. Look for the tracks. If he hit the woods, he'd know he'd gone wrong.

He went right. Every step was a jolt of pain. After the pain, he would stand a moment balanced on his right leg, scanning the snow hungrily for tracks. Then another step forward, like a knife through his leg. He cried out every time.

Then suddenly, there it was in the snow, blue-shadowed and deep: the print of a boot. "Oh!" he cried out, a pure sob of relief; but the wind caught it and carried it away, tiny: a tiny voice in all that immensity of white. Desolation found him. *Now what? Oh, God, now what?*

"God," he whispered. "Help. Help." The memory rose in him of his hand slamming the note on Pierre's desk; of his arrogant fantasies, Pierre lying bleeding by the road; of his white rage over ink on his homework. "I'm sorry," he whispered. "Help."

But then he put his left foot down, and the pain shot up through his leg. And instead of mercy, instead of his father's voice on the road up ahead, came a buzzing in his ears. The white womb of the snowstorm around him was darkening, turning grainy and black. Dark shapes were pouring past him, and he was falling, falling, through a wilderness of white and rushing wind.

When he woke, he could not think where he was. Softness under him; for one blessed moment, he thought he was in bed. Why was everything white? And cold. So cold. Pain in his ankle. He was lost in the snow.

He gritted his teeth and pushed and fumbled his way upright again, resting his left foot carefully on the snow. But the pain spread higher and higher in his leg, crept white-hot into his thigh, and the buzzing returned, and darkness around the edges of his sight. He fell.

He began to crawl, dragging the ankle behind him. The snow came up to his chest. He forced his way forward, hands in the snow, tears freezing on his face. His hands and knees were numb. He crawled. The buzzing came again, the darkness creeping in on him. He lay down on his side in the snow to wait.

This was it. No *boches*, no heroics, no tanks. Just snow and wind and stupidity. And God. Through the white haze came back the image of his sister's laughing challenge to the sky: "Hey, Old Man Winter! We're not scared of *you!*"

What a foolish thing. Not to fear the powers of the world.

Was it true—everything he'd been taught? Would Jesus step through that blinding white curtain to take him home? He felt a strange warmth in his limbs, but his eyes hurt, and the tears on his cheeks were freezing. It was getting darker. He wished Jesus would have the kindness to come soon. He wished he didn't have to die in the snow. *I was going to grow up. I was going to be a pro soccer player . . . or something.* He'd never know what it was like. To grow up, be a man. He hadn't even *done* anything.

He was so tired.

His mind broke free of the white haze—it had been floating in whiteness forever, quiet and warm—when he felt something hard lodge behind his knee. Then a heavy weight crashed down on the injured ankle, and he screamed.

"Wha'? *Qu'est-ce qui s'passe?*" said a muffled voice, and the weight rolled off him, leaving him sobbing with relief, and the face came up within inches of his own. The surprised eyes and heavy jaw of Pierre Rostin.

No. Tears welled in Julien's eyes. Pierre blinked twice, snowflakes falling from his lashes. "Julien Losier," he said softly. The *burle* blew a bitter breath between their faces. "What are you doing here? On the ground—in *this*—" His eyes were incredulous. "Get up!" He grabbed Julien's coat sleeve and pulled. "Get *up!*"

Julien's tears spilled over. He stirred and pulled back against Pierre's grip. "I can't," he gasped. "I sprained my ankle."

"Oh," said Pierre. "Oh. Crap. What're we gonna do?" He looked around at the storm, then down at Julien, a frown on his heavy face. "Okay. I'm going to see if I can carry you. But first you're gonna have to get up. *Now.*"

Julien gritted his teeth. Pierre pulled on his sleeve, and in the snow he struggled up onto his right knee. Pierre grabbed him under the armpits and dragged him to his feet. "Okay. Can you walk at all? Try it."

Julien put his left foot down and winced. He didn't dare rest his weight on it. "No. I . . . I can't . . ." More tears spilled out, helpless child's tears. "I'm sorry—"

"It's okay, Julien," Pierre said quietly. Julien felt a hand on his shoulder. "It's gonna be okay," said Pierre, and his eyes were steady. There was no scorn in them. "I bet I can carry you. We're not that far from my house, you know."

Julien opened his mouth. There were so many things he wanted to say, but his mind offered no words. Not even *thank you.*

"See if you can get on my back," said Pierre. "Here—" He knelt in the snow. Julien climbed on, clumsily, gasping in sudden pain as his ankle caught Pierre's coat. "You okay?" Pierre put his hands under Julien's knees. "Does that hurt?"

"No," Julien whispered. Pierre stood, slowly, and began to walk, his gait labored, forcing his way through the snow. There was no sound but the swish of his boots and the keening of the wind; no world but the broad back and strong arms holding him, and his head on his enemy's shoulder.

He woke with a jolt. Pierre was squatting, trying to put him down. He slid off onto his good foot.

"Gotta stop a minute," Pierre gasped. "Get my breath."

"Yeah. Sorry . . ."

"Oh, it's all right." Pierre stood for half a minute while his labored breathing slowed. He looked at the darkening sky and at the snow up past his knees and muttered, "*Merde*." Then with a sideways glance at Julien, "Sorry."

"You don't have to apologize for cussing when you're saving my life!"

Pierre laughed. Julien did too. They looked down at the snow.

"Guess tomorrow's off," said Julien.

"Yeah." Another pause. "You wanna call it off or do it when you're better?"

Oh, what a stupid fight it would be. "Maybe it should be up to you."

Pierre grunted.

"Um. But. Listen." *I want you to know the truth.* That's *what I want.* "I really didn't tell on you. Honest. Either time." Pierre gave him an unreadable glance. "Okay, the first time there was a kind of accident–"

"*Accident?*"

"I came home, and your mom was in my living room! And man, she's *really good* at jumping to conclusions."

Pierre snorted. "Tell me something I *don't* know." He looked away into the white for a long moment. "She gave me double my share of chores for a month."

"That's not right. When you didn't even start it. I told her you didn't–"

"Oh, if I didn't deserve it this time, I will next time. Ask *her*."

A lump was forming in Julien's throat. *No. You deserve . . . something else.* "You sure she's right about you?"

Pierre looked at him. In the dusk, in the snow, it was hard to see his eyes.

"I really didn't tell on you, Pierre. I swear."

Pierre held out his big hand. Julien took it in his numb fingers, and they shook.

The swish of skis on snow woke him, and voices. "I'm sorry, sir. I just went for a walk. Yes, sir." A man's deep voice, indistinct. Then, "He's hurt his leg." A circle of golden light on the snow. A stocky figure, his legs lit by the lantern in his hand, his face dark.

"I can carry him now," said the deep voice. Monsieur Rostin. "Anyone looking for him?"

Julien lifted his head with an effort. "My family—I fell behind . . ."

"Headed to town?"

"Yeah."

The lantern light bobbed crazily as Monsieur Rostin bent down. "Here." He was pushing his skis toward Pierre on the snow. "Go into town. If you don't meet the Losiers before your uncle Maurice's place, get him to come with you and go tell them the boy's safe with us. But don't come home tonight. D'you hear? Stay with Maurice."

"I can make it back—" Pierre began, but his father cut him off.

"Sure you can. But you do what I say. I want you back tomorrow. Understood?"

"Yes, sir."

Julien felt himself lifted, laid across Monsieur Rostin's powerful shoulders like a sack of potatoes. A chaos of white and dark and bobbing lantern light, silence; then warm windows, all golden brown, and a door opening, light spilling out, the crackling of a fire. Hands shifting him, arms under his body. Then he felt himself falling, not into light, but into darkness.

He was floating in the sea, the warm sea, in Italy. No. He was lying on the shore by a driftwood fire. What was that sound of pots and pans clanging? The slamming of a cupboard door. Julien opened his eyes.

He'd never seen this place before.

It was beautiful. Small, full of lamps and firelight, warm. A little kitchen with a big iron stove, a shape in a gray dress bending over it. He was on a rug. His fingers brushed old stone. He turned his head and saw the fire, and tears welled up in his eyes. The red and the gold and the little blue flames licking the wood, washing the whiteness from his mind; life flaming bright against the great dead world outside. He had never known what beauty was before.

"Where does it hurt?" It was Monsieur Rostin. He was beautiful too.

Julien's wet coat and sweater were pulled off; the fire was warm on his bare skin. Monsieur Rostin prodded and squeezed his leg for where it hurt, got towels full of snow from Madame Rostin, whom he called Ginette. Imagine. Ginette, like a little girl in pigtails. His leg was packed with snow that stung with cold and wrapped with towels; he was given a swallow of something fiery, then a bowl of warm milk. "*Mon pauvre petit*," said Ginette.

He slept.

Julien woke in the dark with a single thought: *I'm alive.*

It was quiet. The fire was banked and barely glowed; there were deep shadows. The hush was unnerving. The *burle* had moaned around the house and rattled the shutters for hours, and he'd hardly heard it; now it was still. It was the silence that had woken him.

He was alive.

He had been rescued. And he had cried. In front of Pierre Rostin.

Julien closed his eyes again and pressed his palms against them. In front of *Pierre*—

Pierre who had looked at him and said, *It's going to be okay.* And said, *I think I can carry you.*

For a moment he writhed.

In that moment all was clear as day inside him, unbearable. The dim fire-glow warmed and softened the bare room around him, but in his head was a horrible brilliance that lit, with sharp-edged shadows, *everything.* How he'd prayed and hated, how he'd hoped to win, and how he'd lost. How it shamed him that Pierre had carried him, Pierre the Good Samaritan, safe as in the arms of God. And what that meant about *him.*

Julien swallowed, a trail of broken-glass pain down his throat. He tried not to swallow again, and failed.

He turned away from the shadows. He propped himself on one elbow and reached for the woodpile, got another log onto the fire. A shower of sparks rose, and the flames flared and lit up this place he was alive in, this bare little house.

A table with two benches. Against the wall, a wooden hutch with doors; no other cupboard in the room. In the far corner, a woodstove with a sink beside it; and on his right, four straight-backed chairs. The living room. Bare walls. No books that he could see. No radio.

No, there *were* books on the hutch. Two of them. A big family Bible and a brown almanac; and two framed pictures. One old daguerreotype reflecting the fire in its metal surface; two dim figures, sitting stiffly upright. The other was André in his tank-driver's cap and leather jacket, standing tall.

The truth rested on Julien's shoulders, waiting, like a huge and heavy hand. The truth was it shamed him, that Pierre had saved his life; that Pierre had spoken to him gently, as he cried; that Pierre had been, most truly, the hero. It shamed him because he had already decided who was who in this story, and Pierre was the bad guy, and Julien was the hero with the weapons of love. Because he'd wanted to come out on top. Because that was what he'd thought God's weapons were good for. The truth whispered itself without sound; the truth filled the room like the fire's light. *You cannot attack with the weapons of love.*

He bowed his head.

The fire breathed warmth on him, and he lifted his eyes to it, the blue and red and gold. God was stranger than he had ever known; strange and terrible and kind.

You carried me. He whispered aloud the words that stuck in his throat. "I was wrong. I am sorry." The firelight danced in his tears, and the world was red and golden, and he raised his head. "God. Can you forgive me. Please."

And the fire burned, and the dark hung over him in the rafters just out of reach, like someone looking at him from the shadows, where he could not see. Gentle as a mother, more commanding than a father, wild as the storm, and wise as Grandpa's eyes. Warm eyes deep with years, the strength of ancient days. God. Could God be like Grandpa? Someone he could come to—before it came to this—someone to whom he could say, *I need help*, and sit down and tell the truth about himself and—and learn to carve?

Oh God. Will you teach me?

Because he wouldn't do it right, not next time either. Because the weapons of love were too big for him. "That's a pretty advanced project, *mon grand*," he whispered into the silence. The log popped in the fire, and its two halves fell apart from each other, each one dancing, flaming with life against the dark.

Pierre came at dawn with the doctor and Grandpa and a sled. Papa came after to haul him up the hill toward home.

Monsieur and Madame Rostin stood at the door of their little house, its walls muffled deep in snow, so bright in the sun he could barely look. "It's nothing," Monsieur Rostin was saying to Papa, who was shaking his hand again and again, not letting go.

Julien lay wrapped in so many blankets he could hardly stir, watching the snow-powdered branches move past against the deep blue sky. He could hear the heavy breathing of Benjamin and Papa pulling, and Pierre pushing from behind. The branches ended; the sky broke free into endless blue; they were almost home. Julien leaned back till he could see Pierre's cloudy breath and whispered hoarsely through the pain in his throat. "Hey, Pierre. I always wondered." He couldn't see his face. "What's it like being a hero?"

He heard an odd noise behind him. "Not too bad," said Pierre.

From over Mama's wild crushing hug at the door, Julien caught a glimpse of Pierre before he turned away. He was grinning from ear to ear.

Chapter 16

Woman

The younger of the dark women was Marita. Strong cheekbones and flashing black eyes. Then there was the old one, whom everyone called Grandmother, and obeyed. Gustav was in awe of her. When they'd first come to get Niko, Grandmother had slung her over her shoulder—"like a sack of potatoes, Nina!"—and carried her to the camp.

It was Grandmother who brought her the dress.

She laid it on the foot of the bed and stood there, fixing Niko with a sharp look from her good eye, and said something extremely commanding in Romany. Then in Italian, which didn't help. Still, the voice and the dress said it: *You're all better. Get dressed. Now.*

"Gustav," Niko whispered. "What's Italian for *pants?*"

"Bit late to fool 'em now."

"Gustav, I mean it. I'm not wearing that thing."

Gustav cleared his throat, said something halting in Italian. The old woman snapped out something in Italian or Romany or both about how she'd have no girl wearing pants in her wagon or some such thing and dropped a commanding finger at the dress, and Niko folded her arms and the old woman started shouting. Niko sat up in bed and shouted back in Yiddish. "My father is dead! You hear? He's dead, and he told me to cut my hair and burn my papers and call myself Niko, and you people may have saved my life, but you're not my father and you're not my mother either! I've done what my father told me since the day I left home, and *that* saved my life too, so I don't want to hear what a nice girl does or doesn't wear, *I want my pants!*" The old woman was looking at her with hard, shocked, angry eyes, and Niko's eyes blazed back at her. Gustav was staring at Niko, his mouth open, something oddly like joy in his face. The children were staring too. Marita stood in the doorway, her dark eyes bright. Then she was gone.

Marita came back with Niko's old pants, clean, off the line. Grandmother turned and left. Gustav left too. Marita gave Niko a long look, opened a drawer, and pulled out the long band of cloth Niko had used to wrap around her chest. Clean and folded. Her mouth fell open at the sight.

Marita smiled.

She was well. She was Niko. She walked on her crutches beside the wagons with Gustav, hearing the horses' harnesses jangle, breathing the cold clean air. She sat inside the wagons, rocking with their movement, playing with the children. "What's this?" she would ask in Italian. "*Cos' è?*" And Drina and little Mari would laugh and tell her, and she would repeat it and they would laugh again. She shared their mattress at night; Marita was their mother; Marita, with her deep black eyes and her loud laugh, who had showed her how to tie the cloth round her chest twice as tight as before. Marita who had saved her life.

When the wagons stopped, Marita would clap her hands and marshal her children: Gustav and the boys to go fetch firewood, Niko and the girls to chop potatoes, vegetables, anything—meat if they were lucky—into the big soup pot over the fire. And it was by Marita's campfire they sat when they were done, and warmed their feet and ate their fill. And people came and went around them, dozens of people old and young, sitting on folding chairs and logs and the ground, laughing and talking in Italian and Romany and both, interrupting each other, slapping each other on the back, their laughing faces lit by the fire. And then maybe someone would start singing. And the women would jump up and dance, fast and faster, graceful and wild. Sometimes they almost made Niko want to be a girl.

Chapter 17

End of the Line

Julien spent his first week in bed, burning and freezing, his throat raw as meat and almost as bloody. He'd never felt so awful in his life. He tossed and rolled through fever-dreams of white, crawling through snow toward lantern light that receded into the night. Then he was in his room again, Mama bending over him, saying, *Drink this.* Then he was gone again.

Then he was back. He woke, and blinked, and outside his window were huge clouds lit brilliant white against the blue of the sky, and he stared and stared at them. He was alive.

He spent his second week in bed getting very bored.

Mama said she was glad his fever had broken but he wasn't healed yet, and he was going to *stay put.* Benjamin brought him the homework from school and sat on his bed and helped with his math. Grandpa brought up a knife and some wood and started him carving a cat rolled into a ball. He carved, he did homework, he wrote to Vincent. He prayed.

Will you teach me? he'd said. As if he believed for a moment that

God would talk to him, that praying wasn't like sending a letter at all. Maybe God had been talking to him, in the snow, in the fire, in Pierre's face; maybe the storm was God's terrible speech, the warmth of the fire his love. But what was he saying now, in the blue bedspread, the white walls, day after day?

Still, there was something there. He wasn't eyeing God across the room anymore, like him and Benjamin the day he'd arrived, wondering what they could possibly have to say to each other. Now there was something to talk about.

He read the gospel of Matthew, then Mark. By the time he'd finished, he knew one thing: Jesus was cool. Wore himself out healing people and walked on water and wasn't afraid to say anything to anyone. All that yelling and flipping tables in the temple, and the next week they killed him—was that what they killed him for? Was that loving your enemies? Confronting them and not caring what they did to you? He'd imagined something . . . nicer. Not that Jesus couldn't do nice with sick little girls and all. He wondered if just anybody could do the yelling part, or if you had to be the Son of God.

He prayed, *Teach me*, still, like a letter, like renewing his application. He prayed for Pierre, that this time they'd actually end up friends, and for Henri, that . . . that anything. Whatever God had in mind. He didn't know.

By the third week in bed, Julien had run out of things to talk to God about. He'd finished his cat carving, he'd finished the Gospels, and he wanted out of this stupid bed. He told Mama this. She smiled. "Sounds like you're going to live."

Downstairs, Magali and Benjamin had their homework spread out by the fire. "Hello, long-lost brother!" said Magali. "What news?"

"What *news*? My walls are white, and there are four of them."

"How's the leg?"

He pulled up his pant cuff and showed the ankle. The network of angry, reddish-purple bruises had died down to faint dark-brown and yellow, fading away under the skin.

"Ew," said Magali.

"How 'bout you?"

Magali vented a long sigh. "Rosa's not talking to me. 'Cause according to her I like Lucy better. She could try letting *me* say who I like. You know what she said to me yesterday?"

"I thought she wasn't talking to you."

"Hush. She said, 'Go to–'"

"She *didn't!*"

"'*Go to Ireland!*'"

Julien and Benjamin burst out laughing. "It's not *funny*," said Magali. "I don't know what to *do!*"

"Can't you invite her to hang out with you and Lucy? Can't you all be friends?"

Magali shot him a look. "Oh, I forgot how much you know. Mister 'girls are *different* and that's why you have to help them.'"

"Oh," he said, his face warm, "shut up."

Roland came by and stood in the doorway, wiping his boots and looking awkward till Julien offered him a drink of Grandpa's strawberry *sirop*. They sat at the kitchen table, watching the reddish swirls of concentrate dissolve in their glasses, and began to talk. Julien told his story from start to finish; the story of how he'd learned that he could die. Roland was nodding soberly. "Heard your fight's off."

"Yeah."

"Speaking of . . . all that. I wanted to tell you." Roland looked out the window. "I feel stupid. About, you know, not hanging out with you in homeroom. It was . . . stupid."

Was stupid. Julien's heart lifted, just a little.

"Hey," he said. "Don't worry about it. Please."

And Roland smiled his shy, quirky smile.

On the night of the church Easter pageant, Julien stepped out of the house for the first time since his accident and breathed the fresh air deep into his lungs. It had that lightness, that tiny touch of warmth, and flocks of swallows flew round and round overhead, crying, black against the sunset. Spring had come when he wasn't looking.

"Julien Losier! Julien's back!" Gilles shook his hand and clapped him on the shoulder, Léon and Antoine wanted to see his leg, and then suddenly Pierre was there, grinning broadly, his eyes alight, shaking his hand with such a powerful grip it was all Julien could do to match it. "Hey, man. Long time. How *are* you?"

Julien laughed. "Fine. It's so good to be *outside*."

Inside the church, he sat for once not with his parents but with his—friends. Yes, friends. Roland and his family showed up as they were sitting down—his mother short and plump, his father thin and weathered with Roland's exact same crooked smile. And Louis, grinning. And they were together again—Roland and Louis and Julien and Benjamin. And Gilles. And Pierre. They sat together and watched the passion play, and Mama came on and sang "A *Toi la Gloire*," her voice rising pure and lovely as when she'd sung it the night the war began. Benjamin had come just to hear it, and who wouldn't? Maybe the Thibauds had too. "She's *good*," Gilles whispered. Pierre nodded. Julien grinned.

They made their way round the refreshments tables; Julien shook hands with half the church and told them he felt better and lifted his pant cuff to show his leg. Monsieur Thibaud shook Benjamin's hand and said he'd like to have them over for supper sometime, and Benjamin gave him his rare smile. Then the smile dropped as Monsieur Bernard's low voice cut through a lull in the conversation, speaking to Monsieur Moriot: "God loves Germans, God loves Poles, and a good *tanieusard* does too and invites them all to the big Tanieux party. Why keep anyone out? God even loves Hitler!" Henri beside him was nodding, a wry look on his face.

Benjamin was looking fixedly at the back of Monsieur Bernard's collar. Julien grabbed his shoulder and steered him firmly the other way. "D'you see they've got real hot chocolate over there?"

"Don't listen to that guy," Julien whispered to Benjamin as they got out of earshot. "Like father, like son. They wouldn't know God if he smacked them in the face." Benjamin's scowl split into a sudden, helpless grin. "You're crazy," he said.

The sun was shining the morning Julien went back to school. The sky was a pale, luminous blue, and the frozen earth in the schoolyard was mud again. On the tree were tiny buds, the merest dabs of yellow-green. The muddy yard was full and loud with boys. It was spring.

Julien walked in the gate and hesitated.

"Hey look, guys!" cried Gilles. "Julien Losier's back!"

The in-group of his class stood under their tree, its budding branches trembling a little in the breeze. He was being beckoned over. Roland was grinning, and Pierre. "Hey! How are ya!" He walked slowly toward them. Benjamin followed.

They greeted him warmly, shook his hand and Benjamin's; they wanted to know how he was, how was the leg. He showed it to them, the faintest traces of dark yellow under the skin. "Used to be this sort of glowing red and purple. There, and there. When it happened, I thought I'd broken it, I swear. It hurt that much. I thought there were bones sticking through the skin." He laughed. They were all looking at him.

"Well?" prompted Jérémie. "Then what did you do?"

"I kept walking. I had to. And then it started to hurt so much I passed out and fell. And then I started crawling." *I had to,* he almost said again, but he could see it in some of their eyes as they nodded soberly, that they knew what had looked him in the face. In their eyes was something like respect. He glowed.

They pressed Benjamin for his story, and he told it, looking a little surprised at being asked to speak. It sounded kind of harrowing, being out in the dark, searching for someone lost. "And then Pierre skied up to us and told us he was all right. He *didn't* tell us he'd mangled his ankle and was going to half die of fever," he added with a wry smile at Pierre, who grinned back.

"You wouldn't believe how I felt when he tripped over me out there," said Julien. "I swear, I thought he was Jesus."

"So you can imagine what he said when he saw it was me," Pierre tossed back with a straight face. Julien laughed. They all laughed. Except Henri Quatre.

The days grew warmer. The long rains of spring came, and the courtyard was pure mud, and the boys stood under the *préau* in little groups, looking out at the rain. The royal court broke up and shifted, without its tree; Julien stood in a corner with Gilles and Dominique, talking spring and soccer, or sat with Roland and Benjamin against the wall, reading one of Benjamin's books. Jean-Pierre talked math with Benjamin. Julien helped Pierre with his history.

Henri watched with stony eyes, and said nothing. Julien prayed for him. Or tried. Mostly, *You know what to do, I guess.*

Vincent wrote. He couldn't believe Julien had almost died. He wished something that exciting would happen to *him*. He was failing math, and he wished this Benjamin guy would come live with him, and honestly, if Benjamin had let Pierre copy a few things off his physics homework at the get-go, maybe there wouldn't have been so much trouble. Julien smiled crookedly and wrote back to Vincent that *that* would be the day and that it was weird having almost died; everyone was nicer to you. Almost everyone.

He sat with Benjamin at the dining-room table, doing homework; and Benjamin—Benjamin who had walked in here with his head so far down you had to talk to the tops of his glasses—looked across his homework at him just like a normal person. Like a friend. And they walked down to school together, and Julien's chest did not grow tighter with every step down the hill, and at the bottom of the hill, he waved and called to Roland and Louis.

The river rose under its stone bridge with the snowmelt and the rain, and the grass along its banks grew green and thick. The *genêt* bushes on the hills, once the only green against the pale dead grass, grew dark as the new growth outshone them, and the young leaves opened, and there were violets against the black stone schoolyard wall. They laid new lines out on the soccer field and gathered the teams. Julien convinced Benjamin to come watch the first game.

Henri's team won. By one goal.

The trumpeting music that began the nine o'clock news played in Julien's head during the day. Fighting in Norway, Denmark in defeat. The announcer's fruity voice made it sound far away, a story; but it wasn't. Mama stared at the radio; Papa ran his hands through his hair. They were waiting. Spring was the time for war, Papa said. At school, Pierre bragged on his brother André and his tank, his eyes a little too bright; they traded stories they'd heard about the Great War, the trenches. They wondered out loud how long it would last.

Julien sat at the table and listened to Papa's devotions: Joseph forgiving his brothers, saying at the end of his life that what they'd meant for evil, God had meant for good. "That's how I know I didn't invent God. A God I invented wouldn't let evil men have their way. The real God does. And works it for good. Lets it look like he's doing nothing—and comes through in the end. I believe this: he always has, and he always will come through, with good, in the end." *In the end. When's the end?* The clock began to chime nine o'clock, and Papa turned sharply toward it. In a moment, he was on his feet, switching the radio on.

The fanfare played, the look-at-me music; Julien settled back in his seat, rubbed his finger on the smooth wood of the table as the announcer said the usual words in the usual tone. The tape cut like a fracture to the same voice, its fruitiness gone, speaking quickly with an undertone of fear. "Dramatic developments. Since yesterday, German troops have been pushing deep into both Holland and Belgium, in complete violation of these countries' neutrality." Julien looked up, his eyes wide. Holland. Belgium. His father's hands were gripping the edge of the table, hard.

"German tanks and infantry have met heroic resistance from the Dutch army. The Dutch and the Belgian governments have dropped their efforts to stay neutral in this war and have called for help from British and French troops to push back the Nazi tyrant." They were straining toward the radio. The *boches* were bombing Holland and dropping paratroopers everywhere; an "impregnable" fort in Belgium had been taken in less than a day. *Holland*, whispered Julien's mind. *Belgium. They're coming here.*

"There are unconfirmed reports tonight," said the announcer more slowly, "of a strong push by several divisions of German tanks onto French soil. They are reported to have crossed the Ardennes hills," he said, "bypassing the end of the Maginot Line."

Time stopped as they sat staring at each other. The room became vivid, suddenly, the shadows sharp-edged: the dents and scars in the smooth golden pine of the table were etched into Julien's eyes as he stared. It had come. The lamplight bloomed like a rare, precious flower, and the faces around the table, the faces of the people he loved, in that wide-eyed moment filled with fearful beauty. The sound in his head echoed above the stumbling voice of the radio, a high, buzzing echo speaking the words again and again. *The end of the Maginot Line. The end of the Maginot Line.*

His mother's face was white and frozen, her hands knit together, the knuckles pale. Julien looked at Papa. He would go and comfort her now. He always did.

But he didn't. His face was buried in his hands.

Chapter 18

Stones

The wagons were stopping, but it was before mid morning. The children were excited, jumping up and down and looking out the windows, calling out "Sondrio! Sondrio!" They saw a stream and a little wood, and a town in the distance. It was lovely.

Marita stepped out of the wagon and looked around with an air of great pleasure and set to work. Before five minutes were gone, she'd laid a fire, strung a clothesline between two trees, and was sorting through an enormous pile of laundry. Niko had enough Italian now to understand her when she called to them: "Gustav! Niko! Go into town for me, would you, and tell me what you see?"

"Yes, Marita," called Niko. "What . . . uh . . . do we see?"

"If the people are friendly. The children like this campsite. I hope that we can stay. Here, take some bread. Be back by noon. Go!"

They took the path to town slowly. The sun was shining, and the air was light, almost warm; the wheat fields were furred with pale green shoots against the dark earth. They were walking a road together with the sun on their shoulders, neither cold nor hungry nor afraid. They walked, saying nothing. Happy. They sat on the edge of the road and ate, and then went on.

They came to a country lane between farmhouses. Children squatted on the dusty ground playing with apricot stones. A bright-eyed boy, a kid with an apricot stone in his hand, looked up at the strangers, pointed, and yelled.

And then threw the stone.

It hit Niko on the arm and stung like a bee, and she stared at the boy. Bright black eyes full of anger and scorn—the children were all shouting, another stone hit her. "Let's get out of here," muttered Gustav, and Niko turned, swung her crutches out and ran. An apricot pit bit the back of her neck. *You got her*, she thought bitterly. *Happy, Friedrich? You've got apprentices.*

Children. Boys. Even Friedrich. Evil boys become evil men. *Why do you let them?*

"Even here," she said bitterly.

"They got no idea we're Jewish, Niko. Don't you know that word? *Zingaros?*"

She looked up sharply. She hadn't caught it. "Gypsies?" she said. "Gustav—Marita—go back and warn them, *run!*"

"I'm not leaving you, Ni— Niko—"

"Then *keep up!*" She swung her crutches and began to run, fast. And she could run—Friedrich hadn't taken that from her—she could run in the dark, crashing through the woods, evil behind her, always, always there . . . As she turned the last corner, out of breath, a sharp stitch in her side, she saw that she was too late.

The clothesline was broken, a pair of pants still hanging from it; underneath, a white shirt trampled in the dirt. Cook fires smoldering, a black pot lying on its side. Where the wagons had been, deep wheel-ruts in the mud. She could see it—the women ripping laundry off the lines, snatching up their children, the men whipping the wild-eyed horses into a gallop, pulling out just in time ahead of—What? Who? Had they come with guns? Oh Marita.

Marita standing at the wagon's window, grief in her eyes, looking back at the town. Where she had lost two children. And they had lost her.

And everything. This time. They had nothing but the clothes on their backs; not even food.

It was so quiet here.

Marita's voice singing in Romany, shouting orders to her children—never again. She mustn't let Gustav see her cry.

"Nina. It'll be okay. Look, there's some soup in this pot that didn't all spill—there's pants, and a shirt, and I bet there's a blanket or two if we look around, and it's almost spring, Nina—"

"Niko," she said harshly, and covered her mouth with her hand. She sank down on the ground, shaking her head, her throat tight with tears.

"Niko," whispered Gustav. "We can make it, Niko." He knelt by her, looking into her face. "We can do it again, like in the mountains. I'll work at farms, and if I can't find work, we'll steal milk and eggs, and God will forgive us because we're hungry. And then we'll find a town—I'll find another house like in Trento. We'll make it. We'll make a life for ourselves, Niko."

She looked at him, and saw that he believed it.

Chapter 19

The Time for War

"What happened to our army, Papa?" Julien asked. "We had the strongest army in Europe, didn't we?"

"One of the strongest, Julien." Papa leaned his head on his hands. "We still do. They're just–it's–war's all about position, Julien." He shook his head. "They did something we didn't expect, that's all."

Something we didn't expect? That was what it came down to?

Julien said nothing. Papa didn't look up.

The *boches* were in France, the radio said. They had made it through the Ardennes, five divisions or more: tanks. Papa went pale at the number. Half the army was stuck in Belgium behind the *boche* lines, up where they'd thought the fighting would be. They hadn't put troops to defend the Ardennes, Papa said, because they were supposed to be impassable.

Apparently the *boches* didn't know that.

They kept the radio on all the time now. It was all news, spoken breathlessly, no more pompous voice. The *boches* were dropping bombs and paratroopers all over the Low Countries; it was called *blitzkrieg*. The *boches* had bombed Rotterdam and killed thirty thousand civilians. Holland had surrendered. The *boches* had crossed the Meuse and were plowing west, and the radio kept saying some division or other had fought heroically against incredible odds and gotten rolled right over.

Where *was* everybody? Where was the army? Julien knew where the army was: in Belgium and on the stupid Maginot Line where the stupid, *stupid* generals had put them all; how did something like this *happen*? He lay awake in bed, his blood beating in his temples, not believing it. They had this entire army, and none of them were in the right place, none of them were in the *way*.

At school it was like a dream, a dream of another place and time where there was war and it was going badly, and people gathered and talked about it in tense voices. It was like being underwater, the tightness in his chest, his heart beating fast for the moment he'd break out through the surface and breathe.

Henri got down on his hands and knees under the schoolyard tree and traced a map of France in the dirt. "Here, see? There's Sedan. There's Dinant. They're here now. Here's Paris but they're not going for it, see, they're going due west, heading for the coast. Here's Cambrai and Saint-Quentin. There's a river in front of 'em; you always try to stop 'em at a river because it gives you a defensive position." He drew a snaky line in the dirt.

"That's the Oise," said Julien. "It goes into the Seine west of Paris; I've been there."

Henri glanced at him. "See this?" He slashed a line in the dirt in front of Saint-Quentin. "Paper says we've got a division of tanks right there. They'll hold them up. And see how we've got people *here* and *here*?" He stabbed his stick at the Maginot Line, and then at northern Belgium. "See, if we can move fast enough, it's called a pincer movement—" two strong slashes toward the German line, cutting it in half. "And we cut 'em off. See?" He lifted his head, his blue eyes glinting. "You can bet that's what the High Command is working on right now. Of course they wouldn't say so on the radio."

Julien nodded, saw the other heads nodding around him; his mouth was open, breathing in hope. Henri's teeth met in a fierce grin.

In two days the Germans had crossed the Oise.

By May 22, the *boches* had reached the sea. It was on the morning news as Julien left for school; they held the entire northern tip of France. The guys stood under the tree, hands in their pockets, looking down at the dirt map at their feet.

There it lay, their country, like a five-pointed star; a pebble for Paris, a bark chip for Tanieux deep in the south. Quietly, with one finger, Roland traced the last of the German advance: a complete arc to the English Channel, a fault line. Like a star with one point broken off; that was all they held, just that far-north tip. But half the army was trapped behind it. And in front of it lay Paris. Julien breathed in, deep and slow, looking at his country and understanding the truth: this was really happening, after all.

It was a May like none he'd ever known. Blue sky, new leaves unfolding in the sun, flowers bright in the gardens, war maps in the dirt. And in the evening around the radio, lamplight and the smell of fear. Papa's face with the lines in it, carving deeper as he listened; Mama sitting like white stone. Benjamin not looking at anyone, not willing to leave the radio even to study. Listening desperately for hope.

They'd stopped talking about it, at the table or any time. They talked about other things in brittle voices, and no one was fooled. One morning Julien came down the stairs and froze in front of the stairwell door, hearing his mother's voice on the other side, high and brittle and scared. "And they were shooting—they were shooting—there was blood in the water—there were *children*—"

"Sh, Maria. Sh. It was a dream."

"Thirty thousand people, Martin—*thirty thousand*—"

He slipped back up the stairs.

That night, Papa beckoned Magali and Julien into his study while Mama cleared the table, and asked them quietly not to discuss the war in front of her or turn on the radio when she was there. They nodded. "I don't know what's going to happen. But . . ." Papa looked down, shaking his head. After a moment he looked up at Julien. "I've got to be strong now for your mother. And you, I think, for Benjamin." Magali was looking down at her knees. Julien looked up and nodded, trying to see his father through the pictures in his head: tanks on the Champs-Elysées. Tanks in the Rue Bernier, under Vincent's window.

"Has Benjamin talked to you—" Papa started, and Julien said, "No." *Are you kidding?* As soon as Papa switched off the radio, Benjamin always went up to his room and shut the door.

"Do what you can for him, Julien. I don't know what we *can* do . . ." He shook his head. "It must be awful." His voice cracked. "His parents, Giovanni . . ."

An image hung in Julien's mind, the same image that had appeared to him so vividly the night the war had begun: a kitchen sink full of dirty dishes, strewn with shattered glass and shrapnel. The scrape of glass shards against sink enamel; he could feel it in the back of his neck.

There was a long silence.

"Papa," said Magali in a small voice, "have we lost?"

"No, Lili," Papa whispered without looking up. "But we will."

Julien and his classmates stood in the schoolyard, a crowd of boys with whispers moving through it like wind in the woods. Monsieur Astier raised his megaphone. Silence fell.

"You don't need me to tell you," the principal's deep voice began, "what is going on in the north. I think it safe to say that for all of us now, facing this emergency is our priority. That is why," he said, "we are closing school early this year."

Astier raised a hand for silence. School would end on Saturday, he said. They were to try to concentrate until then; to learn was to believe in the future. Were there any questions? A hand shot up in the front, and Henri's firm voice asked whether school would open again in the fall.

Si Dieu le veut. God willing.

Julien felt strange—strangely empty, strangely free, like a boat cut loose and floating. They all felt it; it was in the air, in the eyes all around him. Fear, exhilaration, the ground fallen out from under their feet. They'd sat in classrooms listening; they'd eaten and slept and played soccer; and all this time the world had been changing under them. Even as they made their maps, tried to make sense of things as best they could, the walls of the world they knew had crumbled around them. Now anything could happen.

He sat—they all sat—in classroom after classroom for the rest of that day and heard not a word the teachers said.

Benjamin sat through supper, looking at his plate. Not even pretending to eat. When Mama stood to clear the table, he looked up and spoke.

"I can't wait till Saturday. I'm leaving for Paris tomorrow. Can I leave my books and winter clothes here?"

For a moment no one moved. Then Mama put down her plate and said flatly, "No. You cannot go to Paris. The Germans could be there before you."

"I know," said Benjamin in a low voice, "but I've got to try."

"I guess you've been thinking about this for a while," said Papa carefully. "Tell me how you're going to do this."

"Catch the morning train to Saint-Etienne. Find out what's running north."

"How do you know there's anything running north?" Papa asked.

"They haven't shut down all the trains!"

"You don't know that any more than I do." Papa's voice was firmer now. "There may be a few running–troop transports. You might get as far as Lyon. Maybe even Dijon. After that . . ."

"I've got to try," said Benjamin, looking at the wall behind Papa.

"And when the trains won't take you any farther, then walk? The Germans are bound to beat you there at that rate. And when you get there?"

Julien held his breath. Papa was looking Benjamin straight in the eye.

Finally Benjamin dropped his head. "I don't know, sir. But I've got to try. Don't I have to try?" He looked up, as if pleading for Papa to agree.

"What would your parents tell you to do?" Papa asked.

"Stay." Benjamin's voice was a hoarse whisper.

"Then stay," said Papa. "Try to think. What happens if they've already left Paris? What happens when they send word for you to join them somewhere else, and I have to say, 'He left for Paris'? How could I face your father if I let that happen?"

Benjamin stared at his plate. Picked up his fork, put it down again. He looked up at Mama. "May I be excused? I'm sorry–it's good–I'm just not hungry."

"Of course," said Mama, giving Benjamin a long look.

"Wait." Papa laid his hand on Benjamin's arm. "I want to hear you say you're not leaving tomorrow."

"I'm not leaving tomorrow," Benjamin said in a low voice.

Julien saw Papa's hand tighten on Benjamin's arm. "Believe me. It's the best thing you could do for them."

"Right," said Benjamin, and got to his feet.

When he was gone, Papa sat back, shaking his head, and murmured, "Lord preserve us." His hands on the table in front of him were clenched, one inside the other. "Did you–have any idea about this, Julien?"

"He hasn't said two words to me all week," Julien said, suddenly beginning to breathe again.

"Look out for him, Julien. Please. If you can." Papa pressed his hands against his eyes. Julien shivered, although it was not cold.

In the morning when Mama sent Julien down for the bread, the door of the little *boulangerie* was locked. A handwritten sign on the door said, No Flour, and underneath that, Shipment Delayed, and underneath that, each word underlined by a forceful hand, That's All We Know. Julien couldn't help but smile.

But when he looked again, the smile dropped. Through the window, he could see the bread racks, tall metal baskets with open fronts that covered the whole back wall of the *boulangerie*. Every morning, those racks were filled with loaves, bushels of tall brown and golden loaves stacked upright and leaning, a whole golden wall of bread. But not today.

Today that wall was completely bare. The racks hung like empty cages, and the chipped white paint behind showed through. He had never seen them empty. They looked so strange.

Chapter 20
Wrong

Gustav looked around the convent courtyard. Chimney smoke rose in the morning air; sheets billowed on the clotheslines in the warm spring wind, shining pure white against the sky. Workmen repairing the courtyard wall joked with the nuns as they passed by.

Maybe his luck was changing.

He had been scared, these last two weeks. Turned away from one farm, then another. After a day without food, he'd stolen three eggs from a henhouse and almost been caught by the most savage farm dog he'd ever seen. Then it started raining. He'd found Niko a goat shed outside Menaggio; but he could find no work.

He'd been begging in front of the church when the nun had found him. Sister Theresa. She'd promised a hot meal at the least for him and his brother, and maybe she could talk to the Mother Superior and see about more.

A convent. Niko was smiling. It was beautiful to see.

Sister Theresa vanished into the broad stone building. Another nun lugged a bucket of water across the yard; a second brought out a chair and beckoned Gustav to sit down.

"I cut your hair," she told him. "Mother Superior doesn't want *pidocchi*." She scratched her head, and he laughed.

"But *signorina*, I will miss them. The *pidocchi* and I, we have been friends for so long!"

She laughed, throwing her head back. She pulled off his shirt and began to cut; the scissors were cold against his head. Niko sat on the bench, gazing at the blossoming trees. Gustav's bare head was wiped with a rag that smelled of turpentine, and stung. This Mother Superior knew what she didn't want, all right.

The other nun took Gustav's hand and led him to a shed with a tub of water in it, soap, and clean folded clothes. He went in and shut the door and began to undress.

He was just putting his foot in the water when he heard the scream.

He lunged for the door, fell back, and jerked his pants on, grabbed the handle, and bashed his head against the door. He turned the handle one way, the other way, jerking the door back and forward—it was locked. Locked! He pounded on it, yelling, but there were so many voices crying outside—a flurry of shouts, Nina's voice rising in shrill, panicked Yiddish—"Get your hands off me, get your hands off me, *no!*" *Oh no, Nina.*

They took off her shirt.

He was screaming, pounding on the door, but no one heard him. *I didn't think—why didn't I think—they took off her shirt, in front of the men*—he could hear through his cries a loud voice shouting orders, and Nina's high-pitched sobs. He pounded till the door shook on its hinges. But no one came.

Outside, the shouting died into silence.

Niko lay in the dark, weeping.

She had thrown herself at the door and shaken it, but it hadn't budged. She had beaten on the shutters, run her fingers over the walls for a light switch, but there was none; she had found the bowl of soup on the desk and thrown it against the wall. She had slumped on the floor, wanting to scream, wanting to rip her fingernails into that woman's face. They had tied her up, tied her to a chair and shaved her head, they had locked her in the dark, and all without a word to her, like an animal, like a—she knew, she knew what they thought—

Crazy.

Crazy, said Uncle Yakov. *Nina, your father has never been the most sensible of men, and I think you know that; but now he is very, very sick. He's not thinking right.*

She screamed.

Long and loud. The shrieks of the insane cripple, echoing through the convent halls. What would they do with her? What had they done with Gustav? He was gone—gone—she was alone in the dark and everyone was gone. Father had run on ahead of her in the dark woods and would not turn back for her no matter how she called—*Oh, Father, Father, come back!*

A harsh sob tore from her throat, then another, and another; her whole body shook; her fingers clawed at the stone floor; she convulsed. *I did everything—everything—I kept my promise, Father, I did everything you said and WHERE ARE YOU?* The white heat of anger shook her, and she screamed at him, her father whom she'd loved, who had shrunk down to nothing in his bed and died, and left her; and left her nothing but orders. *How dare you, Father, how* dare *you leave me alone!*

She hit the stone wall with her closed fist and hit it again and again till her knuckles began to bleed. But he did not come.

She had lain in the dark for hours, her fingers feeling her bare scalp, her mind wandering a dark maze. Father. Uncle Yakov. Herr. Alone in the dark on the border, under pine trees tall and black as fear.

Uncle Yakov's voice saying *madness, Nina, madness.* She hissed aloud, *It's Niko,* then fell, her face against the ground, dry sobs shaking her chest, because she knew he was right. He was right and she was wrong, Father was wrong: there was no escape—the world would eat her and all the innocent, the trusting, the fools—and everywhere there were evil men. She should have listened to Uncle Yakov.

She had never tasted any thought so bitter.

I listened to my father. That's why I'm here.

The door scraped as it opened. Bright light hurt her eyes. A figure stood dark against it, holding a bowl in a hand that shook, and set it on the desk. The door shut, the key turned in the lock. Niko lay on her bare mattress, looking up at it; a hot bowl of soup, white steam rising into the thin lines of light the shutters let in. She did not move. After three days, you didn't feel it anymore, the hunger. She hadn't been even one day in the dark yet, but already she knew.

After three days in the dark, she wouldn't feel anything anymore. She would be gone. Like him. Like her mother. Gone.

A dark silhouette stood against the light in the doorway: a nun. She stood; not shaking, not turning to leave. Looking at Niko. Sister Theresa from the marketplace, who had promised them soup and a bed.

Slowly Niko stood, and looked back into Theresa's steady eyes. She felt something give in her chest; her mouth opened. *You do not think I am an animal. Sister. Do you?*

Non sono . . . she didn't know the word for crazy. The word for sane. She didn't know.

She stood a long moment; then with her hand, she touched the bowl on the desk. *Zuppa,* she said. Soup. She pointed to the mattress and said *letto.* She touched the door, said *porta.* Then she looked Theresa in the eye and said *luce.* Light. "*Per favore. Luce.*"

"*Non sei pazza,*" said Theresa. "*Vado a chidere.*" Ask, that meant. *I will ask.* "*Vado a chidere luce.*"

And Theresa set the bowl on the desk, looked at Niko and stepped out the door. It swung shut behind her, and Niko heard the key turn in the lock.

She waited for hours. But no light came.

Chapter 21

The Straight Path

The teachers didn't even try to teach the last three days. Nobody would have listened.

The *boches* were sitting on the Somme River; the troops in Belgium were trying to evacuate to England. That was all they knew. Julien's class stood under the tree, looking at their little map in the dirt, and said nothing. On Saturday Henri knelt and erased it, carefully.

They walked out the gate, all of them quiet, all of them glancing back. Their school looked strange and empty and small as they crossed the bridge; the world around them was widening. The sky hung huge above the hills as they stepped out into their new life.

He didn't know what to do. He tried going into town, to see if any of the guys were around. He met Gilles and Lucien on a street corner, but the second time Lucien said, "We'll drive those *boches* out yet," in a tone of brittle insistence, Julien lost it. "You know my father?" he said, leaning in. "The history prof? You know what he says? 'We haven't lost yet, but we will.'"

That was the end of *that*.

At home, Mama was weeding the kitchen garden in the yard where he used to kick his soccer ball. "Want help, Mama?"

"This is my work. Find your own."

He tried. He pulled Benjamin off the radio and went down to the farm, but Grandpa didn't want them. They stood in the garden, a vast spread of dark tilled earth and green shoots, and Grandpa took off his hat and wiped his forehead and said he couldn't train them. This growing season was too important, what with the prices and the war. "Sylvain and Jean-Luc have worked for me for years; they know exactly what they're doing"—the two men moved down the rows using short-handled hoes as if they were their own hands—"and they're what I need for now. Come back in a month when we start picking. For now—" He glanced up at the hills. "Go walking. Get to know the hills. Could come in handy."

Benjamin looked up for the first time.

That evening, Grandpa walked with them and showed them how to find food. Dandelion leaves for salad and roots for coffee; wild thyme and mint and marjoram; nettles—stinging nettles—for soup. One of the most nourishing plants there was, he said, smiling at the looks on their faces. They weren't going to waste any of what God had put out there for them. Not this year.

There was no bread. Breakfast was potatoes. Lunch was potatoes and cheese. There was no sugar. There'd been meat only on Sundays for months, and this week it was a beef bone in the leek soup. "I'm sorry—" Mama started. Papa cut in, "You will absolutely not apologize for this soup, Maria. Nor for the prices, nor for the war."

Julien and Benjamin walked. Belgium had surrendered unconditionally. The *boches* were coming. They didn't talk about it. They knelt in pastures between *genêts* in golden bloom and grubbed up dandelions, and Julien watched Benjamin get dirt under his fingernails and on his shiny leather shoes. He watched Benjamin pull on gloves and step carefully into a ditch, and grasp his first nettle, and pull till it came up by the roots. He stuffed it whole into his bag.

"Um," said Julien, "we're supposed to get just the young leaves?"

"We're not wasting anything," said Benjamin.

Julien stood at the crest of the hill, the *genêts* blazing yellow around him, and wondered when a letter would reach Paris if he sent it now. Whether it ever would. The white clouds raced through the blue, and the hills sang with bloom, and he thought of the Rue Bernier, and the park, and Vincent; the way he'd look now, sixteen years old and thinner, a fire in his dark eyes. *We'll drive those* boches *out yet.*

Julien stuck his hands deep in his pockets and watched the cloud shadows flow over his hills.

He didn't know what had happened to him. The chestnuts were in bloom, their long feathery flowers spreading like a pale yellow dust over the distant treetops; his eyes traced the thousand greens of those woods, the dark chestnut leaves and the deep green of scrub pines, the vivid leaves of the oaks and the light, living green of pasture. And everywhere the *genêts*, the dark, dull, tough *genêts* covered in gold.

He'd learned somewhere, and he didn't know where, to love this. The curve of the hill that lay behind Grandpa's farm—he loved it, and the low mountains in the distance, and the high wooded ridge that hid the road north and stood like a bluff above the Tanne. And the flash of the Tanne itself, down below, the river that had flowed there when his grandfather was a child. It would flow there still, singing the same liquid music to itself, when all of them were gone, and he was glad.

They walked the north road beside the train tracks at the foot of the ridge; they walked east where the hills grew low and rolling.

They followed trails into the woods and dirt roads between pastures fenced with black stone walls. They were hungry. Mama packed them potatoes with no butter, and they wolfed them down as if they had never tasted food before, and they were wonderful. But not enough. They walked, feeling the unfamiliar edge of hunger in their bellies.

In the evening, it was still the same: the radio, the cluster of faces around it. In the daytime, there was peace somehow—in the green of the land, in the strength of his legs, in the mass and solidity of the hills they climbed. But in bed at night, Julien tried fumblingly to pray and found no words. What did God have to do with German tanks overrunning the earth, with bombers pounding Rotterdam to blood and fire? What did God have to do with the blitzkrieg?

He didn't know.

He crept downstairs in the dark, wishing there was something, anything, he could eat. Wishing for warm milk to help him sleep; milk that he'd taken for granted in the old days, when there was enough.

There was candlelight in the kitchen, and Mama, a cup in her hand and her back to the door. She turned.

"Mama," he whispered, "I can't sleep."

She nodded.

"Is there—anything I can have?"

"Sit down," she whispered. "I'll make you chamomile."

He sat. Her Bible lay open on the table, in the wood-and-canvas cover he had made. The page it was open to was torn. He looked into the candle flame.

"Mama?" he whispered finally. "What was it like? The . . . other war?"

Mama looked at him, her face half in shadow. She put his cup of tea on the table and sat by him. "What do you want to know?"

He took the cup, hot against his fingers. It would warm his stomach. Fool it awhile. "Were you . . . were you hungry?"

She was looking straight ahead. She was looking at the candle as if it was the last light on earth. "Yes. Your grandmother. Your grandmother died of hunger."

He stared at her. She did not look at him.

"They took our goats. We hid the best three, but they found them—they were hungry too—but they had guns. Julien." He could feel her shaking. "Julien. I'm sorry. I can't talk about this." Her voice had lowered. "I pray you'll never understand."

They sat for a long time, watching the candle quiver in the dark. Listening to her breathing grow slower. "I've never been back," she murmured. "It was so quiet. Without Mamma singing."

She looked at him, and her mouth lifted in the ghost of a smile. "She sang off-key," she said.

They walked south. Benjamin suggested it. Benjamin, who never spoke.

Benjamin wanted to make a map. They found a slate and some chalk and traced the roads they'd walked. Julien marked where they found nettles or blackberry brambles. Benjamin traced the south farm track and its lanes and the roads to Le Puy and the Rhône Valley, a full morning's walk south. He marked the field near that same crossroads, where they found the bees.

A whole field of white clover, buzzing, alive with them; and in the woods behind, a dead tree golden with promise. He could taste it already. That feeling of sweet fullness after a meal, of having eaten *dessert*—he'd almost forgotten what it was like.

"Monday," he said. Benjamin nodded and almost smiled.

That night there was news, finally. The Germans had captured forty thousand French troops at Dunkerque, and they were on the move again. Headed south.

Then the power went out.

"Though an army lay siege to me, my heart will not fear," read Pastor Alex. Everyone was listening. "Though war break out against me, I am still filled with confidence." *And if they're bombing Paris right now?* "How could David be confident?" asked Pastor Alex. He described David's situation. He could have been describing theirs. Every eye in the room was on him. Julien saw Monsieur Bernard in the next pew, his face still as stone, tightening ever so slightly when Pastor Alex used the word *defeat*, the word *refugee*.

"This man can speak to us," Pastor Alex said. "Let us listen."

Julien listened. David wanted only one thing in his defeat, Pastor Alex said. Only one, but he had to have it. "He wanted God. 'Do not abandon me, do not hide your face from me.' In God, he says, he has a light, a stronghold, a shelter. If God is with him, he says, 'I will not be afraid.'"

Not afraid. Were Mama and Papa afraid, was Pastor Alex afraid? Was God with them?

"Show me the road you want me to go," read Pastor Alex. "Lead me along the straight path." Then he leaned forward in his pulpit and paused. A hush fell over the crowd.

"Friends," he said, "we know what is happening. The time has come to say it. France is defeated." The words fell slow and heavy. "The straight path is to walk, without closing our eyes, into this defeat. To know that the presence of God is not, for all this, taken away from us unless we choose to despair of him. To ask him to show us the road he wants us to go—now—" He said the next three words in a slow and level voice: "under German occupation."

Julien opened his mouth, and tears were in his eyes. His parents were holding each other. Benjamin had his head down. Julien put an arm over his friend's shoulder and sat looking up at the pulpit, the tears running down his face, grieving for his country.

Pastor Alex came that night to talk to them.

"I wish I had spoken about this sooner. I'm sorry. I didn't expect all this." *Really.* "We all know the Germans will probably be here before the end of June. What–what do you know? About the Nazis? And . . . the Jews?"

"I know there's persecution," said Papa. "I know there's prejudice–maybe hatred."

"Hatred. Yes. Listen. I have relatives in Germany. I traveled there before the war, while Hitler's power was rising. Martin, Maria, hatred is a mild way of putting it." He looked down at his hands, which were clasping each other tightly. "I believe that if the Nazis could find a way to make people accept it, they would kill them all." He swallowed. "I believe it is very dangerous now to be a Jew in Germany. And soon . . ." He looked at them.

"Germany will come here," Papa finished.

"Yes. It would be best if very few people knew that Benjamin is a Jew."

"It's a little late for that," said Papa quietly.

Julien and Benjamin carried coals in a pot, feeding them with twigs, a full half-day's walk to where the bee tree was. They carried a hatchet and the two biggest buckets they could find.

They lit a fire under the tree, a small one, the ground around it cleared. When it was big enough, they threw wet leaf mould onto it and blew the thick gray smoke into the tree. The many-voiced hum of the bees rose to a massed and angry buzz. Bees boiled out of the top of the tree; Julien grasped his hatchet in both hands and struck.

Once. Twice. The third time, a great rotten piece of wood came away, and honeycomb came with it.

The rest was mad and sticky and golden; there was honey on their gloves and honey on their shirts; and in the buckets, there was beautiful, beautiful honeycomb to the brim; and they were licking it off their dirty gloves and laughing as they ran. They got to the road and looked back, and Julien held his bucket up and whooped. Benjamin's face was smudged with black, and there was a bee sting by his eye; there were two on Julien's neck and one on his stomach, and the boys were grinning wildly at each other.

The sun was setting by the time they made it home, tired, dirty, and very happy. They were late for supper. They didn't care.

When they opened the door, they stopped. The power was on. No lights. But everyone huddled tightly around the radio.

They set the buckets among the dirty dishes on the table. No one turned to greet them. They began to take in what the newsreader was saying.

Thousands upon thousands of refugees choking the roads of France. The Germans were headed straight for Paris. Every soldier France still had was being rushed to stop them, but there was no hope. The government, from the prime minister on down, had fled south. Military sources said it was inevitable. Paris would fall.

The buckets sat forgotten on the table. Papa's Bible lay forgotten on his lap. No one moved or spoke. They sat in silence, while outside the open window, the evening sky darkened slowly into night.

Chapter 22

Gate

Gustav stood by the convent wall, waiting for his sister. For Niko.

He *hated* calling her Niko. Nina was his fierce-eyed sister, who had walked home one day on a shattered leg, her teeth gritted, not a single tear in her eyes. Who had said so fiercely, "We have to do everything he told us." Who had made him cut her hair. But Niko—Niko was this strange, new, sad person. Niko was someone who lay on the floor with empty eyes, looking at something he could not see. Something that was eating her. Ever since the border. He knew. But he couldn't make it stop.

They never talked about that night. He hated it. Hated that there was nothing he could do.

He'd tried so hard. He'd learned to split wood, milk goats; he'd learned rough Italian and the alleys of Trento to get food for her. He'd tried so hard to make her laugh. She'd laughed. Sometimes. And with the Gypsies, she'd been almost herself. But he'd never imagined *this*.

"Gustav," Sister Theresa had told him, "you have to get your brother out of here. I went to Mother Superior about it, I told her I don't believe he's crazy—just frightened—but she wouldn't listen. She keeps saying she saw with her own eyes—Gustav, she's written to the bishop about sending him to some kind of 'home'—I don't know . . ."

He knew. He knew he had to get her out now.

They were letting her out once a day for a couple of hours; Sister Theresa had gotten that much. Soon. If they let her out soon enough, her chance was sitting in the driveway.

A delivery truck. Men unloading it, manhandling huge sacks of flour through the double kitchen doors. A truck that would be driving out the convent gate when it was done.

The far door opened, her door. He heard the click of her crutches on the stones. He stood waiting as she walked toward him, and when she reached him, he looked her in the eye. "Niko," he said quietly, "do you want to get out of here? Now?"

She took a deep breath, standing a little taller. "Yes," she said.

Niko woke when the truck stopped, her cheek on a hard bag of flour, her mouth open. It was almost pitch dark.

"Got your crutches?"

"Ready."

He was peering out the tiny, side window. Beneath her, she felt the engine cut out.

"Now," said Gustav. She heard him slide to the back and open the door. In the red glow of the taillights, she slid forward between the flour bags, set her crutches on the ground and swung down. Cold air met her. "Behind that rubbish heap," whispered Gustav, and she followed him, quietly—they heard voices ahead, people standing far off in the light of the headlights, a low square building with lit windows—she ducked behind the heap and breathed quietly in the dark.

The sound of the engine again, the truck moving off toward the building. Then voices in Italian, the thump of the huge flour bags being unloaded. She looked around, but it was deep dark. Thick clouds hid the moon. Then the truck was coming back, and in the light of the headlights, she saw it and cried out. Gustav jumped to his feet as he saw it too: a tall gate swinging open, framed by high, chain-link fence topped with razor wire. In the red glow of the taillights they saw it swing shut; closed by two uniformed men.

Gustav sank to his knees. "Oh, Niko," he whispered.

Niko said nothing. There was nothing to say.

Chapter 23

What They're Like

When Julien woke, he had a moment of peace, watching the sunlight sift through his white curtains, before he remembered Paris.

He knelt by his bed and tried to pray, but he had no words. Only pictures, only memories and names: Vincent and his sisters, Uncle Giovanni and Aunt Nadine; the Kellers; his friends, Renaud and Mathieu and Gaëtan. He knelt and said nothing, thought nothing, felt nothing, only saw them. He hoped God understood.

For breakfast, there was real bread with honey. He had never tasted anything so good in his life. They ate ravenously. The power was out again. None of them spoke.

Benjamin went up to his room, and Julien walked alone. He walked between pastures, between brambles thick with hard green blackberries, not seeing the hills. Green as they were, and solid, they could not change news from the north.

They were probably bombing right now.

Papa had a new radio someone had given him. A shortwave. Benjamin and Julien helped him carry it into his study to hide it from Mama. He said he wanted the BBC.

"You boys know what really happened up on the Belgian coast?"

He knew. He knew the *boches* had captured forty thousand French soldiers.

"Three hundred forty thousand of our guys got away, that's what."

Julien blinked. "To where?"

"England. Don't look at me like that. They're still free. As long as England stands, there's a chance for us." He told them the story: the troops huddled on the beach like the Israelites by the Red Sea, the boats on the horizon. Every boat England had: yachts, fishing boats, rowboats. And the rear guard holding the Germans off—the rear guard, who would go down in history too. Papa swallowed. "Um. Benjamin. Something I've been meaning to tell you. No, stay, Julien."

Benjamin's eyes were on the floor.

"Benjamin. Look up. Benjamin, Maria and I want you to know that we consider you part of our family. We're counting on your staying here for the summer and the next school year and as long as you need."

Benjamin swallowed, looked at the window, at Julien, at the history books on Papa's shelf. He swallowed again. "But. But I can't pay my room and board. There's no word from my parents and I don't know when they'll be able to send money. I've been saving what's left of my allowance but it's not nearly—" Papa was shaking his head.

"No, Benjamin. That's what I mean when I say you are part of the family," he said firmly. "We don't ask Julien for room and board, and we will not ask you either."

"But . . . but it's not fair to you. You're *hungry*—"

"Benjamin. Look at me, please." Papa's voice was commanding.

"If we are hungry, we will be hungry together. But until your parents are able to take you back in peace and safety, you are staying. Please tell me you understand that."

Papa and Benjamin stared at each other, a very long moment.

"Yes, sir," said Benjamin, and lowered his eyes.

Thursday the power came back on. They sat in the living room, around the radio that crackled with static; they looked at each other, and then away. The room grew quiet as the announcer began to speak.

"Since Mussolini's declaration of war on France two days ago, Italian troops are pushing west–"

Mama was on her feet. "The thief!" she hissed. "The backstabber, the *coward!*" Her face was red. Everyone was staring. She sat down.

Papa looked at her. "Saw his chance, I guess."

"He's a shame to his nation," Mama snapped. Then they heard the shift in the announcer's voice and turned sharply to the radio.

"German troops are approaching Paris at a rapid pace. As we speak, the vanguard is reported to be fifteen kilometers from Versailles. This will be our last broadcast for a while."

They did not look at each other. The silence was total.

"Today Paris has been declared an 'open city.' Our military will not defend it. This decision was made to avoid bombardment and the great destruction and loss of life that it entails . . ."

Julien realized he had not been breathing. It was an amazing thing, breathing. Tears shone in Mama's eyes.

"They won't bomb Paris," said Papa quietly.

"They won't bomb Paris," Mama whispered.

Benjamin stood, his face very still. He walked slowly to the door and took the stairs.

Julien waited, breathing, seeing Paris; seeing Vincent and his mother look up out of their second-floor window at a clear blue sky.

He waited until the news ended, until they had read a psalm that said *The Lord has delivered.*

Then he followed Benjamin.

Benjamin's door was closed. Julien hesitated, biting his lip, and went into his own room.

He looked out the window in the fading light. They wouldn't defend it. This was it, then. What Pastor Alex said was true. German tanks would roll down the Champs-Elysées for real in just a couple days. Then the *boches* would come here. And they would stay.

He pulled Vincent's last letter out from under his nightstand. *I can't believe you almost died*, it said. *That's crazy.* He got up, and went and knocked on Benjamin's door.

No answer.

"Benjamin? You all right?"

"Fine."

Julien opened the door. Benjamin turned quickly, scowling.

"Did I say you could come in?"

"Well *sorry*," Julien growled. *How am I supposed to help when he's like this?* "Just wanted to say good night."

"Good night then."

"Look, it's not as bad as it could have been, okay? They could have bombed the place to shreds like Ro—" He bit his tongue.

"You're right," said Benjamin, looking away. "That's good for your relatives. I'm glad."

"And your parents!"

"Nothing's good for my parents." His voice was toneless. "Look, Julien, we can talk about this in the morning. I need to go to bed."

Julien knew when to quit. He turned away. "Sleep well."

"You too."

But he couldn't. He turned and turned in his bed, twisting the sheets.

He got up and looked out at the crescent moon and the stars high over Tanieux, so white, so far, always the same; they would still be there when the Germans were here; they would still be there all his life. They were still there over Rotterdam too. It didn't make any difference.

When he finally slept, he dreamed: Paris on the fourteenth of July, the fireworks, bursts of blue, of gold, of red above the city. A whirling rocket going up with a hiss and a bang. Then a louder bang. Then a bang that threw up a great shower of dirt and stones, and people screaming, people running as the shells began to fall—

He woke, and lay shivering. He got up to close the window. The stars shone down like cold eyes.

He heard a faint scratching. Mice maybe. A floorboard creaked. He listened.

And he heard it. Very slow, stealthy footsteps going down the stairs.

He sat up slowly. Magali or Benjamin. Tiptoeing down the stairs to the kitchen, wishing there was something to eat . . . He got out of bed and leaned out the window, watching for the faint light that would come through from the kitchen. No light came.

But on the ground floor, the heavy front door opened, and a dark shape slipped out into the street. A shadow with a suitcase in its hand.

He ran across the hall and threw open Benjamin's door. A neatly made bed, a letter on the pillow. He grabbed it, ran back to his room, jerked his pants on over his pajamas, and ran downstairs in his socks. He'd catch him. Benjamin was on foot. He had to catch him. He scrawled on the flip side of the note, *I've gone after him*, pulled on his shoes and jacket, and flew down the stairs and into the dark.

He raced down the shadowed street and stopped at the corner, heart pounding, looking both ways. North, over the hill: the road to Saint-Etienne. A train to Paris, like he'd said? There were no trains now. Or south—south to where? *Oh Lord, help, if I choose wrong I'll never find him.*

Think. What would he do if it were him? He'd go south—north was suicide, but—he didn't know, he didn't *know* Benjamin. Who did? Nothing is good for my parents, he'd said—he didn't seem to even care that Paris wouldn't be bombed—

Because his parents weren't in Paris.

Julien turned, suddenly sure, and ran.

The Kellers had left Germany because of Hitler and his people. Would they stay in Paris and *wait* for them? "Let's walk south," Benjamin had said—and that stupid *map*—he should have guessed.

He ran, breathing hard, his eyes on the dark road ahead. *Oh God. Oh Jesus. Don't let me miss him please—please—*

He broke free of the houses; the Tanne gleamed in front of him under the splintered moon, cut by the dark curve of the bridge. He froze. He ducked into the shadows and breathed.

There on the bridge was a slender figure leaning on the parapet, looking down at the dark water.

Oh God. Oh Jesus. Now what?

Benjamin turned and took a long, last look at Tanieux. Then he adjusted his backpack, picked up his suitcase, and walked away.

Julien slipped out of the shadows and up to the bridge, his heart beating *help me Jesus help me*, his mind searching for words. *Come home.* And if he said no? Drag him? *Help me Jesus.* He was across the bridge, ten paces behind Benjamin; he broke into a silent run on the grassy verge of the road. He caught up to him. Laid a hand on his arm.

"Benjamin."

Benjamin whirled, eyes wild in the moonlight. They stared at each other. "Why," said Julien. "Tell me why." His voice was angrier than he meant it to be.

"Let me go."

"No." He tightened his grip on Benjamin's arm.

Benjamin tried to pull away. "Julien, let me go. You have no idea. You have no idea what they're like."

"The *boches?*" This time his voice came out small.

"The *Nazis*, Julien. Ever heard of them? Yeah, you heard they don't like Jews—I don't think *any* of you people understand." The sweep of his arm took in the school and the sleeping town. "Your parents are great, Julien—offering shelter and all—they really are. But they don't know. *Yet.*"

But they do. They know. "Know *what*? What'll they—do?"

"I'm not waiting around to find out." His face was white and deadly serious. "Trust me on this, Julien. They are coming here and when they do, it's better for you if I'm long gone." *I believe it is very dangerous to be a Jew in Germany. And soon—*

Julien stood silent. The night wind touched his face; the hills were shadows on the horizon where they blotted out the stars. Suddenly he felt how large the world was, how huge the night, how small they stood on the road in the light of the waning moon. Ahead, the road bent into the pine woods, and in his mind, Julien saw Benjamin walking away, a small form carrying a suitcase into the darkness under the trees. His fingers bit into Benjamin's arm.

"I don't care," he said savagely. "Where would you *go?*"

Benjamin said nothing; the moonlight quivered in his eyes as they filled with tears. He turned his head away. "I don't know." His voice shook.

Julien caught him by the shoulders, gripped him hard. "Well I do," he said fiercely. "You're coming home." He was shaking too.

"No. No." Benjamin was breathing strangely, too fast. "No."

"Come on." He picked up the suitcase. He took Benjamin by the hand. "I know a place we can sit for a minute. No one'll see. Come on."

Benjamin came. Slowly at first, but he came. They crossed the bridge, the water murmuring under Benjamin's ragged breathing, and made for the little chapel. Manu's chapel, whose door was never locked.

The heavy door closed behind them. It was so dark they might have been blind. Julien felt his way to a stone bench, and they sat. Benjamin's breathing was slowing. The darkness closed round them, deep and quiet. Safe.

"How on earth did you find me?"

"I woke up," he said, surprised at the memory.

"I should've been quieter."

"It wasn't you. It was a nightmare. About Paris."

Silence.

"I'm glad it didn't get bombed, Julien."

Julien sat looking into the dark. "Me too," he whispered.

Another silence.

"Benjamin. You've got to stay. They do know—Pastor Alex came to talk to us—I mean none of us knows the future but they know it's a risk. They're—okay with that."

Benjamin was silent. Julien sat in the dark of Manu's chapel, the stone bench cold beneath him, groping for what Grandpa would say. "Anyway," he said slowly, "maybe it was God."

"That *woke* you?"

"Yeah that *woke* me," Julien flared. "You think that's stupid? Going off God knows where in the middle of the night with a suitcase is what's *stupid*. You wanna laugh at me talking about God, go ahead, but *God* put you here because *God* knew what would happen to Paris and it's *God's* business whether it's safe for us or not. You hear me?"

"Your parents think that?"

"They do. I don't care what you think; I *know* they do. And so does Grandfather, and Pastor and Madame Alexandre, and—they're not the only ones. And anyway it's true."

Silence.

And in it, he felt something move in the darkness around him, felt something open, though he did not know what it was. He only knew that Benjamin's shoulder slowly began to lean on his, slowly, until finally Julien leaned his weary head against Benjamin's and closed his eyes. He heard Benjamin's tiny, quiet whisper in the darkness: *Ribbono Shel Olom*. He took the words in. He did not ask what they meant.

They sat a long time in the ancient chapel, leaning on each other in the dark.

The night was pale above the eastern hills when they left the chapel and walked up through silent streets toward home. The air was cool. Julien felt the knocking emptiness in his head that came from a sleepless night: wide awake and utterly drained.

They crept inside, held the big front door back so that it latched with barely a click. They slipped up the stairs in silence. Nothing stirred. Julien pulled off his pants and crawled into bed, shivering. He wanted to sleep till noon. But his parents . . . Benjamin wouldn't want him to tell. Maybe he should go get the note. That was his last thought before he slipped into sleep.

Mama's eyes were red around the edges. She was still holding the note in her hand.

"Because it isn't safe for *us*?" she said. "He said that?"

Julien nodded. Mama's eyes welled with tears.

"He's fifteen," she whispered. "He's only fifteen."

Yeah. Me too.

Papa looked at him across the desk. They were in Papa's study, in the straight-backed chairs. Papa looked at him without smiling, but Julien felt warmed by the look.

"Papa," said Julien. "Is he right? That it wouldn't be safe for *us*?"

Papa looked down at his hand clasping Mama's hand. He looked up into Julien's eyes. "Maybe."

"But"—his eyes swept them both—"that doesn't make a difference, right? He has to stay here, right? That's what I told him—that you thought that."

Papa didn't speak. He was looking at Mama. As if she knew something he didn't know. Mama looked Julien in the eye and said nothing. Just looked.

"Julien," she said finally, "what do you think?"

He frowned. "What do you mean?"

"Is this a risk we should take?"

He stared at her. "You're asking me?"

Papa was nodding. Both of them—what were they *saying*—"It's your risk too, Julien. It's your life. We can't decide it for you."

"We— Wait. What's the question?" He looked from Papa to Mama and back. "We can't send him away—after I brought him back—" His eyes were hurt and blazing. "That's not what you mean! We can't!"

She put her hand on his shoulder and looked into his eyes. Her eyes were warm. "So," she said, "you're willing?"

He looked at her, and he saw his life. He saw hard-eyed men with guns; he saw the other end of those guns, the small dark eye of the barrel. They would come, and they would stay. Fear lay like a lump of iron in his belly, unchanged by the pride in Papa's eyes, by the warmth and lightness of the morning air; but through the open window he felt joy enter the room like a shout.

He looked back at them, his eyes clear. "Yes."

Chapter 24
Kid

It was their second night in the army camp when Private Lorenzo picked them up.

It had rained all day. Gustav was soaked to the skin; Niko was shivering uncontrollably. The rubbish heap gave no shelter. Gustav crawled out into the dark, looking for something—a tarp, some boards, anything—to cover them with. It was so cold. He was crawling on his hands and knees when the flashlight beam found him.

He was marched to the guardhouse, throat tight and heart hammering, by a shadow whose face he couldn't see; only that blinding beam of light in his face, the pistol shoved in his back. In the guardhouse, he was shoved up against a wall, looking down the dark barrel of that pistol; he saw the man's black eyes look him over and hesitate. Saw the pistol lower just a little.

Then Gustav's stomach growled so loudly that both of them jumped.

Gustav saw the pistol jerk back up, saw the soldier realize what the noise had been, saw the smile that began to fight for possession of his face. And relaxed. He clapped his hands to his belly and said in a stern voice, "Shh!"

And Private Lorenzo of the 19th Infantry Brigade began to grin.

When they went to get Niko, her face was white as snow where Lorenzo's flashlight shone on it, and gleamed with tears. Gustav told her it was all right—he had a feeling about this guy—but she looked at him with wide and wounded eyes and did not answer.

In the guardhouse, Lorenzo sat them down by the oil stove and began pushing and pulling boxes on the concrete floor, making a row of them under a cluttered table against the wall. Testing the width of the space behind, studying it from all angles. Finally he smiled.

"You'll sleep there," he said.

And that was how it started.

They slept under the table during the day, in a nest of blankets Lorenzo brought them. At nightfall, Lorenzo came.

They'd stuck him on night guard duty alone for a month, he said. They'd caught him selling the regiment's coffee in town, and man, the sarge knew how to stick it to him. Nothing he hated worse than being alone.

But it meant he could hide them.

He came each night with a pot of soup. Apparently the cook owed him one. It was Gustav's and Niko's breakfast, lunch, and dinner; they ate and ate. He sat watching them, grinning, reaching over to ruffle Niko's nonexistent hair. She cringed, and his face fell. After the first couple of nights, he quit touching her entirely.

She ate the soup he gave her and said, *Grazie.* She warmed herself by the oil stove. Then she crawled back under the table.

Gustav sat with Lorenzo and played cards—pinochle and *a la copa*, and poker with candy for counters. They played for hours. Lorenzo told him about pranks or deals he'd pulled, ways he'd fooled the officers. Gustav told the story of their journey. Lorenzo's eyes grew wide, listening. He clapped Gustav on the shoulder. "You've seen a bit of life, kid. You're a man." Gustav looked down, feeling warm inside.

Lorenzo taught him things. How to slip a bag over a hen's head so you could steal her quietly. How to get into places you weren't allowed to be just by acting like you belonged there. How to make sure there were enough guys who owed you one, and you'd be safe anywhere. "I want you two to be safe, kid. I want you to be okay. My month's gonna be up, and I won't have anyplace to hide you. I gotta figure some way to get you out without my CO knowing–I'd get the court martial if they knew. But I'll figure it. When you get out there, you remember what I've taught you, okay?"

"Okay."

"Yeah. You can do it, kid, if anybody can."

"See, it's like this, Gustav. We're movin' out, the whole brigade. West."

"To France?"

"Y'see why I couldn't let ya go? Yeah, to France. Too sharp for your own good."

"Can we come, Lorenzo?"

"Kid, this is an invasion. You can't just–"

"But Lorenzo, France is where we are going. Our father said we should–"

"Even if it's under attack? No, listen, kid. It might work out okay for you–it's like this. You can't come with us–they might not even fight, with all the trouble they got up north, but they might and it's not safe for you–but you just follow us. We drop you at the border, and you come along after us. With your Italian, you could do okay for yourself. Messenger boy at least, maybe even run a little business with the troops just like I do here. They'll love ya. Heck, maybe we'll meet up again." Lorenzo's grin was a little shaky. He swallowed. "That'd be great. Wouldn't it?"

"Yeah," said Gustav, looking up at him. "Yeah. It would."

Chapter 25

Kingdoms Fall

Julien and Benjamin stood on the hillcrest under the morning sun, looking north. The mountains were hazy in the distance. The ridge cast a deep, black shadow over the north road, the road to Saint-Etienne; it passed out of the shadow and far away, winding between hills in the haze.

"That's the road they'll come down," said Julien.

Benjamin nodded.

That day, there was no news. When they switched on the radio, it played music; the same music over and over.

Mama worked. She washed the baseboards, she scrubbed behind the stove, she weeded the garden; now and then she stopped, looking at nothing with wide eyes. Papa walked around like a man in a dream, pale, spending hours in his study. Julien and Benjamin walked all day down paths they hardly saw, through woods that were a blur of green, saying nothing.

Saturday. Potatoes for breakfast, eaten silently—the only sound the squeaking of Magali's chair on the floor. Benjamin went upstairs and shut his door. Julien went down into town.

The headlines were posted on a board outside the *Tabac-Presse*. It should change its name to just *Presse:* news, that was all there was to be had now. News no one wanted and everyone got. German Army Enters Paris, said the headline. Yesterday. A swastika flag flying from the Arc de Triomphe. People stood around the board, looking at it. Nobody spoke.

Back at home, Julien walked in circles in the living room—*where are they, where are they now*—until Mama took pity and made him weed. He knelt on the damp earth, pulling savagely at dandelions, leaving broken roots in the ground. Papa came out the back door and said quickly, "BBC says they're moving south. Almost to Orléans by now." The door slammed behind him. Mama stood, her face white, a spot of mud on her cheek. She went in the house without saying a word.

Sunday, he sat in church not hearing Pastor Alex, thinking: from Paris they got almost to Orléans in what, a day? So maybe eighty kilometers. From Orléans to here, maybe three or four hundred kilometers.

Four or five days.

They turned the radio on that night. Triumphant music poured out, and then a voice. A new voice, calm and self-assured; no trace of a German accent, just a touch of smugness, as it told them serenely that the Germans were moving south with unstoppable force. They had reached Dijon today, the voice said.

"They wouldn't lie about that," said Papa. "People would know." He ran a hand through his hair.

Dijon. Julien revised his calculation.

Three days.

Julien stood at the hillcrest and looked up at the north road and shut his eyes. It would be dust on the horizon first, a small cloud;

then larger; then perhaps, tiny in the distance, the low-slung crawling silhouettes of tanks. In two days. The Germans. The conquerors. *You don't know what they're like.*

That night, the walls crowded in as they cleared their plates from the table. The triumph music cut the silence like a knife. A special announcement, said the voice. Marshal Pétain, revered by all Frenchmen for his heroism in the Great War, would speak to the nation. Marshal Pétain, who in 1916 had won the Battle of Verdun.

The Germans were in Verdun. They'd been there for two days.

A new voice spoke in measured tones, full of force and dignity: the marshal. "Today I have taken over as head of government," he said. "I am offering to France the gift of my person. It is with a heavy heart that I am telling you today that we must stop fighting. I have spoken to our enemy tonight to ask if he will seek with us, as one soldier to another, after a valiant fight and with all honor, the means to ceasing this conflict."

They looked at each other. "Papa," said Magali, "are we surrendering?"

Papa swallowed, ran his hand through his hair, and swallowed again, nodding slowly. "Yes, Lili," he whispered. He switched off the radio. The crackle of the static died into silence. They sat looking at each other. It was over.

It had been over long ago.

"Julien." Papa's voice was very quiet. "Will you read tonight?"

He nodded. Mama handed him the Bible.

"'God is our refuge and strength,'" he read. "'A very present help in trouble. Therefore we shall not fear . . .'" He felt dizzy. The words were falling into the silence like the notes of a bell, like tiny stones thrown into a very deep well. He dared not sound, at this moment on the edge of time, as if he doubted them. "'Though the earth may change, and the mountains slip into the heart of the sea. Though its waters roar and foam, though the mountains quake at its swelling pride.'" He didn't need to doubt anything. This was no promise that all he had known wouldn't drown in the tide.

"'There is a river whose streams make glad the city of God, the holy dwelling of the Most High. God is in the midst of her, she will not fall. God will help her when morning dawns.'" *She will not fall. The city of God—won't fall.* "'Nations are in an uproar. Kingdoms fall.'" Faraway, long-ago Sunday school kingdoms, names ending in *ite,* he'd thought. "'The Lord of hosts is with us . . . He breaks the bow, and shatters the spear . . . Be still, and know that I am God . . . The God of Jacob is with us.'"

He closed the Bible. No one spoke.

"Papa," said Julien, not quite looking at his father. "What's it like? Being . . . occupied?"

His father looked at his hands. "I don't know, Julien," he said quietly. "I suppose you could ask your mother."

Wednesday morning, Julien went out alone, early. It was the third day. At the hill's crest, he took the north road; he climbed the ridge, slipping on brown pine needles, scrambling over rocks, wet green needles lashing his face with dew. He sat on a rock at the north end; from there he could see far off to where the road vanished on the broken horizon, to where the soldiers would come.

He sat and kept watch as morning faded slowly into day. He ate the potato and cheese he had brought, his eyes fixed on that distance. He sat till the sun was low over the western hills, the pine shadows lengthening eastward. Then he stood.

They hadn't come.

He almost wished they'd hurry.

"You're not going to the Santoros's today," Mama told Magali.

"But Mama!"

"I want you in the house with me till they get here. Till we know what we're dealing with."

"Mama, I'm not scared!"

Mama's hand flashed out and her fingers dug into Magali's shoulder and shook her. "Then you're a fool," she grated. Julien stared.

"Say yes."

"Um. Yes, Mama." Magali's eyes were wide.

Mama turned away and walked into Papa's study and shut the door behind her. They heard voices. They looked at each other, and found nothing to say.

Magali stayed inside. Benjamin stayed inside. Julien went to the rock on the ridge again, telling no one where he was going; his eyes on the green horizon, an ache in his throat. He would run down the hill, calling out that they were coming. And what would that change?

On the news, the smooth-voiced announcer said not a word about where the *boche* army was; spoke of things returning to normal, of how impressed the Parisians were by the discipline and honor of the German soldiers. Of how movie theaters and dance halls were opening again. Papa switched the radio off.

Then Friday night, worse. The terms of surrender, the voice said with pleasure, were being presented to the French generals right now in the very town, in the very same railroad car—brought out of its museum by Monsieur Hitler, specially—where Germany had signed its surrender in the Great War. In that very place now, Monsieur Hitler would accept the surrender of France. Julien's eyes burned.

He lay in bed that night a long time, twisting the covers in his fists, hating. Hating him so much.

On the ridge the next day, Julien squatted on the rock, and the clouds flowed by, great hulks and mounds of white, their underbellies a dark and lowering gray. The horizon was erased, a long bar of gray with no beginning and no end: the north, from which the conquerors would come. The wind twisted the clouds and blew Julien's hair into his eyes; it chased the tears in strange, cracked patterns across his face. Hot tears of shame and bitter fury. He had simply never thought, in his wildest and most terrible dreams; he had never thought of this. He hugged his knees to his chest and laid his face on them and wept, and shook with his weeping.

It began to rain.

He lifted his face to the dark wild sky, and let the rain fall.

His heart felt hollow and oddly clean when he came home. Mama fussed over his wet clothes and made him take a bath. Supper was potatoes and beans. It tasted so good.

Papa turned on the radio. Julien shut his eyes.

Monsieur Hitler had accepted the surrender of France today, the voice said; the armistice had been signed. The full terms would be published soon. They included, among other provisions, German occupation and control of the north of the country and the western coast, but left the south as an unoccupied zone.

It took him several seconds, but finally he understood the voice had really said it.

Unoccupied zone.

Benjamin was on his feet, his mouth open, blinking with tears in his eyes. Papa was gripping Mama's hand. Mama was crying. Julien was breathing hard, *they're not coming, they're not coming!* He stood, his eyes wide open, and suddenly he laughed.

"Mama?" said Magali. "Can I go to Rosa's tomorrow?"

"Hey, Julien!" Gilles called across the *place du centre*. "Julien Losier! How's life?"

Julien laughed. What a question. It was Sunday morning, and the sky was blue, and men were clustering around the *Tabac-Presse* to read the headlines about the armistice. "Fine," he shouted.

Everything is fine, just fine, except, you know, little stuff like Hitler personally stomping all over our nation's flag . . . But we'll never set eyes on him, never see a German with a gun here in the place, they're not coming!

"How're *you*?" he asked Gilles, returning his ironic smile.

"Hey, we're alive, right? That's a lot better than it could be. Did you know they're in Saint-Etienne looting the munitions factories right now?"

"They said the south—if they think Saint-E isn't the *south*—"

"My father says they'll leave when it's official, they're just taking what they can till then. *Sales boches*. Did you hear about André?"

"André Rostin? Is he okay?"

"Yeah—he's alive and all. It's just they're keeping him. The Rostins heard somewhere they're gonna keep all the guys they caught—in prison camps, making bombs for them or whatever. You should see his mom this morning—all in black. Pierre says it's awful at their place. He says she wishes it was him instead. I think he's thinking of running off."

"Running off? Would he really?"

Gilles shrugged. "If anybody would—"

A shout came from the crowd around the *Tabac-Presse*. "He's a hero," someone was shouting. "He's a true Frenchman, and he's saved our honor—and he won the Battle of Verdun, *Verdun* mind you, and that's a lot more than a lot of those politicians can say. Those pansies that ran south with their tails between their legs as soon as things got hot in Paris." The men around him chorused agreement. "Give me a military man any day. He knows what honor is."

Dr. Reynaud said impatiently, "Of course he won Verdun and he knows what honor is. Whether he's qualified to run a country is a completely different question. All I asked was what happened to our government. The one we *elected*."

They were all over him. "You say another word against our marshal—" "He's the honor of France! He's our *savior!*" "Elections at a time like this?"

"Yeah," muttered Gilles. "Honestly. 'Hey the *boches* are overrunning the country, would you all please show up to the *mairie* to vote?'"

"He got them to stop before they got here!" said Julien. "What more does he want?"

Dr. Reynaud pushed past them, his brows drawn down in fury.

"Aren't you ashamed?" someone threw after him. He turned and said crisply, "The day I am ashamed of asking a simple question, Monsieur Moriot, will be a dark day indeed."

Julien watched him walk away across the *place*, his back very straight.

But the bells began to ring, and he and Gilles took off running for the church service.

Pastor Alex, as he walked up to the pulpit, looked very serious.

He spoke of humiliation and repentance. The head of their denomination had called for a collective repentance and humbling for all the things that had brought their nation where it was today. "But we must know," he said, "when not to humble ourselves. When humbling ourselves would be disobedience to God. Let us not humble our faith, not before anyone but our God."

He spoke of the "totalitarian doctrine of violence," known to the world as fascism. It had gained prestige in the world in these days, Pastor Alex said, because it had, from a human perspective, wonderfully succeeded. Julien bowed his head; he understood that. *They conquered us.*

"To humble ourselves before such a doctrine, friends, is not the humility of faith. I am convinced that this doctrine is akin to the Beast in Revelation. It is of the spirit of Antichrist.

"Let us gather around Jesus Christ," the pastor said, "our living Head; and let us draw our thoughts and our words and our actions from his gospel, and only from his gospel. Ungodly and terrible pressures will be imposed on us in the days to come, on us and on our families; this ideology will demand our submission. Our duty as Christians is to resist the violence imposed on our consciences, resist it by the weapons of the Spirit."

The weapons of the Spirit, Julien thought. Pastor Alex had said that before. But what violence was he talking about, what pressures?

To love and to forgive our enemies is our duty, said Pastor Alex, but we will do it without cowardice. We will not give in to them. We will resist when our enemies demand from us obedience that is contrary to the gospel. Something in Julien leapt up, a sharp sweet pang, at the word *resist*. "We will do it," said Pastor Alex, "without fear, without pride, and without hate."

Fear and pride and hate. Julien's eyes stung. Who in the *world* was without fear and pride and hate? And did he mean– What did he mean?

Well, he meant the *boches* of course, the Nazis–they would impose, he was saying, they would demand . . .

Papa looked at him as they walked out together into the sunlight. "I'm afraid he's right, Julien," he said quietly. Julien looked up.

"They said unoccupied," said Papa. "They didn't say free."

The full terms of the armistice were in the paper the next day. The flag on the *mairie* was flown at half staff.

The Germans would occupy the north and the west coast like they'd said. The line was drawn north of Vichy in the middle of the country. The demarcation line, they were calling it.

The *boches* would decide who could cross it, and what. For now, nothing at all; and no mail.

The government of the unoccupied zone would pay a tax each month–an amount of money Julien couldn't imagine–to cover the costs of the occupation.

And they were officially forbidden to call it the free zone.

Chapter 26

West

Niko lay under the bench in the army truck, hidden behind footlockers, trembling. The ride up the Valle d'Aosta had been a steep, jolting nightmare—scrabbling for a grip on the bare truck floor, being thrown against the knees of soldiers, suddenly. Men's grinning faces around her in a terrible blur; loud, rough laughter; men's big hands. Gustav saying, *Niko, it's all right.* All those eyes. Lorenzo's voice slicing through the laughter: "Cut it out guys. He's not all there. You're scaring him."

She couldn't look at him. Lorenzo who had fed her every night for the last three weeks, who'd hidden her—she didn't know him, didn't know what he'd have done if he had known. What he would still do.

Gustav loved him. He'd lit up at the sound of his footsteps. She'd lain under the table and heard their loud laughter, and felt a leap and plunge in the pit of her stomach. *Oh Gustav.* He trusted him. At the thought, longing rose up in her—and terror.

Lorenzo came for them at dusk, alone, his lean face serious, and walked them to the road.

"This is it, guys. You're on your own from here on out."

"We'll be all right, Lorenzo," said Gustav. Niko nodded.

"See that old barn down the road? There?" Its roof stood out black against the fading sky. "It's empty. Good place to spend the night. Hang around here tomorrow and then cross after dark. Won't be any guards at that border, not after tomorrow. Maybe go off the road a little ways. They might leave a couple of our guys behind, but they won't watch real hard. Here, I got blankets for you, it'll be real cold at night, you wanna get down out of these mountains quick—there's rations in this bag here, a little money too—you take care of yourselves, okay?"

"Yeah, Lorenzo," said Gustav. He swallowed. "Yeah. We will."

"Well. Um. Bye then. Always land on your feet."

"Yeah. Yeah. We will." Lorenzo put out his hand, and Gustav shook it; he glanced at Niko and made a funny little motion toward her, then stopped. She looked up at him. His eyes were wet. She put out her hand. He took it in his big rough palm and shook. Then turned away. She watched him walk away into the camp, a tall shadow of a man.

She turned toward the road and filled her lungs with the free air.

"He was a good guy, y'know, Nina."

They were sitting together on the grass between huge, sun-warmed rocks; below them, a valley full of deep blue haze. Mountains all round them. Huge. The highest peak stood snowcapped and blinding against the blue sky: the Mont Blanc. France.

"Yeah," said Niko quietly. "I know."

"Well"—Gustav was tearing up bits of grass—"You'd've known a lot sooner if you'd ever looked him in the eye."

Anger flared in her. "Oh yeah. I should've looked him in the eye and told him the truth so all his friends could find out there's a teenage girl under the table right in the middle of their army camp." How could he not know? "Didn't you learn *anything* from what happened on the border?"

"Nina! It didn't happen! We got away!"

"Oh yeah, someone tried to get me alone in the woods and rape me, but he didn't quite manage it, so now I should trust every man I meet because I'm invincible. Gustav, I'm gonna tell you this now and you remember it: that was *pure, blind luck.*"

"You trusted your instincts, Nina. You grabbed your chance. Lorenzo says that's the absolute best way to get away from someone in the woods. Run like h—like mad—until you're well out of sight and then freeze."

"*You told Lorenzo?*"

"I told him he tried to rob us. Started acting funny and playing around with his knife. I'm not *stupid*."

"I panicked, Gustav. I just plain panicked and ran. And then I tripped. That's not gonna save me next time."

"There's not gonna be a next time, Nina."

She turned on him, grabbed his collar, and hissed into his face: "Yes, there is. And *quit calling me Nina*." His eyes were big. She let go. "You think I call myself Niko for fun? I just felt like cutting my hair? There's more like him out there. Everywhere. This is what it means to be a girl in this world, Gustav."

"It's *not*, Nina!" Gustav yelled. "It's not what it means! How can you *think* that!"

"What's it mean?"

"It means . . . it means—you're my sister, it means someday you'll have a husband and children, I— it . . . I dunno, Ni— Niko . . . Niko I mean . . . aren't you ever gonna be Nina again?"

The force of her anger left her suddenly. She was staring at him. A husband. Children. It was completely unimaginable. A house. A door. One that locked from the inside. Oh, if she could have a door again! She turned from him violently and threw herself down full length with her wet cheek against the grass, her eyes filling with tears.

"Niko? Are you all right?"

"I'm tired, Gustav. I'm so tired." She felt a blanket laid over her. One of Lorenzo's. It was warm.

She woke to a world she had never seen before. She lay on a little grassy ledge above a deep valley ringed with mountains, a bowl filled to the brim with clear air and light. Every blade of grass stood out as sharply as if it had been chiseled; she could see every leaf on every tree. It was the quality of the light. Not bright like midday when colors swim together under the hot sun; this light was dim, but with the absolute clarity of pure crystal. Niko lifted her eyes and cried out with surprise.

"Gustav," she whispered. "Wake up. Look."

Towering above them, so close she could almost reach out and touch it, the snowy peak of Mont Blanc had caught rosy fire from the setting sun. They watched in silence, their backs against the sun-warmed rock, while the glow grew stronger, deeper, until even the rocks and trees blushed rose with the mountain. They watched in silence, aware of nothing but the light, as the mountain faded slowly into glowing, icy blue, and the sky grew dark.

"Niko," Gustav whispered, "I'm sorry."

She looked at him. She could still see his face in the dim light. "I'm sorry too."

"I– Niko– What I meant to say . . ." He fell silent.

"Yeah?" she whispered.

"Well, I'm bigger than I used to be. Aren't I?"

He was. She had noticed. He was as tall as she was now, thin and wiry. Stronger than he had been. She could not say to him, to his face like this under the vast dark sky, that it was not enough. "Yes. You are."

"I– Nina– Niko–if I can–I'm not gonna let anybody hurt you."

She said nothing. Above the mountain, a star had come out, a faint point of light against the deep blue.

"And we'll find a place where it's safe. Another house maybe, like in Trento—maybe I can get a job, I'm fourteen now. After a while we could have a place that's really ours—I mean, I really think we could do it, if we just found a place where people . . . left us alone. Y'know?"

Niko nodded. "Yeah," she whispered.

"Niko?" said Gustav after a moment, in a very low voice. "Do you still believe in God?"

"I don't know," she whispered. They had whispered the Sh'ma together, and walked out the door into the world. The terrible world.

"I don't know either," said Gustav.

There was a long silence. The mountain was barely visible now, a huge blue shadow against the night, under cold stars.

"We're free now," she said quietly. "We can go wherever we want."

"Where do you want to go?"

"France," she whispered. Her father's last command. "And down out of these mountains. It's getting cold."

Gustav pulled the edge of the blanket toward her, and she took it and wrapped it around both of them. "Well," he said quietly, "let's do that, then."

They crossed into France through the trees, barely a hundred meters from the road, in the cold dark after nightfall. They walked down the mountain for two days. On the third they found a railroad, and a freight train stopped on it, and they climbed into a boxcar. It took them to Lyon.

Chapter 27
The Homeland

Things changed. There were things he couldn't have imagined a few months ago, and they were there, and he got used to them. Listening to Papa read aloud the terms of surrender, Julien had felt a hardness forming in the pit of his stomach, a weight of shame and helpless anger like a twisted lump of lead; he carried it with him through his days and nights; and he got used to it. He was a boy from a conquered country. He was not allowed to write to his cousin or hear if he was alive or dead. His friends' brothers were prisoners of war.

There was bread again. There was no meat.

There was work. Half-grown squashes and pumpkins hung on the garden wall, and he helped Mama tie them up with rags so their stems wouldn't break as they grew. Grandpa wanted them on the farm now. They walked between rows of beans or turnips, chopping at the weeds with long-handled hoes. Benjamin wore his oldest pair of dress pants, threads dangling from the cuffs. Things changed. Benjamin sweating, taking Grandpa's old hat off, and wiping his brow, Benjamin with dirt under his fingernails. And Julien too—digging a pitchfork into a cartload of manure and lifting with all his strength. Their hands blistered, then toughened. Their backs ached. They ate their lunches ravenously.

Potatoes and beans, potatoes and lentils, potatoes and cheese. Carrots and leeks and spinach. Bread with a little precious honey scraped across it. But mostly potatoes. The hunger followed them, a tiredness in their blood; no amount of potatoes could chase it away. Sometimes it hit out in the field, and he dropped his hoe and sat down on the ground. Sometimes he thought of what Mama had said about his grandmother. Then he picked up his hoe and started again.

He dreamed at night of meat. It had been so long. Mama's spaghetti sauce, all that ground beef. A chicken roasted with tarragon, a drumstick and a thigh—he could feel the flesh between his teeth. He needed to stop thinking about this.

Mama said when the ration cards came in, the prices would go down; they'd have meat again on Sundays, and butter. Sometimes sugar. She didn't mention chocolate.

He remembered chocolate, the dark sweet richness of it, the buttery taste of a croissant, the smoothness of cream. They were still so vivid to him. Sometimes he wanted to ask Benjamin if he remembered those things too.

But he knew better.

He and Benjamin still walked once or twice a week; Benjamin silent, an inward look in his eyes; Julien looking at his hills. The variegated greens of them, the sunlight resting on them like a visible presence, the height of summer's glory. He pointed out the marjoram and the wild thyme, and Benjamin knelt and gathered them with him without a word. Hard, red blackberries hung on the brambles, beginning to shade toward purple; the yellow *genêt* flowers lay withered on the ground, and dark seed pods hung in their place, pods which in the fall would twist and burst open to their silver-white lining and scatter their seeds. Then it would all wither, and pass into the long, terrible winter of the hills.

And the hills would remain.

On the fourteenth of July, a quiet gathering was held in the *place du centre*—no flags, no fireworks, just the mayor playing a recording of Marshal Pétain's words about the armistice. People stood in the *place*, farmers with their worn cloth caps in their hands, listening to the marshal praise the fallen who had fought so valiantly against overwhelming odds and saved their nation's honor. It was like listening to Grandpa—the gentle, dignified voice saying things that made sense in the depth of your heart. "You have suffered. You will suffer still. Many of you have lost your homes, your work. Your life will be hard. I refuse to tell you comforting lies. I hate all the lies that have done you such harm.

"The land does not lie. She is still your help in need. She is the homeland itself. A field left fallow is a piece of France dying. A meadow new plowed is a piece of France reborn." Old, weather-beaten men of the land stood with tears in their eyes. Julien too. He could see it, the view from the crest of the hills—the wheat fields in the sun, the green of pasture, Grandpa's endless rows bearing food for his children and grandchildren. *That's France: these hills, this land, these roots. That'll never die.* He felt like saluting.

Papa sent him into town for the day's bread and the paper. Julien walked home slowly, reading as he went. He read the paper every day now. A couple of weeks before, the headline had been British Fire on French Fleet! and Betrayal at Mers-el-Kébir. Apparently most of the French Navy had been at anchor in North Africa and the admiral had gotten an ultimatum from the Brits: give them the fleet or they'd fire. They'd kept their word too. Papa said they must have figured the Nazis would seize the ships for themselves. The marshal said nothing could justify such an act. Julien agreed with the marshal.

Let Us Be French! read the title on the editorial page. *Foreign influences have weakened our nation.* France had been defeated, the writer said, because it had slid into cultural weakness and decadence; as our good marshal put it, the spirit of enjoyment had trumped the spirit of sacrifice, and the French had abdicated responsibility, had been taken in by foreigners who claimed to have their good in mind—had let them take over important positions in the government, journalism, the arts . . . Why only a few short years ago, a Jew, Léon Blum, had been the prime minister of France! What other proof was needed, the writer wanted to know, of our nation's criminal apathy or of the dangers of socialism, gateway to international communism? This movement, determined to break down all borders and wrest the land from those who had held it in sacred trust for generations, this movement, also led by Jews, had gained a foothold in France . . .

Julien folded the paper and tucked it under his arm with the bread and walked home slowly, even more slowly than before.

They were invited to dinner at the parsonage. Benjamin was home sick, which was just as well because suddenly the Alexandres were hosting a refugee family who'd just arrived. From the north.

They looked terrible. He was unshaven, a bruise on his cheek. There was mud in her wild hair. She was holding her baby like someone might steal it from her. A stunned-looking toddler sat on the floor.

Their names were Régis and Juliette Granjon. They were from Paris.

After supper, they told their story. They'd heard the Germans were coming, had packed their car, and gone. But the roads were jammed with cars and buses and people and carts, and they'd run out of gas. All the money in Régis's wallet would hardly buy a liter—gas was worth its weight in gold, and that was the asking price. "So we left it by the road. Abandoned cars were everywhere—people like us thought they'd get away easy. Turned out farmers were the lucky ones with their hay carts and horses . . . We kept one suitcase and carried the children and started walking. Walked for a couple hours. It was getting hot—it was about noon—when they came."

He stopped.

"They?" said Pastor Alex.

Monsieur Granjon nodded, looking straight ahead. He swallowed and spoke lower. "Planes. German planes. Over the road ahead of us, full of people—three planes flying low—" He looked up as if he could see them now; there was fear in his eyes.

"Michel. Go upstairs." Madame Alexandre's voice was sharp.

"But Mama!"

"*Now.*"

Michel dragged his feet up the stairs. When he was gone, Madame Alexandre leaned low over the table. "Monsieur Granjon," she said in a low voice, "are you about to tell us that the Germans bombed those roads?"

Granjon looked into her eyes and nodded.

"God have no mercy on them," she whispered.

Mama stood. "Excuse me." Her face was white. She went into the bathroom and closed the door.

For a few moments, no one spoke. Then Pastor Alex said quietly, "We thank God that you have come to us safely." Madame Alexandre said, "There's only one bed—I hope it's all right—" And then everyone was talking about rooms and beds and ration cards, and Mama came out of the bathroom pale and dry eyed and was asked if she could think of anyone in the church with houseroom. "The Bonnauds. That apartment his mother lived in, it must seem so empty to them now." Julien didn't know how she knew this stuff.

"You're brilliant, Maria. Would you be so kind as to ask them for me?"

"Of course," Mama said softly.

It was hot. The hills were baking in the sun. Under the pines, the air was still, without a breath of wind, and insects hummed over the forest floor, a carpet of tiny movement and sound. Benjamin sat down on the brown, springy needles, and Julien opened their lunch: lukewarm potatoes and goat cheese. *Well-aged* goat cheese. As the smell filled the clearing, Benjamin wrinkled his nose and said, "What died?"

He had spoken. He had made a joke. "Think we should give it a proper burial?" Julien asked.

"We can't waste food."

"Maybe there's some other use. I would've thought bug repellent, but . . ." He waved his hand and scared up a cloud of gnats. "Maybe some sort of weapons application. Just think, Benjamin, if we'd had this cheese a few months ago—"

Benjamin gave a resounding—almost an echoing—snort. The look of surprise that passed across his face made Julien crack up completely. Suddenly, they were laughing helplessly, uproariously, as they hadn't laughed in weeks, falling on the pine needles, holding their sides. It felt wildly good to let go, after weeks and months of defeat and hard work and not talking and *getting used to it.* It was freedom, it was— Benjamin was gasping. Too loud.

Benjamin was curled on the pine needles, breathing hard and fast, his gasps growing to great tearing sobs. His body convulsed, his hands curling like claws, his face distorted. Julien knelt by him staring, his stomach tight. What could he do? He put out a horribly awkward hand and laid it on the shaking shoulder. He could think of nothing to say. Except "It's all right."

But he knew better.

Benjamin was mad at him for days after that. Julien walked alone, kicking rocks. There was nothing he could have done. Except not be there at all. Not be there, not see him finally crack. There was nothing to be done about anything. Nothing but hoe rows of beans and potatoes till his arms hurt, and eat beans and potatoes, and do the dishes, and get up in the morning and do it all again.

He turned sixteen. He had Roland and Louis over and celebrated with wild blueberries and a goat *saucisson* they'd bought from Monsieur Rostin. He tried to invite Pierre too, but Pierre was gone.

He'd done a *fugue*, as they called it. Run off, just like Gilles said. Julien didn't blame him. Lots of country boys did it, Grandpa said. "He'll be up in the Tanières probably—lots of caves up there."

"Tanières?"

"Those hills on the west side of the Tanne. Good place to hide."

Julien stood on the bank of the Tanne and looked over at the western hills, a tumble of green and rocky places; then he took off his shoes and waded across and climbed into the most beautiful country he had ever seen.

Great jutting rocks and boulders, tilted ridges where lichen and moss grew on the layers of rock, and growing from every crack, tall southern pines with their papery bark that glowed rust red in the slanting sun. It stirred his blood. He climbed deer paths onto high outcroppings of rock; he slid down into a steep ravine with a tiny clear stream at the bottom and drank deep of the cold water. He ate his lunch on a small cliff, a fifteen-meter drop to the bushes, dangling his legs over the edge. This was the place. If the *boches* ever came here—if they ever got the chance to fight them here on their own ground—this was the place all right.

He went up to the Tanières every day he could get free. He was looking for Pierre; Monsieur Rostin badly needed him on the farm. But he was looking for something else too. At home, he would kneel by his bed and try to pray, and it was like pushing a boulder up a hill, like that guy in the Greek myth, all the time knowing it would just roll down again. War. Defeat. Work and waiting and nothing he could do. What had God changed about *anything* this year because Julien had prayed for it?

It was only here he could pray for Pierre. For Vincent. For Benjamin. Only here in the hills where all that weight lifted off him like a bird springing up into flight.

Chapter 28

Down

In Lyon, Niko learned to beg. There was no other way.

They searched for a hiding place and could not find one. The hiding places were full. Skinny kids, whole families with shell-shocked eyes, they were in the crumbling buildings around the train tracks, under bridges, on park benches. Standing in long lines on the streets with desperate faces. They found a place at nightfall under a bridge, crowded with bodies. Men, women, children who whimpered in the night. She was glad of their presence, the safety in their numbers. She slept.

When morning came, the numbers weren't so safe.

Gustav went round to the back doors of restaurants, came back to her empty-handed, taught her the French for, *We have nothing. Go away.* There were too many hungry. Looking for help, looking for work. Gustav stood in line all day. When he got to the front, he tried Italian, Yiddish, Romany; the man behind the desk looked at him blankly. In desperation, he tried German. The man spoke sharply and gestured for him to go.

"I'm so stupid, Niko. They've gotta be from the north, the Germans invaded . . . Lorenzo told me France was in bad trouble, I don't know why I didn't put two and two together, Niko, I can't believe I was so stupid. I'm sorry . . ."

"It's not your fault," Niko whispered. "It was my idea."

Niko took their bundle and made herself a place on the steps of the cathedral, among the other beggars. Since there was nowhere to hide. She spread out the army blanket and knelt on it, held out her hand. She said what the other beggars were saying. "*S'il vous plait, monsieur, madame. Pour manger.*" Something about food, she thought. Most people looked away. Most people looked like they didn't have food either.

They were going through Lorenzo's money as slowly as they could. One loaf of bread was food for a whole day. But the money would be gone soon.

They had to get out of here.

They talked about going on the road again. But there were so many refugees. They might walk days and find themselves somewhere just the same, or worse . . . They went back to the railroad yard where their boxcar had come in. It was their only chance.

Gustav climbed the chain-link fence, quietly, in the dark; he was hoisting Niko up when hoarse yelling broke out of the shadows, and she fell, landing on both feet with a cry of pain. A guard shouting, striking out with his club—Gustav scrambling—the nightstick clashed against the fence as he jumped down.

They limped home to their bridge. Niko felt tears clogging her throat. "It's all right, Niko," Gustav whispered. "We'll try again."

When they tried, two nights later, there was a dog. A wiry German shepherd, spine bristling, growl heavy with menace.

They stayed in Lyon.

Chapter 29

Peace, Peace

"Good news," said Papa. "Monsieur Gautier's renting us that place of his, after all. Apparently he needs the money. Now we've got exactly a month to fix it up."

Julien looked up from his beans. "*Le père Gautier*? The one who wouldn't rent to you after that . . . meeting?"

"You remember that?"

"Yeah."

"We'll need a lot of help. There's a call out for volunteers. Your grandpa says he can let you and Benjamin go from the farm. If you'd like."

Julien looked out the window at the sun on the rooftops. "Yeah. I think I would."

"Hey Julien," Louis said out of the corner of his mouth as they scrubbed blackened baseboards. "Y'hear the one about the toilet paper?"

"No . . ."

"Well the *boche* says, 'You French and all the lies you print about our führer, you wanna know what we use your newspapers for? Toilet paper!' And the French guy says, 'Hey, I don't mind, but I'd be careful with that if I were you. You don't want your butt ending up smarter than your head.'"

Julien snorted, and Roland and Jean-Pierre roared with laughter. Even Benjamin cracked a smile.

The work at the Gautier place was hard and hot, but it had its compensations. Julien still went to the hills on Sundays, but the rest of the week, he threw his strength and his heart into the work. He sweated, scraping ancient grease off floors; he scrubbed behind toilets. It was something he could do. In the fresh mornings, they laughed and told stories or sang songs; Gilles and Roland taught him old Huguenot songs from *le désert*: "*We have nowhere now to say our prayers, only a little wood behind Les Ollieres . . .*" But mostly they talked about food. What they'd like to have, what they did have, where they got it.

Roland had caught a rabbit in a snare.

"A snare?" Julien leaned forward, and Jean-Pierre did too. "How d'you make those?"

"Well, wire's best," Roland said, his eyes lighting a little, "or you can get a strong piece of string and wax it and then grease it . . ." Julien paid attention. This was good.

It was August, the height of summer's heat; they showed up at seven and broke for lunch at eleven. Baskets and old blankets covered the grass; everyone shared their potatoes and cheeses and melons. Like a huge, rotating village picnic, everyone was there: Pastor and Madame Alexandre, the Raissacs and the Bonnauds, the Astiers, Monsieur Barre, Madame Laubrac, Madame Rostin, the Michels—with two beautiful college-student daughters that Julien tried not to stare at—the Souliers, from the Fellowship, and sometimes Madame Thibaud, Roland's mother. And Régis Granjon, who was going to teach math at the new school, talking calculus with Benjamin.

And the guys. They'd have lunch together, all of them: Julien, Roland, Louis, Gilles, Jean-Pierre, and Benjamin—sometimes Jérémie or Antoine—then a swim in the river in their shorts, splashing and wrestling in the water, in the sun, seeing who could stay under longest. The only thing that could have made it better was Pierre. But Pierre wasn't there. Nor Henri. Nor his father. *Count your blessings*, thought Julien.

La France nouvelle! said Marshal Pétain on the radio. A new France would emerge from this defeat, returned to her roots and her values, her honor restored. Political parties had promised disaster if they were not elected, and heaven on earth if they were—how empty all those words seemed, he said, now that true disaster had come upon them.

"We have to return to our fundamental values," Monsieur Faure had told Julien yesterday, sweeping plaster dust off the stairs. "Pétain understands that. We were sliding into selfishness, individualism, abandoning our nation—that's why we were defeated, not some tactical mistake. And just like the Bible says, Julien, if we repent, we can be saved. He is a truly Christian leader."

It was called the National Revolution. The new motto of France was Work, Family, Nation. A return to real values—hard work, duty, loyalty, faith. Implementing practical measures like seed distribution to help the farmer, the backbone of the nation, alleviate hunger. Purging the administration of those who had failed through incompetence, laziness, or even deliberate sabotage, including those who had been French for only a short time yet had slipped into government positions. There would be youth camps to teach France's glorious tradition to her young people, her best hope.

"Well," Grandpa said. "Heaven on earth, eh?"

Julien and Magali both stared at him. He didn't sound impressed. "Grandpa," said Magali, her voice rising in surprise, "you're *against* him?"

Grandpa laughed. "A bit early for that, isn't it? He hasn't done anything yet!"

Papa smiled at Magali. "It takes time, Lili. Don't be in such a hurry. Did I tell you all what I keep hearing on my other radio? The shortwave? I hear De Gaulle saying our best hope is to go on fighting. Refuse to accept the defeat. He's calling for volunteers—gathering an army in England." He shook his head. "I don't know. I just don't know yet."

Magali was grinning. "Can I go?"

Julien snorted. Then looked at his grandfather.

"Soon Pétain will have to act," said Grandpa. "Then we'll know."

"I can't *believe* it," Monsieur Raissac bit out, shaking the newspaper.

"Oh, I can," said Monsieur Barre.

Julien sat cross-legged on the grass with the men, sweaty with hard work, feeling like a man. "Can't believe what?"

"You've heard what the *boches* have done, haven't you, young man?"

He knew. They'd annexed Alsace and Lorraine. French territory. *Annexed* it.

"Well, we stole it from 'em in the last war, what d'you expect?" said Monsieur Bonnaud.

"They broke the armistice! It was written, black and white—"

"What I don't understand," drawled Monsieur Barre, "is why anybody ever expected them to keep it. Don't people realize who we're dealing with here?"

"The marshal cut a deal. This wasn't some kind of unconditional surrender. That's why the *boches* aren't here in Tanieux. There were *terms*."

"And see what they do with them!"

"The marshal's doing the best he can," said Monsieur Michel. "I'd hate to be in his position, but we need someone like him."

"We need a leader," said Monsieur Astier slowly, "and we need hope . . . but I wonder. He *is* in a difficult position. And so are we. I notice that he doesn't speak very much about that."

Heads around the circle were nodding. *Honor and glory*, Julien thought—*but he does, he talks about the defeat*—

"The marshal cut a deal, and the Germans have broken it. What can the marshal do?"

There was a long pause. Eyes were on the ground. Finally, Monsieur Barre bit out, "Not much, that's what."

Monsieur Astier nodded. "So I ask myself, why is the marshal trying to make France feel powerful when she has no power right now against Germany? I'm not sure. But when I ask myself, is that a good thing . . . I think the answer is no."

"'They have treated the wound of my people lightly, prophesying *peace, peace*, when there is no peace,'" said old *père* Soulier softly. He had been sitting quietly at the edge of the group. Julien looked at him in amazement.

"Yes," said Monsieur Astier.

The *boches* were bombing England to pieces. The BBC went on about courage and solidarity; Radio Vichy made it sound like half of England was rubble. Papa said it might be true this time. "The Brits don't dare tell it as bad as it really is. They have to keep their spirits up."

They'd invade England soon. Then there would be no one left.

Julien and Roland walked up into the Tanières, and Roland showed him how to place the snares he'd made. They went there again in a couple days, but the snares were empty. "There's not so many this time of the season," Roland said. "Better in June when they're young and stupid."

"Like us," said Julien.

Roland grinned. "I hear Pierre's getting a pretty good catch," he said. "He always did know the good spots."

"Pierre? He's back?"

"Nope. But *someone* put two dead rabbits on his parents' doorstep this week."

"Really?" He remembered standing on a boulder up in the Tanières and asking God what he'd ever changed because Julien asked. Dead rabbits. Huh.

"Wish the dumb guy would just come back."

"Yeah," said Julien.

September. Two weeks before the first day of school. The place was rewired, painted, spotless. They had a huge picnic, half the village, to celebrate with toasts to the new school, to the revitalization of Tanieux, to defeat for the *boches*—that last from Monsieur Raissac who might have had a drop too much. "Nothing like shutting the barn door after the horse gets out," whispered Louis. Benjamin snickered.

They went down to the river, Julien and all the guys, for a loud, splashing, water-wrestling swim before the party broke up for the summer. Julien looked around at his friends. Only two weeks, and they would all be back in school. Henri would be there. But so would Jean-Pierre, and Louis, and Roland.

In the hills, three days before school, Julien caught a rabbit. It lay in a gap between the tough, green *genêts*, its legs kicked up awkwardly, its neck in his snare. He stood a moment, looking at this small life he had taken, then gave a whoop that echoed through the hills.

Roland showed him how to skin it, took the skin and promised to tan it for him. He had meat. Soon he'd have leather. He'd gotten it himself. Roland slapped him on the back.

Mama outdid herself that night, chunks of rabbit in a savory sauce with thyme and wild mushrooms. It was heavenly. He ate till he was completely full, mopping up the last of the sauce with a crust of bread. Even the potatoes tasted good.

"Look what they've done, Julien," said Papa.

"New commission to review foreign-born citizens," Julien read. "Protecting our nation against foreign influences . . . a commission to review the cases of all foreign-born citizens naturalized after August 1927 . . . the foreigners in question may have been . . ." The usual. France must be French. Foreign influences, Communists, undesirables let into the country with too few restrictions. Kick 'em all out. The journalist seemed to think they were going to.

He looked at his father.

"They're only reviewing, right?"

"True. We may not even know . . . what they've decided. Till we try to get Benjamin a ration card. Don't tell him. Okay?"

Julien nodded slowly. Picturing Benjamin's face. "But Papa, does the marshal—"

"Does he what? Approve?"

Julien shrugged. *Does he know about it?* What a stupid question. But—honor and glory—fundamental values—foreign influences, *corrupting* foreign influences, purging foreigners out of the new Vichy government, was that what "fundamental values" meant? Being French? French by blood?

The marshal, the beloved, heroic marshal, who sounded so noble on the radio, who wanted to give France a new birth of honor and virtue—he thought he could do it by throwing Benjamin out? Julien felt the bile rise in his throat.

"It's like your Grandpa said," said Papa. "Now we know."

Above the *place du centre*, the swallows flew, crying, turning against the red sky. Julien watched them and felt a deep, sweet sadness rise in him. It had been a good summer. In spite of everything. He was still full—both heart and stomach full—from the meal they had just had with Roland's family. One of those meals where awkward conversation slowly gives way to loud talk and laughter, and by the end of the night, everyone is in a warm bubble together, the world outside forgotten for the circle of faces and the light in them. He'd never seen Benjamin so happy. They'd asked him so many questions. Julien had learned what the words meant that Benjamin had whispered on the night he ran away. *Ribbono Shel Olom*: Master of the Universe. God.

There were guys around the *Tabac-Presse*. Julien headed for them.

And saw too late who they were.

Henri, Lucien, and Gaston. "That's why I put the sign up at the *mairie*," Gaston was saying. "The papers won't report it! The Jews own them all! The marshal can change the law, but someone's gotta . . ."

Julien turned, walked casually across the *place* toward the *mairie*. A notice board stood there, glassed-in and locked. A paper was taped outside the glass.

Marchandeau Law Repealed. A law against racist and anti-Semitic speech in newspapers or on the radio. Repealed. By the beloved marshal, naturally.

He began to pick at the tape.

He heard them behind him, but he did not turn. He had one corner of the tape off when Henri spoke.

"Hello."

Julien turned. Henri was alone.

"Censorship?"

"This is an illegal notice."

"Because there's a law against the truth?"

Julien looked Henri in the eye, took the corner of the notice, and pulled. It came off, and he held it up by its corner like the dirty rag it was.

"I'm proud of you, Julien. Striking a blow for liberty and justice. And free speech and truth."

Julien almost couldn't speak. "You think *truth* is what's gonna come of this?"

"Listen and see. The marshal just might know something you didn't know. How many Jews own radio stations in this country?

Don't know? Hm. And you'd like for nobody to be allowed to tell you, right? How many Jews are Communists? How many of the Jews in this country are from Germany? Oh wait," said Henri with a little smile. "Maybe you know that one."

Julien opened his mouth. Nothing came out. He was dizzy with rage.

"You don't want that thing, right?" Henri said, and snatched the paper out of his hand. He turned toward his friends across the square and saluted; and Julien forgot the paper. Forgot everything.

It was a stiff-armed salute, hand pointing up into the evening sky. He'd seen it before in newsreels. They used it in Germany.

When they saluted Hitler.

His rage dropped away, fathoms and fathoms down, into the void of pure shock.

"Henri," he said, almost breathless. "Do you know what that salute means?" He couldn't know. Even Henri—*especially* Henri—

"It's the new salute of the National Revolution. It symbolizes strength and pride in our nation," said Henri with calm pride.

"*No it doesn't!*" Julien half roared, his voice cracking. Henri stared at him. "It's the salute they do in Germany! The Nazi salute! Don't you understand, Henri?" He had to catch his breath. "It's Pétain, he's giving them what they want, they want to turn us into *Nazis! French Nazis!*" His eyes stung. The swallows wheeled and cried above them in the darkening sky.

Henri's little smile was back. "Julien, Julien. Maybe you should go home and lie down. You've had a hard day. If we use the other salute, does it make us Brits? Or Americans? The Germans have one thing right, and that's pride. We could use some too. That's why we're supposed to salute the flag every morning at school now. Marshal's orders. And"—he snapped out the salute again—"*That's* how we're supposed to do it."

Henri turned on his heel and walked away. "And Julien," he added over his shoulder, his voice growing colder, "when you're in my presence, could you *please* refrain from calling the marshal a Nazi?"

School would start in the morning, but Julien hardly slept at all.

Chapter 30

Help

Gustav stood on the main street of Lyon, between expensive shops and restaurants, looking around at the people: men in suits, women in beautiful dresses. The people who still ate.

He didn't want to do this. But he was so hungry. And Niko, every day by the cathedral, pleading with strangers—in three days getting maybe enough for a loaf of bread. Her collarbones stood out; there were hollows in her cheeks.

It scared him.

They had fallen to searching garbage cans, eating moldy bread, cracking bones for the marrow. Lying in wait on market day to find the smashed tomatoes and broken carrots when the merchants packed up their stalls. But even there, others were before them. Yesterday he had fought a man over half a cabbage. His ribs were bruised. He had come home empty-handed.

So he had to do this.

Lorenzo said purses were the easiest. Then wallets in back pockets. *I know you're not the type, kid, but if it comes to life or death,*

I want you to live, okay? I want you to do what you gotta do. You got a brother to take care of, don't forget that.

He watched the people go past. They watched him. Women in fur coats, clutching them closed. Men's eyes darting round, back pockets empty. He watched for an hour and saw not a single chance. He dared not try for an inside pocket. He'd be arrested. Nina would die.

Even today he could bring her nothing.

"I saved you this, Gustav—a nun gave it to me. I ate half—and this man gave me fifty *centimes*, with another fifty we'll have enough for—"

"You eat it."

"Gustav. It's for you."

The woman came out of nowhere, before he could move, screaming. Her face distorted by rage. She grabbed Niko's crutch, and Niko fell. The woman swung wildly, caught Niko a hard crack on the ribs that made her cry out—Gustav grabbed for the crutch, grappled with her, but his grip broke, and she swung again, and sharp pain hit the side of his head. He heard his own wild voice yelling curses in Yiddish as he plunged toward her, and then someone grabbed him from behind and pinned his arms, and a male voice was shouting in French, and a big, bearded man had the wild-haired woman by the shoulders and was shouting in her face. Gustav went limp, and the arms released him. He fell to his knees beside Niko. She was moaning in pain. Gustav felt her ribs, gingerly. She cried out.

"Is he all right?" said a voice. Gustav looked up sharply. It was the bearded man.

He had spoken in German.

His name was Herr Buhle. A refugee from Alsace, near the German border. He carried Niko in his arms to the train station, where he and his wife lived until tomorrow. Tomorrow they were leaving for Valence, they'd bought the tickets with the last of their money, but his wife was a nurse, he said, and could at least examine the boy—he was sorry he could offer so little help—

"It's all right," Gustav whispered.

The woman had thought they were German, Herr Buhle said. She'd heard their Yiddish and taken it for German—hardly more than a month ago the Germans had been here in Lyon, the swastika flying over the city, and they'd left so much anger behind. "Please believe that this is not normal here. I don't know how to tell you how sorry I am."

Gustav nodded. They were entering the station. Herr Buhle led the way to a dimly lit hallway by the bathrooms, where a tired-faced woman sat on a blanket.

He left them with her, and she began to feel Niko's ribs beneath her shirt. Niko's eyes followed her, but she didn't move. Only a sharp intake of breath told him Frau Buhle had discovered the truth; her eyes flicked over to Gustav, but she gave no other sign. "I'm afraid he may have a cracked rib," she said quietly. She gave him a small bar of soap to wash Niko's wounds where the skin was broken. He hadn't seen soap in months. She said when the body was weakened, risk of infection was high.

Herr Buhle came back with a small tin pail; when he opened it, Gustav's stomach cramped with hunger. Cabbage soup. Still lukewarm. It tasted incredible.

He drew Gustav a map to the soup kitchen he'd got it from and put a French note into his hand. He'd gotten him permission to bring a second serving of soup to his brother every day. He should show them the note. He hoped it would help.

Gustav swallowed, and couldn't speak.

"I will pray for you," Herr Buhle added. "Is it all right if I pray for you?"

Gustav nodded.

Chapter 31

French Nazis

Julien walked in the school gate; a *troisième* for the second year in a row. They were making them repeat their semester on the theory that half a semester spent watching their country get conquered hadn't prepared them for lycée very well. Good point. Magali was at the new school now, but thanks to Julien, and Henri's father at that stupid meeting—and Hitler, he supposed—the *Ecole du Vivarais* couldn't take *troisièmes* till next year.

So there they were, the old guard, still the kings of the school. Henri, under his tree again, and the royal court too—looking a little thin. Pierre wasn't back. And there weren't as many followers around the edges. Julien glanced around hopefully.

There they were. His friends, sitting on the wall. Roland beckoned.

Benjamin followed him, and they shook hands all round: Roland, Jean-Pierre, Louis, and his friends. Roland gave him his crooked smile. Julien grinned.

Maybe it wouldn't be such a bad year.

Monsieur Astier with his bullhorn gathered them, and called

the roll, and announced the new, ah, *activity* they would be doing this year at the suggestion of their good marshal. It had been, ah, *instructed* that they salute the flag. He didn't mention the Nazi stiff-arm bit. "This ceremony," he continued in a much surer voice, "is, as far as the school is concerned, voluntary. Those who participate may, if they choose, use an alternate style of salute with the hand over the heart."

Up at the front, Henri's head snapped up, and he said something to Lucien in a furious whisper. Then he was speaking to Ricot—Ricot was breaking away from the class, walking up to Astier. Astier lowered his bullhorn. They conferred. Then he raised it again. "Monsieur Ricot has volunteered to lead the ceremony."

Ricot stared at him.

"What're they so worked up about?" whispered Roland.

"It's the kind of salute they want us— We don't even *do* flag salutes in France, we never have—"

"Follow me," Ricot was blaring with his high-pitched voice in the bullhorn. The rows of classes broke up into confusion. Henri and his friends were right on Ricot's heels, the *petits sixièmes* right behind them. Others were hesitating, looking at each other. *What's going on? Are we really supposed to do this or not?*

"Form a circle around the flagpole. Don't you people know what a *circle* is? Form a circle!" People were flinching away from the voice. In spite of everything, Julien laughed.

Slowly, the chaos shaped itself in a shifting circle. Guys breaking in, guys breaking out, *sixièmes* looking scared, Ricot getting redder and redder.

Julien didn't move an inch from where he stood. Neither did his friends.

Ricot said a few shrill words about the glory of France. The janitor, looking annoyed at all the attention, raised the flag. As the blue, white, and red rose up above them, Monsieur Ricot threw his arm out stiffly to the sky.

Julien watched Benjamin's face turn white.

Henri Quatre and his crew saluted proudly. Most of the others saluted too. Gilles's friendly face creased into a troubled frown as he lifted his arm. Antoine and Léon put their hands on their hearts. They weren't the only ones.

"Have I seen that salute somewhere?" muttered Roland. He gave the white-faced Benjamin a look of concern.

"You might've seen it in a newsreel," said Julien in a flat voice. "A whole bunch of Germans at some kind of rally saluted Hitler like that."

"Yeah," said Jean-Pierre slowly. "I think I saw that one too. The—"

Benjamin cut in. "I'm going home."

"But it's the—"

"Tell your father, would you?" His voice was completely expressionless. He turned and walked away, across the schoolyard, his small form growing even smaller in the distance.

"Does he . . . need help or anything?" asked Roland.

"No," said Julien. "I think he'd rather be alone."

At supper, Benjamin said nothing. He ate steadily, looking at the spot just beyond his plate as if he had never seen anything so fascinating. After supper, Julien followed him upstairs.

"Only half of them even did it, Benjamin. You saw that, didn't you?"

Benjamin turned from his windowsill where he was leaning, looking out into the evening sky. His face was very calm. "Can you keep a secret, Julien?"

Julien blinked. "Sure. Of course."

"Astier fumbled it on purpose. And your mother knows."

"She told you?"

"She wouldn't say it right out. But she wanted me to know. Don't ask me who told her."

Julien felt a wry smile spread across his face, slowly. "Huh," he said. "Huh."

Mama sang while she did the dishes; then stopped, for a minute, to tell Julien and Magali about their new ration cards.

She'd stood in line at the *mairie* with all five of the family's identity cards, wondering if she dared show them Benjamin's. If they looked him up in the records, they might find he wasn't a citizen anymore. Anything could happen. They could send him back to Germany—

"They better not," Magali growled.

"Hush now. So I thought I'd hold his card back. But I just can't feed the five of us on four ration cards, even with what your grandfather gives me—"

"We'll manage, Mama. We'll—" *Eat less . . .*

"Let me tell my story, you two. So I got up to the front of the line, and I couldn't do it. I dropped his card back in my purse, and I handed the woman our four. And she says, 'Is your husband in the army?'"

They stared at her.

"I'd dropped the wrong card. Your father's card. So I gave it to her. And you know what she did?"

They looked at each other.

"She gave us all ration cards. That's what she did." And Mama opened her mouth and picked up her song again, her voice rising lightly, effortlessly as a bird.

"Haven't you heard?" Philippe was saying to Jean-Michel. "That's a *boche* salute!"

Julien, behind them, threw Benjamin a wink. "Toldja they'd listen," he said under his breath. A rare smile bloomed briefly on Benjamin's face.

"No, it's not," hissed Lucien from across the aisle. "Not when it's *our flag.*"

"Well doesn't it look a little funny? And then getting all worked up about the Jews—the *boches* started that, y'know—"

"The marshal's only saying the *truth!*"

Papa's ruler rapped twice across his desk. "Lucien, would you care to share with us whatever it is you find so fascinating?"

Lucien reddened. "Uh, *non m'sieur.* Sorry, *m'sieur.*"

Too bad, thought Julien. Papa would have told him a thing or two.

They'd been telling everyone a thing or two, he and his friends. Telling everyone the truth. Some of the farm kids had never seen a newsreel in their lives; how were they to know? Somebody had to tell them.

Even Roland had never seen one. They'd stood by the wall at break that first day, as the whole school buzzed about what was wrong with Astier, and Julien and Jean-Pierre had described that newsreel of a Hitler rally, with massive, frenzied crowds all saluting and screaming "*Heil!*" over and over for what seemed like hours.

He also told Roland, privately, how Benjamin could have lost his citizenship. "Don't tell him, please," he said. "He doesn't know. And it's already bad enough for him."

"Sure." Roland's eyes glinted. "Some other people are gonna hear it though. I can't *believe* that."

Everyone they knew, anyone who would listen to a word they said, heard the message. Everyone in their class, everyone from last year's soccer teams. Roland repeated the description of the rally to all his friends on neighboring farms. And to his parents, who told it in their Fellowship meeting. Roland's brother, Louis the schemer, raised his hand in his history class to ask Papa why he didn't salute the flag, and the next morning, a good third of the *cinquième* class descended on Julien's group at the wall during the flag salute, hollering that Pétain was a traitor. Julien had to laugh. He wondered if he'd been like that, too, at thirteen.

After class that day, as boys poured out the doors into the fall sunshine, Philippe turned to him. "Hey, Julien," he said. "We gonna do any soccer this year?"

"Open games," said Julien. He and his group stood by the wall in the sunshine, ignoring the last flag salute of the week. "Eleven men on each team, but mix 'em up every time. Or every other time. Whaddya think?"

"Yeah," said Dominique happily.

"Where're we gonna get twenty-two guys?"

"Half the *quatrième* class would jump at the chance, I mean last year—"

"Half the *quatrième* class is ten people!"

"What's wrong with the guys we had last year?" said Philippe. "Are we doing this without Henri? It's his *ball*."

"You know he won't go for the open-game thing."

Julien felt light-headed. Floating. He heard his own voice speaking quietly.

"I have a ball."

Silence fell. They were all looking at him.

"Then," said Roland softly, "we don't need him."

Dominique was looking over Julien's shoulder. Grinning. "Hey, Gilles," he said.

Julien's head whipped round. Gilles sauntered up to them, dropped his *cartable* on the pile, and sat on the wall.

"Hey, Gilles, *ça va*?" He glanced over at the flag salute. "You're not going?"

"I'm late."

"They're not done yet."

Gilles shrugged, then looked Julien in the eye. "Okay, if you really wanna know, I don't like that salute."

"What's Henri gonna say?" asked Roland with his crooked smile.

"Y'know," said Gilles, "I don't really care."

Philippe snorted. "Yeah. Mister King of France needs to get off his high horse these days. He wants us all to follow him around telling the *sixièmes* they're unpatriotic if they don't salute."

Gilles nodded. "I'm tired of it."

Julien and Roland looked at each other. "Well," said Julien, "I don't know if you want to join *us*, then."

"Yeah," said Roland. "We've been going around telling the *sixièmes* they're unpatriotic if they *do* salute."

They laughed. The French flag was snapping in the breeze, and the circle was breaking up. Julien glanced over. Sure enough.

"Here he comes, guys," said Philippe.

"Watch out, it's the king."

"Make way! Make way!"

"Hey, where's his white horse?"

There was laughter; but Henri was close now, and his face was set.

"Gilles," said Henri crisply, ignoring the rest of them. "We missed you."

"I was late. And it's voluntary."

"*Voluntary!*" spat Henri. "I don't know what's come over this school. I've never seen such a limp bunch of little girls in my *life*. Come on, Gilles. Tell me the truth." His eyes were hard with challenge, cold as ice.

Julien watched, not breathing. Gilles looked away. Then he stood a little straighter and looked at Henri again. "It's a *boche* salute, Henri."

Henri's lip curled. "You wanna see a real enemy of France?" He pointed at Julien. "You're looking at one right there. Cowards that won't stand up for France, that go around whispering rumors, undermining the marshal—why do you think we were defeated? The greatest nation in the world—*conquered*—because of cowards like him."

"We were defeated because the *boches* violated another country's neutrality," said Julien quietly.

"We were defeated because the *boches* violated another country's neutrality," repeated Henri in a childish singsong. "I don't wanna know what your daddy says. I want to know what *you* say, coward."

"I say you're slipping if you think calling someone a coward'll make him do what you want. You can call me a coward three times a day, and you won't make me a fascist."

Henri's jaw tightened. He didn't answer.

"Is that what you want me to be? And the *petits sixièmes*? Is that what you are?"

"If you can't be proud of your country anymore without being a fascist," Henri bit out, "maybe that *is* what I am."

"You and Pétain both. That's your National Revolution–if you can't lick 'em, join 'em."

They stood facing each other, eyes locked. There seemed to be more faces around them than there used to be. Cold winter air came back to him, and blood on the snow.

The bell rang.

Chapter 32

Go

Gustav had never been so afraid.

My sister is dying.

She was cold when he touched her. Heavy and cold. She lay on Lorenzo's blanket, not moving, looking up at the bare flickering bulb. When she wasn't cold, she was far too hot, feverish, talking strange things like she had in Trento when he went to the Gypsies. There were no Gypsies here. Only the soup-kitchen people, who let him wash bowls for a cup of milk a day. He gave it to Niko, but she said she wasn't hungry. It took him an hour every day to make her drink it, make her eat her share of soup. She said she wasn't hungry. He could see her bones.

"Niko. Eat."

"Gustav, I'm telling you the truth. I can't eat. I'm not hungry at all. It's like . . . like I've gone on past hunger. Left it behind me. It's just gone."

"Niko. No." *No.* He tried to force the spoon into her mouth. Soup spilled down her chin. Something broke in his chest–his hand jerked, and he flung the spoon hard against the wall. He wanted to strike her.

She just lay there. Not looking at him. Slowly, she closed her eyes.

She felt so still. So heavy and still. She didn't feel hunger. She didn't feel anything except the stillness. The letting go. She wished Gustav would eat the soup. Drink the milk. She understood her father now. His fierce desire for her and Gustav to get out, to live. *It's only Gustav now, Father. He'll live for you. He's a fighter, Father. I was a fighter. But I'm done.*

She didn't really think there would be anything, after. She didn't really think there was a God. *Death the thief*, she had thought once, but it didn't seem that way anymore. There would be darkness; it wouldn't hurt. If you didn't exist, you couldn't hurt.

And if there is, her father had said. And if there is anything after—will I see you, Father? What will you say? For having sent your daughter to her death for a dream of safety? What will I say to you, for having lied to your son and led him into danger. Father. Father.

"Gustav. I have to tell you something."

He was kneeling over her. "Niko? How do you feel?"

"Gustav. I lied to you."

"You feel too hot, Niko . . ."

"I lied to you. Before the border. When we couldn't find the rabbi. I said Father'd told me what to do if the rabbi was gone. He didn't tell me a thing, Gustav. I'm sorry."

Gustav's face went still. "Nina. Why are you telling me this?"

"Because I'm going to die."

His eyes were wide. "Nina. *No.*"

"I'm not getting better. I'm getting worse. Gustav, I'm so sorry—I don't know how you'll find a way to bury me, here." She stopped. A boy with a suitcase was standing by the entrance to the toilets, looking at her.

"Niko!" Gustav's eyes were fierce. "Don't you dare think like that, don't you—"

"Sh, Gustav. There's someone listening. He might think we're German too."

The boy was gone. Gustav's head was in his hands. Above her, the light of the bare bulb flickered and dimmed, and she watched it; the last light she would ever see. She heard with a detached ear the shallowness of her breathing. Not long now. Days.

Voices woke her. Gustav, a strange voice speaking Yiddish. The boy with the suitcase, sitting on the floor beside Gustav. Talking.

"My train leaves in the morning—at eight. I could spend the night here with you. Will your brother be able to make it onto the train?" What was he talking about?

"Niko," said Gustav. "This is Samuel Rozengard from Grenoble. We have a plan."

He had heard them talk about her dying. He had thought about it for an hour, and come back.

He was on his way to boarding school in a little town in the hills. He would sleep here with them tonight instead of in a hotel and use the money to buy them tickets. To this town, where there was food. Tickets out of here.

He reached into his shoulder bag, and brought out something round, blotched in gold and red. It took her a moment to recognize it. A peach.

"We have a tree in our backyard. This one is for you."

She stared at it. Its unbelievable color. In this dim place, it glowed like summer, like the sun. He put it in her hand. It was round, and heavy as life.

She couldn't. He wanted her to live, stand up, get on a *train*. She couldn't even face crawling to the toilets. He didn't understand how tired she was. *The time comes, Gustav. It comes. When you can't load all that hope and fear onto your back again, and keep walking. When you have to put it down.* She would never love a boy, she would never read a book again, or sit at a table and eat. She had accepted it. She sat leaning against the wall where Gustav had propped her, looking at the peach cradled in her hand, and did not move.

"Niko. Eat." Samuel was gone. Gustav was looking at her.

"I can't do it. I can't do any of it. Gustav, it's too late for me, I'll die on the way—Gustav, you should keep the tickets, wait a few days, you can go on your own . . ." She pulled feebly away from the anger that swept out from his eyes like a blow. He spoke in a low and furious voice.

"You are getting on that train if I have to drag you."

"We should never have left home. Father was— Gustav . . . Gustav, Uncle Yakov was right . . ."

"Do you think I don't know that?" Gustav hissed. "We left. We're here. We're alive. We are—both—still—alive. Now you eat that peach or I will hit you."

"Gustav."

"So help me I will."

He wouldn't. She knew he wouldn't. He was beginning to cry. His eyes red, his mouth open, twisted, a wail without sound. She was doing this to him. But she couldn't. She couldn't. To turn around like that in an instant—and live . . .

"Gustav, just give me time. I need . . . a little time. I need to sleep . . ."

His red eyes held her, hard. He was afraid she would die in the night. She slid down against the wall to the ground and lay on the blanket, exhausted. The room was getting dark. The last thing she saw was the peach. He had put it by her head.

The smell of it woke her in the night.

She opened her eyes, and it was there, filling her vision: one perfect peach, its deep red blush glowing like a jewel against the grimy floor beyond. It smelled like life. Her stomach cramped with a hunger she had forgotten.

Beyond the peach lay Gustav's sleeping face, his mouth open, slack with weariness. He was tired too. And here she was asking him to go on alone.

She'd just take a little bite.

Sweet. So sweet. She had forgotten, she had never known, that such sweetness existed; sweet as sunlight on grass, as a morning when you wake into the light knowing all is well. Sweet as everything she had lost.

She licked her fingers. Took another bite. Another. Her teeth met in the tender flesh, the richness of life in her mouth. She swallowed, and tears sprang to her eyes.

Words rose in her mind, words she had heard Uncle Yakov say at Shabbat dinners with the family: *Blessed art thou, O God, who brings forth bread from the earth.* And peaches, O God. Blessed art thou, O God, who brings forth peaches from the earth, who lets us lick the juice of life from our fingers in the hour before we die.

Chapter 33

The Train Man

Julien stood between the post office and station house, listening to the long whistle of *la Galoche* drawing closer, to the hiss and ring of her wheels on the track. Reading the postcard Mama had sent him to get. Preprinted: a space for a name and then "in good health/tired/slightly, seriously ill/wounded/killed." And other options farther down. People were supposed to cross out the ones that weren't true.

It was the only mail allowed across the line.

Mama had sent one to Uncle Giovanni and Aunt Nadine a month ago. They hadn't written back yet.

Today he would lead his first soccer game. He had fourteen guys—seven-man teams, and now Luc was in too. At this rate, he'd have full teams by next week. Henri Quatre didn't even know. Too busy with his fascism. Julien felt the bulge of his soccer ball in his *cartable* and watched *la Galoche* pull in, bright steam rising from her in the sunny air. He watched the back of the train where the mailbags rode, imagined a postcard lying face down in the bottom of a bag, with *in good health* circled after *all* in Uncle Gino's messy scrawl. Or with other things circled. He put his hands in his pockets, watched Monsieur Bernard walk with his clipboard to the back of the train.

From the passenger car, a boy came down, neat dark hair and a suitcase, maybe fourteen. Julien glanced at him as he turned back to help a friend down out of the train.

Then he stared.

The boy's hair was a greasy mat on his head, his clothes stiff and shiny with old sweat. The crutches he rested on were encrusted with grime; the hands and wrists gripping them were sticks. You could see the shape of his skull through the face.

I thought I knew about hunger.

Julien watched, motionless, as a third boy descended, thin and tough and unbelievably dirty, quick black eyes darting around the moment he hit the pavement, like a wary animal's.

He looked at them and knew: nobody was meeting them. Even the one with the suitcase; there was fear in his eyes too.

They were helping the crippled one sit down on a crate, his crutches leaning against it; he sat and did not move. The other two began to walk toward the station house.

Monsieur Bernard stepped up to them. Julien froze.

He listened, not breathing, as the well-dressed boy spoke first.

"Sorry to bother you, monsieur. Could you direct us to the *Ecole du Vivarais*?"

Bernard's back was to Julien, but his voice sounded courteous. "The new school? Oh, it's just about everywhere. Up the hill, down the hill . . . are you enrolling?"

"Yes."

"And," said Bernard in a bland tone, "your friends?"

The boy hesitated.

"Or maybe they're your brothers?"

"Friends," the boy said firmly.

"How long have you known them?"

He hesitated again, looking away from Bernard. The black-eyed boy said something to him in a language that sounded strangely familiar. The other looked at Bernard again. "Can you tell us the way to the school?"

"I can tell *you* the way to the school," said Bernard quietly. "But I have a question for your friend." He turned to the black-eyed boy and said loudly, "Are you enrolling in the *Ecole du Vivarais*?" The boy stared at him.

"He doesn't speak French, monsieur."

"So it seems rather unlikely the answer is yes, doesn't it? I'd like you to translate something for him." Julien looked at him, at the straight back in the blue uniform, and his hand went up to his mouth as Bernard continued. "Tell him that if he heard this village takes in anybody who shows up on the doorstep, he heard wrong. *Je regrette*, but I'm telling you the truth. We are not rich. He'll find people are not willing to give to beggars here like they are in the city. He's made a mistake. But tell him this." Julien bit down on his forefinger. "Tell him I'm willing to help him correct it. They can both have a free ticket back to where they came from, on me."

As the French boy translated, Julien watched the listener, saw his black eyes begin to burn. He snapped out something guttural to his friend, and the friend turned to Bernard and said in a firm, polite voice that didn't give an inch—to *Bernard*, from someone *Magali's* age—"Could you please tell me the way to the school?"

Julien watched, not moving a muscle, as the two looked Bernard in the eye—and in the black eyes hatred burned—and Bernard told them the way to Pastor Alex's house. He watched as the two boys walked back to their crippled friend. He watched as Bernard turned and walked into the station house, and picked up the phone.

Julien stood for a moment, feeling the bulge of the soccer ball in his *cartable*; thinking of the game. Then he stepped out from the shadow of the station house, into the sun.

"What did he say?" whispered Niko. She was light-headed. She could hardly stand.

"Gave us directions to the pastor's house."

"Should—should we go . . . find ourselves a place now?"

"What place?" asked Samuel frowning.

"Well," said Niko, "we usually . . . usually . . ."

"We usually look for an abandoned house or something like that," said Gustav. There seemed to be something wrong with his face. She was so tired.

"No!" said Samuel. "You're coming with me."

"*Bonjour*," said a voice from behind them. Niko turned. A boy her age with messy brown hair and worried eyes. Speaking a stream of French to Samuel—beckoning to her and Gustav—giving the station-house window quick, sidelong glances.

"What . . . does he want?"

"He says he'll take us to the pastor's house. He says not to listen to the stationmaster—they'll help us—he says—"

Help us. The words rolled over in her mind like two nonsense syllables. *Help us.* She closed her eyes and gripped her crutches. She was so tired. It seemed to be getting dark. She was so tired . . .

"Nina!"

Her mouth shaped the word *Niko* as the world blurred and swam around her. She didn't know why it was so dark . . .

"Catch him!"

Julien made a grab for the crippled boy, caught one of his shoulders as he slumped forward; the black-eyed boy caught the other and gave Julien a sharp glance. He was so light. His brother gathered him into his arms like a child. Then stumbled. Julien held out his arms to take him, but the other shook his head, eyes bright with fear.

Julien looked at him standing there, his thin arms shaking under the weight of his brother. *We can't do it like this.* Farm carts and wheelbarrows stood alongside the station house, the ones the farmers had brought their shipments in— There was Roland's father, thank God. "*Excusez-moi, M'sieur Thibaud?*"

Roland's father nodded as Julien explained, and gave him Roland's exact lopsided smile when Julien asked if he'd give Roland his soccer ball on the way home so the guys could still have their game.

They were arguing when he got to them with the wheelbarrow. In that language. He was pretty sure he recognized it. "Here. We can put him in here." He almost asked them, to see if he was right. But he wanted them away from the station house, and the eyes inside.

They laid the crippled boy in the wheelbarrow, legs dangling out the back. Julien bent to take the handles, but the black-eyed boy got there first. *Sure. Whatever you want. Let's get out of here.*

She was rolling. She was lying in a hard bed of some kind, rolling, the world was moving around her; the sound of voices was somewhere behind her, speaking in French. The boy with brown hair—the boy who'd said he'd *help us.* Or had he? The grainy blackness had lifted completely now, but the world was strange. The tops of houses went by against the blue sky above her head.

The rolling stopped. A high black gate. Someone turned a handle and opened a little door in it, and she was being wheeled through. She was set down under a tree with yellow leaves that trembled against a deep blue sky. She did not move. She listened to the boy's voice calling in a language strange to her, as all languages seemed to be now, and ran her finger slowly over the rough, rusty surface under her, the odd curve of it. She was lying in a wheelbarrow.

"He says the pastor's not here. He's going to get his mother."

Niko lay and looked at the yellow leaves and the sky.

"Mama. There's refugees. Young—my age. Just got in on the train. I took 'em to Pastor Alex's but no one's home." She was already putting her jacket on. "Mama, one of them's sick. Real bad—his brother says he's been sick a long time. He passed out at the station—"

"Does he have a fever?"

"I . . . I think so . . ." She was rummaging in a cupboard, pulling out a brown paper packet. She saw him watching.

"Willow. It's good for fever." She put it in her pocket. "You're missing your game, aren't you?"

"This is more important."

She gave him a long look and a moment's smile. "True. What are their names?"

"Gustav and Niko. They're from Austria. They're with this guy from Grenoble—a kid here for the new school—he brought them. He was walking into the toilets in the Lyon station and he heard them arguing about whether Niko was going to die. He says it's terrible in Lyon, refugees everywhere and everybody hungry—really hungry . . . not like us. And Mama."

"Yes?"

"They all speak the same language. I didn't ask. But it's Yiddish."

Samuel almost fell on Mama in relief when she and Julien walked in the gate; Gustav looked up from Niko's wheelbarrow with quick black eyes. Samuel began to blurt out his story again—he just couldn't leave them, he couldn't think what to do except buy them tickets, his parents didn't know, they certainly couldn't afford room and board for three instead of one, but he couldn't have, he couldn't—

"Samuel. It's all right."

"But I don't know what to do. I didn't *think!* And now—"

"You did think. You thought of *them*. Stop worrying. We're going to help."

"What are we going to help with?" inquired a cheerful voice. Madame Alexandre opening the gate. "Hello, Maria, Julien. Hello, young man." Her eyes took in the other two young men, and she sobered a little. "I see. Why didn't you all come in? We never lock the door."

"We didn't think we should—"

"Come in, come in." Madame Alexandre led the way, holding the door open. "And your friend . . ."

"I'll carry him," said Mama.

The wiry boy hovered nervously as she gathered up the thin form of his brother, his closed eyes like bruises in his bony face. She lifted him as if he weighed nothing at all. Julien saw the eyelids flutter, saw the eyes open green and wide with fear. His mother looked into those eyes, whispering to them softly in Italian. Julien listened, and a shiver went down his spine, and music came back to him: the sound of her voice singing in Italian, so long ago. Before everything. Before he had ever heard of war.

She could take it from here.

He took the handles of the wheelbarrow and turned to go.

The dark-haired woman laid Niko on the couch. The pastor's wife sat Gustav down at the table, asked in German with a thick French accent whether he was hungry. He nodded mutely, but she was already speaking rapid-fire French to Samuel, then to the other woman who was moving into the kitchen, opening a brown paper packet. Gustav caught the word *doctor* and started up; Frau Alexandre ordered him sharply to sit down. "You will eat," she said. "Your brother will eat. We'll get a doctor for your brother; he is in terrible condition. We will pay for it. Do not worry."

Then she was speaking to Samuel, and Samuel was holding his hand out to Gustav to shake. "Good luck, Gustav. I . . . good luck."

And they were gone. In the sudden silence they left behind them he could hear Nina's shallow breathing, and the moaning of a kettle; and the voice of the dark-haired woman, low and pure, singing.

"You're *sicuro* now." That's what the black-eyed woman said. Niko knew *sicuro*. Gustav had taught her. *Siamo in un posto sicuro?* he'd taught her. Is this place safe?

The room was rocking gently. She lay on something soft. White walls. Red carpet. The black-eyed woman kneeling by her with a bowl that steamed. How had they found the Gypsies again?

"Marita?" she whispered.

Marita was making her drink something. Soup. It made her warm inside. Then something from a mug, hot and bitter, burning her throat. She swallowed, and coughed. Marita whispered strange words. Romany.

"Marita," she said, her voice cracking. Marita's head turned at the sound of her name. "Marita, you won't tell them will you? Tell them it's Niko, I'm a boy. Marita, can I stay this time? Are you going away?"

"*Sst, sst, calma. Dovete riposare.*"

"*Che cosa hai detto?*" said Niko.

"*Parli l'italiano?*"

"*Un po. Letto, porta, zuppa, luce. Per favore. Luce.* Marita, how did you get to France?"

But Marita was gone.

Gustav looked round. He was at a table. In a house. The woman was setting a plate in front of him, a real china plate, round and white and clean—everything was so clean here: the couch Niko lay on in her filthy clothes, the red and black carpet, the walls—he'd forgotten. He'd forgotten how people lived, in houses. People like these—clean and strong and well-fed—they had let him in here, him and Niko, and now from the kitchen came the sounds of frying, and a smell that made his stomach cramp and his mouth water like a spring.

The woman came out, smiling, with a frying pan filled with not one but two eggs, their yolks golden as the sun, and said, "Here you are," in Italian, and poured them onto his plate. He couldn't speak. She stepped out again and returned with a glass of milk and two thick slices of bread. "I'm sorry there's no butter."

He stared at her.

"Eat."

Tears were stinging behind his eyes. *Eat. I'm sorry there's no butter.* He picked up the fork, and his hand trembled. The smell of fried eggs was stronger than his tears.

He ate.

He had never tasted anything so good—so hot and fresh and golden, washed down with cool swallows of milk—and he could eat every bite and still not take food out of Niko's mouth—Niko had eaten . . . He felt it flooding through his body, the joy of a full belly. The peace.

"I've given your brother some medicine, Gustav, but my friend has also gone for the doctor. And to get you ration cards. You'll need food. Both of you."

"I can work, *signora*. If there is a job—"

"In your condition? No. We feed you first. You get healthy, *then* you work."

"You are . . ." He looked around helplessly, gesturing at the room they sat in, at the plate in front of him from which he had scraped all but the faintest traces of egg. "You are helping us?"

"Yes. Of course."

"The man . . . the train man. With the hat." He gestured to show her. "He say no. He say nobody help us here. He say he give us ticket back to Lyon."

"He *what?*" The woman was on her feet, black eyes blazing. Gustav drew back. "He *what!* The . . . the . . . the *liar!* The *RAT!*" She hit the table, and the plates jumped and clattered as Gustav stared. "The train man? Stationmaster? Brown hair—this tall—blue uniform, blue hat?"

"Yes, *signora*."

"He lied."

"I . . ."

"He lied, I'm telling you!"

"Yes, *signora*. I believe you. Please. I am . . . I am glad." Glad. He looked at her, this fierce-eyed mother staring him down. *Yes, signora, I see. He lied.* He hadn't expected . . . any of this. He was so tired.

"Child, I'm sorry. You need a bed. You and your brother. There's a room for guests—"

"*Signora*, we'll get everything dirty—"

"And a bath. Come with me."

She went to where Niko lay. She was lost again in delirium, muttering to Father. "She's gone, Father, I can't catch up to her, I tried. I tried so hard. Don't make me. Gustav made a campfire in the woods. He'll be okay. I'm going to sleep beside it, Father . . ." Her eyes opened as the woman gathered her into her arms; she gazed at her as if to read some answer in her face. The woman looked at Gustav.

"Do you think it's all right if I bathe him?"

Gustav looked into her dark eyes. "Yes," he said.

"You're not Marita," said Niko suddenly in clear Italian, and the woman paused at the foot of the stairs, looking at her. "Help me," said Niko, and then in Yiddish, "Don't make me, Father. I need to sleep. I can't anymore, Father. I'm so tired." Her green eyes filled with tears. "I'm so tired, Father. I'm going to tell her."

"Not Niko. No. Do you understand?" she said, looking up into the kind, black eyes. "My name is Nina."

Nina was asleep. Clean, and full, and asleep—Signora Losier had sung over her in Italian, sung her to sleep, the afternoon sun spilling light on her wet clean hair, her face relaxing into lines of peace. Gustav hugged his arms tight around himself, shaking his head in wonder. *Nina. My name is Nina. She is going to live.*

He lay on the couch where she had put him under a blanket, with instructions to sleep. But now that he was lying down, he could no more sleep than he could fly. He lay staring at the white ceiling, remembering the bare bulb in the train station, flickering, remembering the hardness of the concrete floor. The woman who had beaten Nina, her face ugly with rage—Signora Losier hitting the table, eyes blazing, shouting *he lied* . . .

He heard the back door open, and voices in the kitchen. Frau Alexandre, the pastor's wife, was home. Speaking French in a low urgent tone. Signora Losier's voice answering her was soft with dismay.

He was on his feet in an instant. "What is it?" He burst into the kitchen. "What? Please, what is happening?" For a moment they said nothing. Both their faces were white.

"Frau Alexandre," he said in German, "what is happening?"

The tall woman looked at him and took a breath. "I am sorry, Gustav. I have made a very bad mistake. I thought that the mayor would help me get you ration cards. I was wrong."

"The mayor?"

"I am sorry, Gustav. I thought—he has normally . . . listened to me." Her face was strained. "He says that you and your brother should be taken to a refugee camp. He says he understands you might not want this, and so you are free to leave town on your own if you prefer."

"A camp—he—Frau Alexandre, my brother—"

"Frau Losier told me. Even if she was a boy she's not going to any camp. Those camps are not for refugees—they are for what those pigs in Vichy call undesirables, and they're hellholes. My husband has seen them. Healthy people die in them." The woman's face was grim. "Gustav, I promise you this. You and your sister can stay here as long as you need. If we have to hide you, then we will."

Gustav looked at her, and couldn't speak. She was turning to Signora Losier, saying something in French.

The two women looked at each other and nodded.

Julien walked out the gate of the school, his heart light, behind Benjamin and Jean-Pierre. He had organized the first soccer game of the year today and then hadn't even been there, and it had gone great. Dominique had scored two goals, and Gilles and Luc had each scored one, and they'd tied, which was perfect, and everyone wanted to do it again, and Antoine said he was in for tomorrow. And he had been at the station at just the right time to help Gustav and his brother and prevent Monsieur Bernard from running them off—*we're winning. On every count.* He grinned. No matter how Nazi the rest of the country turned, Tanieux was going to be different. Henri and his father were going down.

"We should play with those same teams tomorrow," said Roland. "And then mix 'em up the next day. Don't you think?"

"Yeah. That'd be about right . . ." They were at the bridge. "*À demain, alors,*" said Roland, and held out his hand; but as they shook, Roland began to watch something behind Julien's back. He turned.

Mama was crossing the bridge. Her step was quick, her eyes flashed, and her face was very serious.

"*Bonjour,* Roland," she said, coming up to them. "Will you tell your parents I'll be down to their place in a few minutes? I have a favor to ask them. Don't wait for me."

"*Oui, madame,*" said Roland. "Um . . . see you soon then." He turned onto the south road and cast a curious glance behind him as Mama bent toward Julien and spoke in a lower voice.

"Julien," she said, "I need you to do something."

Chapter 34

The Sons of Saints

Monsicur and Madame Rostin sat at a table strewn with spiky chestnut husks, splitting them open with knives and dropping the smooth dark chestnuts into a bowl. Julien sat across from them.

It was only the boy they were being asked to take, he explained. His sister needed to stay in town for the doctor. The boy wanted to work, but he was too weak yet, undernourished. He had no ration card. They were both *sans-papiers*, people without papers, without status, illegal aliens. That was why there had been a . . . disagreement with the mayor.

His heart was beating; he lowered his eyes to his hands and kept them there. When he raised them, they were both looking at him. Madame wore a fierce frown.

"I see," said Monsieur Rostin.

"If I understand," said Madame Rostin, "they're asking us to take this boy and hide him from *Monsieur le maire*?"

Julien swallowed. "Yes."

The Rostins looked at each other. Julien shifted on his bench. He'd ask Grandpa. Grandpa would—

"We'll take him," said Monsieur Rostin. Madame, unsmiling, was nodding vigorously.

"You will?"

"He's in trouble," said Madame Rostin. "He needs help." Julien blinked and looked at her: the broad shapeless bulk of her shoulders, the forehead with the deep creases of a changeless frown, the brown eyes clear, simple, looking at him as if it were obvious. He swallowed again, and whispered, "Thank you."

Night was falling outside, and the Alexandres' house was crowded with people; dense with low voices, planning, tension. Nina slept upstairs, as she had slept for hours, not even waking when the doctor examined her. Gustav sat on the couch, twisting his fingers together, watching. Listening. Catching only a few words: walk, food, work. The Italian woman was there with a black-eyed girl who seemed to be her daughter; the pastor's wife; the pastor himself, blue-eyed and intense; and the boy who had met them at the station, glancing over at him as he ran a hand nervously through his brown hair. Finally, Frau Alexandre beckoned Gustav over, and he jumped up and came to the table. She motioned him to sit.

"Gustav, we've found you a place. But we need to talk to you about it."

Gustav nodded.

"You'll be staying on a farm outside of town, with a family from our church. Nina will stay in town, just a few doors down from here—"

Gustav was on his feet again, shaking his head. "No. No. Frau Alexandre, you don't understand. We can't be separated. She'll die. Do you know what happened last time we were separated? She stopped eating. They fed her but she wouldn't eat. You can't—"

"She stopped eating?" asked Frau Alexandre.

"Yes. They thought—she doesn't speak a word of French—"

Pastor Alexandre nodded. "Gustav, the woman who has agreed to lodge Nina speaks High German."

"Oh," said Gustav. He sat down, slowly.

"Gustav, we don't think we can hide you both together. We must keep Nina close to the doctor, in a place where she can get nursing care—Fräulein Pinatel runs the bookstore, two doors down from the doctor, and she lives above it. And," said Frau Alexandre quietly, "she has very few visitors."

Gustav's hand was over his mouth. Nina in a bed all day, all night, surrounded by the kindness of strangers. The kindest of strangers. He just didn't know. He remembered the Gypsies, remembered watching her delirious, Marita pouring tea and soup down her throat. Like Signora Losier had done today. He was very tired.

"We have planned it this way so that you can both be hidden. We do not know any other way."

Gustav nodded.

It was full dark, the moon hanging low in the eastern sky, when they set out on the road to the farm. They carried no light.

The brown-haired boy walked in front of him. His name was Julien, and Gustav was to follow him carefully because he was going to lead him by a way that would not pass the stationmaster's house. Nina was safe, and sleeping in Fräulein Pinatel's spare-room bed above the bookstore. They hadn't let him carry her. She had stirred once and spoken to Father as they tucked her in. And she had gone back to sleep, watched by the tall, solemn Fräulein Pinatel, by the short, gentle-eyed Signora Losier. Watched by the kindest of strangers.

On the road by the thin light of the moon, he followed the son of Signora Losier.

They were at a fork in the road; the crest of the hill lay in front of them. Julien pointed over it and laid a finger on his lips. "*Le chef de gare, il habite par là,*" he whispered. "*Tu comprends?*" He pointed down the road and shook his head violently. *No.*

Gustav nodded. *The something of the station lives . . . that way.* The road to the stationmaster's house.

"*On prend la route du nord,*" said Julien, and took the left. Gustav followed.

They walked down the road toward shadow. Before them on their right, a high ridge rose, blocking the moon; on the other side, the ground fell away steeply, and far below was the sound of water. The train tracks joined them, two thin threads of silver under the moon, and were cut off sharply as they passed into the shadow.

Gustav watched the boy in front of him, a shadow among shadows, walking with a firm step, a boy on a dark road in his native land. A boy who went to school. Who came home to a family. He wondered if he could ever be in such a world again, if such a boy could be his friend.

He didn't know why he was thinking this. All he had wanted yesterday was a chance to live. For Nina to live.

The bright double thread of the railroad was ahead of them again; down in the valley the singing river wavered and gleamed. Julien was turning to him again, beckoning him to follow, into the woods on their right, where a narrow path led off into dark dappled with dim silver. He followed him into the rustling silence of the woods. They walked. They walked till the woods broke open again on pasture. A field of oats, a barn; two apple trees, and a moonlit garden patch. A house with lighted windows, and an opening door.

"Why didn't you come, Benjamin?" asked Julien.

"I said. I had too much homework."

"No you didn't. You do it twice as fast as me."

"Look, I told you twice now, okay?"

Julien turned away. It was no use talking to Benjamin when he didn't want to talk.

At school, he couldn't stop thinking about it. Monsieur Matthias, in the background, went on about Racine, and Julien thought of yesterday. Of the girl Nina, the stick-thin hands grasping her crutches as she climbed down out of the train; of her still form in the bed, seeming not even to breathe. And the brother, the way he'd held himself, even in the Alexandres' living room—tense, ready, his eyes flicking from person to person. They said he was fourteen.

And the strange moonlit walk; how he'd wished for Benjamin. He'd started out feeling like a commando—hiding a fugitive from the enemy—but the night was so huge and the two of them so small, in the dark of the woods, Gustav's quiet eyes on him whenever he turned around. *Are you okay?* he wanted to ask, but couldn't. *Are you scared? Can I help? Don't ever go down that road. There's a farm down there with an apple orchard, where your enemies live.*

He couldn't stop thinking about it. About Monsieur Bernard's voice cracking like a whip: "*Je regrette*, but I'm telling you the truth." *Liar. Liar. You filthy liar.*

During break Julien wandered away from the group, hands in his pockets, kicking at stones.

"*Ça va?*" said Roland's voice behind him. He grunted. "Fine."

"Heard you did good yesterday. Why didn't you tell us why you missed the game?"

"Um. I dunno." He didn't know. He'd wanted to savor it a little while first—oh, good thing he hadn't blabbed it everywhere—"Who told you?"

"My father. We're sending food up to Mademoiselle Pinatel for the girl. Your mother asked us."

"Food?" His stomach churned, as if it was for him.

"Yeah. Want to come? I'm going up there after school."

"Sure," said Julien. His heart was lifting; there was one person, one friend, he didn't have to keep the secret from. "You know we're supposed to be careful, right?"

"She told us."

"I took the brother to Pierre's place last night. Had to take the north road and cut through the woods so we wouldn't go past Henri's farm."

Roland shook his head. "It's weird. It's so weird."

"It's *stupid*," said Julien, kicking at a stone.

"Yeah," said Roland. "It is."

It was stupid being at school too. There was no *point*. Julien stared out the window at the hills and the flat blue sky, hearing Ricot buzz on about velocity, or Papa about the Revolution, and wondered: Didn't they know? That *now* was more urgent than the Revolution, that the sons of saints and murderers were sitting in their classrooms taking notes?

"One day," said Papa, "there will be boys like you, sitting in a classroom learning about the defeat of France and what came after it. And *they'll* be fidgeting too." The class groaned.

He walked with Roland to Mademoiselle Pinatel's shop, browsed the bookshelves until the other customers were gone and he and Roland could slip upstairs with their delivery. Nina wasn't well enough to see anyone, Mademoiselle Pinatel said. But thank you. Tell your parents thank you very much.

At home, he sat down with Mama over a *goûter* of unsweetened mint tea, and she asked him if he would be a guide again, for Gustav to visit Nina sometimes. He sat up straighter.

On Wednesday after lunch, they had their third soccer game; it was catching on quick, really quick; they had Léon and Jean-Michel *and* Antoine now, and the score was tied one-to-one. Julien was hammering away at it, driving down the field for a clear shot at Dominique's goal, when he heard a clear, scornful voice from beyond the touchline. "Call *that* a soccer ball?"

Someone else had showed up too.

Julien didn't look; but he could see Henri's face anyway. The next moment Philippe had stolen the ball. And Julien played and played and ignored Henri there on the touchline with his arms folded, and missed three more shots. But as they walked off the field, Philippe slapped Henri Quatre on the shoulder and suggested that he join the new soccer games.

Julien saw his back stiffen. "What's so new about them?" asked Henri. "Using an old volleyball to play soccer with?"

"We're switching the teams around now," said Dominique. "Every other game. It's great."

"Well, it's good there's still some kind of soccer game," said Henri. "For those who're still interested in that, with everything that's happening."

Julien picked up his pace, but Roland pulled at the back of his shirt. "Don't listen to him."

"Yeah," said Gilles. "He's just a sore loser. Always was."

Henri talking about *everything that's happening*. Henri talking like he'd outgrown soccer when the truth was the guys had outgrown *him*. Broken free of him. He thought of saying these things to his face; words that had no answer, fighting words. But he wasn't going to fight Henri. He could see his father's face.

Yet for some reason he thought of it again that night, as he walked down the lonely north road with Gustav; Gustav, who could only go to see his sister after dark.

It would have been such a good life for Gustav if only Nina were better. If she could have lived with him in that lovely green valley and woken to see what he saw. He looked through his window at the dew on the long grass in the rising sun, and joy sprang up in him like a flame.

The Rostins fed him all he could eat and wouldn't let him lift a finger. He tried to tell them, in his broken French and Italian and German, that he *wanted* to work, that if he couldn't go see Nina today, he had to muck out the goat barn or go crazy. They let him peel chestnuts, do dishes, but if he tried to go outside, Madame

Rostin stood at the door, shaking her head determinedly, as if wolves were out there waiting for him.

The third night, Julien took him to see Nina.

She was in a white, clean bed in a tiny room with a book-strewn desk, her crutches propped in a corner. She smiled at the sound of his voice but did not raise her head. He sat and held her hand and told her about Madame Rostin and her frown, and the way she heaped his plate high and said, "Good? Good?" And how Monsieur Rostin had clapped him on the shoulder, his craggy face beaming, and shouted "*Tu vas voir Nina*" as if he were deaf. Nina smiled weakly at him, but did not speak.

"It's normal," Fräulein Pinatel told him. "She's come somewhere safe, and her body has let down its defenses. She will seem even sicker to you now, but she needs this time to heal."

He wasn't sure.

Three nights later, Julien brought him up again. She was worse. The doctor had come. She had diarrhea, and they were afraid she was losing too much of what she ate. There was medicine—Gustav swallowed hard at the thought of the price—and Fräulein told him fiercely that *he* certainly wasn't going to pay for it. Nina was delirious, sweating and breathing quickly. She didn't seem to recognize him.

"I wish you could have seen her yesterday," said Fräulein Pinatel. "She was lucid. She kept asking for you. I wish you could come more often."

He suffered through an endless four days before Julien came again. He *made* them let him work; he hit the table and shouted, "*Je veux travail!*"

Monsieur Rostin gave him a shrug and a wry half smile, and said, "*Bon, si tu veux alors.*"

He filled his days as full as he could, picking apples, mucking out the goats, digging parsnips. If he tired himself out, he couldn't lie awake at night, wondering.

She was better. She knew him, and sat up in bed and asked why he didn't come more often. He didn't know what to say. He told her to eat, and take her medicine, and that when she got better she could come live on the farm with him. She promised. "I won't be much use on a farm though, Gustav," she said.

"Yes, you will. You can weed. And cook."

"You know I can't cook!" She laughed. She actually laughed!

Fräulein Pinatel said she was glad he'd seen her on a good day.

The next three days he worked with a will—even scrubbed Madame Rostin's kitchen while she was away at market. Soon, his mind sang, soon; soon she would get up and walk, and he'd work so well Monsieur Rostin would be able to plant more next year, and he'd earn their keep for both of them. They'd live here in the valley, and learn French, and . . .

Saturday night, he was walking light when he started down the starlit road with Julien. Tonight he would bring Julien up to see her too.

"*Viens, viens*, Julien," said Gustav. "*Bitte*."

Julien hesitated. He always stayed down in the bookstore doing homework. He'd figured she wanted to see her brother, not him. But there was no mistaking *viens*, or Gustav's eager beckoning. He followed him up the narrow stairs.

Mademoiselle Pinatel, her face strained, said low words to Gustav, and Gustav answered. To Julien she said, "I just want you to know that she's not like this every day."

He was led into a little narrow room with a bed, and there lay Nina, the girl he had brought to safety and help; motionless, her eyes closed, one stick-thin arm on the cover. Short dark hair hung shiny with sweat around her sunken face. Gustav went to his knees.

"Nina," he said. "Nina."

For a moment, there was no response. Then the eyes opened, slowly, and looked into nothing. Julien had never seen such tired eyes, not even the first time he'd seen her: flat, lightless, shallow pools that no wind stirred. Gustav was speaking urgent Yiddish. Julien heard his name. Nina's eyes settled for a moment on her brother's face, then fell back again into their weariness.

Gustav half turned for a moment, then jerked back; but Julien had seen the tears that trembled in his eyes.

He backed out of the room and shut the door.

In the morning, Julien prayed for Nina, as desperately, as urgently as he had prayed only once. The night before Paris fell. He could not think what it would be like to watch your sister die.

He got up. He had to get away. Somewhere where no one could see him. It was dawn. He'd be back by church time. He slipped downstairs.

He took the road up the hill out of town, but as he got near the hill's crest he stopped, shaking his head. The sight he knew he would see—the green lovely sweep of the hills, and in the foreground an apple orchard laden with fruit and an old stone farmhouse, in which lived a man who had tried to send a young girl to her death. He turned left abruptly, off the road.

The river was calling to him, the clearness of its flowing water, as if it could wash clean the matted tangle of his mind. He ran down the closest alley and out from between the houses; he stumbled and slid down the steep slope and was suddenly alone, shielded from eyes. He could breathe.

The Tanne flowed past him. The hills were green in the sun. Down on his left around the broad bend of the river, he could see his school, its low black wall, the flash of its flag in the wind. He had stood by that wall only a year ago and raged against life because he couldn't get in on the soccer games. And his country had been at war then, but he'd never believed it. Play war, toy soldiers sitting on a border somewhere, nobody he knew. Not his aunt and uncle and best-friend cousin in a fallen city, watched in the streets by German soldiers, forbidden to write to him. Not defeat. Not hunger, and waiting.

So many things he had not believed. *She's not safe yet*, his mother had told him. *If she is sent to a camp, she will die.* He hadn't wanted to believe it. He'd stayed downstairs in the bookstore and pictured Nina up there in her bedroom, sitting up, a little better every day. Someone he had helped. Who'd be okay now. He'd wanted to protect her, yes, he'd done everything he could—he had been careful, walking Gustav into town—but he hadn't believed it. Not until he'd seen.

His mind clawed at the terrible tangle of what he had learned these past two months. Defeat was nothing to this, potatoes for breakfast were nothing; you could get used to them. But to see your own people doing such things—Henri with his arm upraised in a proud and hateful salute, the stationmaster standing tall in his uniform and smart *képi*. Benjamin's face white with fear, Nina's bone-thin arm and her eyes with the light gone from them.

There were some things no one could get used to.

He thrust his hands into his pockets and watched the water, clear and simple, running forever past.

He hated them.

It was wrong. It was wrong to hate. He could hear Pastor Alex's ringing voice in the church: *without fear, without pride, and without hate.*

But God, he tried to send Nina away! And you want me not to hate him?

He clawed up a stone from beside his feet and threw it, with all the strength in his body, down at the river. It fell short in the grass, and bounced, and was caught in the weeds on the bank.

He pressed his hands hard against his face to hide his tears from the sky.

On Tuesday afternoon, Papa came home with the newspaper and spread out on the table the news Julien should have known was coming.

A new law from Vichy. Front page, big headline, no apology: "Jews

Barred from Positions of Trust." They could not hold government jobs. They couldn't be army officers. No Jewish teachers, no Jewish CEOs, no Jewish journalists; it was the law. Papa looked up from the paper, ran his fingers through his hair, and told Julien what the Germans had decreed for the occupied zone.

The Jews had to have JEW stamped on their *cartes d'identité*, just like in Germany. They had to have yellow signs in the windows of their shops that said "Jewish shop" in French and German. And . . . and there were rumors that young men wearing blue shirts and calling themselves fascists were going around Paris, smashing those windows. *French* young men.

Their own people.

"Why?" said Julien, the anger rising in his throat. "Why are they doing this to us?"

"Who's doing it to us?" said his father bitterly. "Looks like we don't need any more help. Looks like we're doing it to ourselves."

The next morning, kneeling on the wood floor beside his bed, Julien prayed again for Nina; and for Benjamin, who had seen the headline and said nothing, had gone pale and left the room. He prayed for Gustav, for Vincent and his family, for Benjamin's parents, and for Pierre still up in the hills somewhere. He remembered how he'd prayed for Pierre when they were enemies. There he stopped. He saw blue-shirted men throwing bricks through windows, men with Henri's scornful eyes. And the heavy knot of anger in his stomach uncoiled itself, and rose up, and blossomed into rage.

Before he left for school, he slipped the newspaper into his *cartable*.

The paper passed from hand to hand in the little group by the wall. The flag circle stood around their flagpole, Ricot and seven boys, their arms pointed stiff and brittle toward the sky.

"Someone's got some explaining to do," said Louis through his teeth.

"Yeah," said Dominique.

"Yeah," said Philippe.

"Yeah," said Julien. He set his face toward the flagpole. "Let's go."

There were ten of them to Henri's seven. They met the flag salute just as it was breaking up. Henri stepped out to meet them, and Julien looked him in the eye.

"We have some questions," he said. "We thought maybe you could answer them."

Henri stood with his feet planted. "Sure."

Julien brandished the paper. "We'd like to know what you call *this*."

"The news."

"We want to know what you call it when your government starts persecuting an entire race. We want to know if you call *that* the honor of France."

"It's your government," said Henri, his eyes scornful. "You seem to be forgetting where you're from. And since when is it persecution to refuse somebody a government job?"

"Would you call it persecution," said Julien, leaning forward and looking Henri straight in the eye, "if they started refusing government jobs to all the *Protestants*?"

It was like delivering a hard blow to the jaw and watching your opponent stagger. Henri Quatre, king of France, with everyone looking on, took a step back, opened his mouth, and closed it again. Said nothing.

"This isn't the honor of France," said Julien. "This is *shame*. I am *ashamed* that my people are doing this. Kissing up to murderers. *Imitating* them."

Henri's eyes narrowed. He stepped forward again. Julien's blood beat in his temples, *I can take him, I can . . .*

"You say that again about the marshal," Henri snarled. "You say that again, and I'll—" Henri's hand was balled in a fist. Shaking.

Julien teetered on the edge of freedom, the edge of danger. *That's right, Henri, hit me.* The flag snapped above them in the wind. He felt light. Invincible. "Say what?" he said quietly. "That the marshal is kissing up to the Nazis?"

Suddenly Gaston was between him and Henri, and Roland had Julien by the arm. Gaston was blustering. "You idiot, Julien Losier! Don't listen to him, Henri. He's doesn't know a thing about the marshal, don't you know that?" Henri shot Gaston an unfriendly look.

"Julien," said Roland quietly, "you might wanna watch out." He gestured with his chin toward the *préau*, where Ricot stood watching them.

"Why didn't you fight him?" said Benjamin vehemently.

Julien turned on him. "Why didn't *you* fight him?" he snarled. "You should talk. You don't even have the guts to visit Nina!" Benjamin's face turned white. He bit out three words in Yiddish, stepped into his room, and slammed the door in Julien's face.

Julien brought Gustav into town that night, answering his broken French in monosyllables. He stayed downstairs with his math.

Thursday morning, Julien woke up late, to rain streaming down his window and a knock on his door.

"C'min," he mumbled sleepily. Benjamin came in. Julien sat up, suddenly awake.

"Hey. You missed breakfast. I wanted to say . . . y'know. Sorry."

"Uh. Yeah. I'm sorry too."

"Your father told me about the citizenship thing."

"He did?"

"Yeah. And there's another thing. Not in the papers, Pastor Alexandre told us this morning. The *préfet*—" he broke off and swallowed. "The *préfet* of each region now has power to arrest any foreign Jews he thinks are a problem and send them to an internment camp."

"Oh," Julien breathed.

"I'm okay. For now. But Gustav and Nina, see . . . I thought you should know. And I'm sorry I didn't go down with you to see them. I . . . I think I was . . . scared of them. Because . . . I'm like them."

Julien blinked. "But your parents aren't–"

Benjamin said in a hard, flat voice, "My parents are dead." Julien stared at him.

"No–"

"Don't tell me you don't know they bombed the roads. My parents wouldn't have stayed in Paris for the world, they were on those roads. And they never got here. They're dead." He was looking straight ahead, out the window.

"Benjamin–"

"Anyway, just wanted to tell you I'll come with you Saturday night," said Benjamin abruptly. He got up off the bed and walked out the door.

The flag ceremony was rained out. Everyone huddled under the *préau* together, voices echoing against the concrete, looking out at the driving rain.

"Julien." A hand on his shoulder. It was Henri Quatre, frowning deeply, beckoning. Julien followed, away from the voices and the scrape of shoes on the concrete floor, into the near-silence of an empty hallway. "Yeah?"

"Julien, I have a question for you."

"Sure," said Julien, squaring his shoulders.

"Who was that you were with on Wednesday night?"

The hallway was tilting. The hollow voices echoed in his head. He tried to catch his breath.

"Wednesday night?" he managed.

"You were with this kid. Black hair, skinny, spoke bad French with a German accent. Weren't you?" Henri looked him in the eye. Julien's stomach cramped as he opened his mouth.

"Yes."

"I'm glad you're not a liar. I saw you. From the window of my aunt's house. You were being kinda careful about staying in the shadows."

Lord God, he prayed. *Oh Lord God . . .*

"He looked a lot like my father's description of that guy the mayor *requested* to leave town. You know who I mean? The two *sans-papiers*?"

Julien closed his mouth.

"Where are they staying?"

He didn't know. Thank God. "Henri," said Julien, without meaning to, desperately, "have you told your father?"

"No," said Henri. "Not yet."

"Henri," said Julien, his mouth dry, "please don't tell your father."

"Where are they staying?"

"Please."

"This kind of thing is supposed to be taken care of the right way. There are camps—"

"Camps?" Julien was breathless, he could barely speak; in a bitter rush he imagined how Henri's throat would feel between his hands. "They can't go to a camp. The sister is sick—"

"What sister?" Henri frowned.

"One of them's a girl."

"A girl? Are you saying they lied to my father?"

"She was dressed as a boy, that's all—"

"Don't you realize you have no idea who they are?"

"Neither do you," said Julien. "I—" Léon Barre stepped into the hall, and Julien snapped his mouth shut. Léon jogged past them toward the toilets, and Henri shot Julien a look of contempt.

"Look," said Henri. "I'm not asking your advice; I'm asking you where they're staying. If you're not going to do the right thing—" He shrugged and looked away.

Julien's knees were weak. He had to warn them— "Henri. Listen to me. The girl is very sick. If she gets sent to a camp, she's going to die."

"Let me make this as simple for you as I can, Julien," said Henri. "I don't believe it." And he walked away. Julien watched him go, feeling sick to his stomach.

Henri disappeared out the door to the *préau.* Julien turned and ran.

Chapter 35

Second Thoughts

"Henri knows about Gustav and Nina."

Papa stared at him. "Does his father know?"

"Not yet. That's what he said. 'Not yet.'"

"Go, Julien. Take my umbrella. Go tell your mother, and then do whatever she says. I'll tell your teachers she needed you home."

"He'll know why I left school."

"What do you think he expects you to do? What difference do you think it'll make? Julien, go."

He pounded up the stairs and threw open the door. "Mama! They know about Gustav and Nina!" He stood, breathing hard, his wet shoes dripping on the floor.

"Who? Who knows?"

"Henri Bernard." *Henri, that swine, that Vichy-loving–*

"He saw me and Gustav Wednesday night. He says they should be 'taken care of' and sent to a camp. I tried to tell him, Mama–he wouldn't–"

Mama held onto the doorframe. Her face was pale. "Does he know where they are?"

"No. He tried to get me to tell him."

She put a hand on his shoulder. "Julien. Here's what you're going to do. Go tell Sylvie Alexandre. Then do my shopping, and tell the grocer I'm not well. Which is true. Then go back to school and tell Roland Thibaud. Discreetly." He was opening his mouth but she went on. "Where you are not going is anywhere near Gustav and Nina, not now during school hours when anyone who sees is bound to notice. You'll go see your Grandpa after school and drop by the Rostins' on the way home. With Benjamin along to translate. Whether he likes it or not."

"He said he wanted to go with me. Next time I went."

"Good," said Mama. "Now go."

Outside Gustav's window, the moon was setting; pale shreds of cloud passed over it, driven by the wind. Benjamin was asleep in the next room, the room that belonged to André, the prisoner of war. Benjamin, who'd chosen to stay the night and skip school to be with him. Why didn't these people tell him anything? A German Jew his own age with fluent Yiddish living with Julien, and they'd never told him. Even if Benjamin was in hiding too—but he wasn't, he'd said.

Benjamin didn't need to hide.

Gustav closed his eyes. He had failed her. He had been stupid, he had grown confident, he had spoken to Julien in the dark street; and now Nina would die. They would be taken to a camp, and separated, and there she would finish what she had started. She would die. It was his fault. If he hadn't urged her to tell the truth—if he hadn't insisted on calling her Nina every chance he got—they would at least be together in the camp. If he hadn't spoken in the street. He imagined the stationmaster's son, a peering face behind a thin curtain, and the taste of vomit rose in his mouth.

And he couldn't even go to her.

But why? Why couldn't he? They thought he should stay hidden here like a mouse in a hole—why? Because the authorities might only find one of them? If they took her, she would die. That was all that mattered. If they took her, let them take him too.

Nina. We came so far. Nina, you've got to hold on. Was he praying? He didn't even know. Could God really let it end like this? Was there a God?

He didn't even know.

He paced and listened to Benjamin's deep breathing and thought of the things Benjamin had said. *You can't go. This is the worst time for you to go.* He didn't care. Fräulein Pinatel would take him; he'd sleep on the bare kitchen floor, he'd clean the whole apartment every day, and she'd take him in because she knew it. Because she was a good woman. And at least they wouldn't come and find Nina there alone—in her bed, asleep, her eyes opening to the sight of men in uniforms—

No.

And so he knew; there was one thing he knew.

At least they would find them together.

For what was left of the night, Gustav slept.

Benjamin translated. Everything Gustav had turned over in his mind, in the dark. Monsieur Rostin didn't wait for him to finish. He held up a hand. "*Oui. Oui. Va voir Nina.*"

The Rostins went outside, left Gustav with Benjamin. They sat across the table from each other, Benjamin turning and turning his water glass, looking down. His parents used to live in Paris. He'd said that last night. Now Paris was taken. He didn't know where they were.

"Benjamin," said Gustav; Benjamin looked up quickly. "Will you—teach me a little French?"

They sat there all morning, heads bent together over three pages of paper, writing. Practicing. *My sister is very sick. My sister does not speak French. Please do not separate us.*

He could hardly keep his head upright. They ate lunch with the Rostins. Benjamin left. Madame Rostin ordered Gustav to bed, and he slept.

Julien woke Saturday morning, certain they had been taken away. They hadn't.

But they would be.

It was torture. The waiting, the knowing, the going to school and pretending it was fine. The flag salute, even though he was deliberately late to avoid it. He'd almost liked it before, he realized: standing there with his friends ignoring, mocking it, being mad at it.

Now the thought of it made him physically sick.

He did not hear a word that any teacher said. He didn't see Henri, either, because whenever the particular shade of blue that was Henri's jacket came into the corner of his eye, he turned his whole head away.

Gilles came to him and asked him why he'd been late and informed him that there were only five flag saluters. "I guess we convinced some of 'em the other day. Don't think it worked on Henri though. I don't know what we expected, you wave a newspaper in that guy's face and he's not gonna go"—Gilles did a mock double take—"'Oh my word, you're *right!*'" He looked at Julien. Finally. "Hey Julien, you okay?"

"Fine," said Julien.

At night, he lay staring into the dark, reliving the scene: him and Gustav on the dark street; Henri at some unseen window. He'd revise it, make them walk tall as if they had a right to be there, make Gustav shut up with his accent. Make it unhappen. Uselessly. Again and again.

He couldn't pray. He tried.

They were not taken that day. But it didn't mean anything. There was day after day after day. There was no knowing which would be the one.

It was night when Gustav woke. His mind was heavy, full of sleep. He crawled out of bed, dressed slowly by the moonlight through his window. Made a bundle of the blankets and sweaters Madame Rostin had given him. Winter was coming. He crept quietly through the house and out the door.

The moon was still high and almost full; the garden, the apple trees, the barn were laid out clear as day in the silver light. He couldn't go yet. It was by moonlight that he'd been seen.

He went into the barn and looked up the hayloft ladder. From there, he'd see everything. The silvery hay field, the dark woods he would walk through soon. He set his bundle at the foot of the ladder and climbed up.

As he began to crawl into the hay, his hand touched something solid—it gave a loud grunt—he reared back and scuttled backward in the dark. "*Mais t'es qui, toi?*" said a voice, deep, sleepy, and angry. "*Mais va-t'en, merde, fous l'camp, c'est ma grange ici!*"

Gustav retreated farther, wishing he'd had Benjamin teach him threats and swearwords. Trying to remember his French. "Who—you?"

"*C'est chez moi, ici,*" said the shadow. "*T'es qui, toi?*" *Chez moi.* "My home!" The farm was his home? Was he nuts?

"I am Gustav," he said calmly. "I work for Rostins. I sleep here."

"*Pas possible,*" said the voice. He could make out his outline now—broad shoulders and a heavy face—he looked a little like—

"*Dis pas à mes parents, hein, sinon . . .*" That meant, *Don't tell my parents . . .*

That was who he looked like.

"They . . . they say you gone—"

"Well I'm not, am I?"

Gustav shook his head, trying to gather enough French to tell this guy to wise up. Living in the hayloft while a stranger slept in his bed. "Your parents are good," he started.

"Oh, shut–" said Pierre, but Gustav cut across his words, leaning forward in the dark. "My parents are dead," he said loudly and clearly. "I have no home. You have parents." What was French for *stop being an ungrateful blockhead?* "I go away now, to the town. I am not in your bed now. Go. Go sleep in your bed. *Va chez toi.*"

"*Va t'faire . . .*" said Pierre, weakly.

"*Au revoir,*" said Gustav, and climbed down the ladder.

An hour later when the moon had set, he took up his bundle in the pitch black night and started down the little path into the woods, south toward the town, toward Nina, toward whatever would come.

Sunday morning after breakfast, Mama beckoned Julien into the kitchen to dry the dishes she was washing. She turned and looked at him intently, her hands in soapy water, and asked, "Julien, will you tell me what you know about Henri Bernard?"

Julien looked at the cup he was drying. "He's a lot like his father."

"How?"

"He's arrogant. What he wants out of life is everybody obeying him. And he talks big about honor. Like Vichy. He's into Vichy."

Mama looked sober. "You're sure about this?"

"Yeah. I've seen him in action. A lot." He could still see him looking at that newspaper, the look in his eyes for a moment–*he knew I was right*–then the narrow-eyed snarl . . . It wasn't about truth. It was about winning. Always.

"Hm. That's too bad," said Mama. "I was starting to think– Julien, we've heard nothing from Monsieur Bernard, not a word. It's not like him. Sylvie Alexandre expected him up at the parsonage yesterday demanding to know where they were. It's almost as if he didn't know."

Julien stared at her.

"And I was wondering—the only explanation I can think of is if your friend Henri is having second thoughts. And hasn't told him yet."

Second thoughts—the king of France didn't have second thoughts. Julien saw it again, that moment, that hesitation, that look in his eyes when they opened for a split second to the truth—and then his own voice, snarling *shame.* Shame.

"He's not my friend." His throat hurt. "And he doesn't have second thoughts."

"I wondered why he came to you about it before telling his father. He must have waited a whole day without telling his father, just so he could talk to—"

"He was giving me the chance to rat on them!" His heart was starting to race.

"Did he really think you would?"

"I don't know." There was broken glass in his throat. "I don't know. I don't know." His pulse pounded in his ears It was not possible. It was too late.

No one listens to his enemy.

Julien sat in church, not hearing what Pastor Alex said, aware of nothing but what he was not looking at: on the far side of the church, Henri and his father in their pew. Henri, who had not told his father for three whole days. Who was wondering what to do, wondering *what was right.* Was he really? Was it even possible? He had seen it—seen, for a moment, doubt in the ice blue eyes. And hadn't even noticed the miracle.

And what had he expected, each with their guys lined up behind them, like—like one *warlord* against another?

He heard Gilles's mocking voice: *Oh my word, you're right.*

He shut his eyes; there was darkness. And in the darkness there was God. He had been there all along. Lying in wait.

Julien shifted on his pew, wanting to stand, to run, to find a place where he could hide. There was no escape. From what he'd done.

It's not about truth. It's about winning. That's true. About me.

He'd thought he was such a hero. Defender of the truth. He who'd asked God to teach him the weapons of love, so long ago by the Rostin's fire—and who'd dropped it, like he'd dropped carving, and neither God nor Grandpa had ever said a word. Stupidity wasn't enough. It wasn't about stupidity at all. *We will resist with the weapons of the Spirit; without fear, without pride, and without hate.*

He'd just liked his own weapons better. That's all.

He turned his head and looked across the church at Henri. He'd picked him for his scapegoat. Acted like it was Henri who passed every vicious Vichy law, like it was Henri who tried to send Gustav and Nina away to die. And he had taken his revenge, oh, he'd gotten him good. He'd stolen his soccer games from under his nose, won over half his followers, laid siege to the palace, and claimed the throne. He was *winning.* Julien, the new king of France.

But God. Gustav and Nina. I thought I was defending them.

The organ began to play, deep echoing notes, but in Julien's head there was silence. God did not answer. God didn't need to.

You cannot attack with the weapons of love. You cannot defend with the weapons of hate. What if he had done it right? What if he had done it like Jesus said, like God and Pierre had taught him in the white womb of the snowstorm: quietly, simply, with grace even for an enemy, even for a betrayer? What if he had pulled Henri quietly aside and spoken to him without pride and without hate; two boys in an empty hallway, speaking in low serious voices? The way Henri had spoken to *him.*

Oh, God.

He sat and looked across the church at his enemy, the brown hair and the thin face, his enemy singing *The darkness deepens, Lord, with me abide.* He sat and watched him, biting his lip until he tasted blood.

"Mama, I have to go do something. I—I might not be able to

make it home for lunch. Mama"—he had never asked this before—"will you . . . will you pray for me?"

"Of course I will," she said, putting a hand on his shoulder. He looked away. He felt sick.

He left his parents and wove through the crowd at the church door. He had to talk to Henri. But he couldn't do it yet; not without help. A hectic energy flowed through his body, almost equal to the weight that pressed on him: the knowledge of what he had to do, and that it would fail.

He would go first to Roland's farm. If anyone could help, Roland could.

The sun was riding high and cold in the sky as he took the south road from the bridge; shreds of cloud were blowing swiftly across the hills. He pulled his jacket close around him, walking fast, hoping, afraid. The clouds had covered the sun by the time he reached Roland's farm.

Roland was not there.

Julien shivered in the wind. He was going to face Henri alone, not knowing what to say. Knowing what Henri would say back. Could he stand there and take Henri's scorn and give back simple truth—and after weeks of hating, not hate? *Oh God, send somebody else.* But there was nobody. *Almost* nobody—

He stopped at Gilles's house. Gilles wasn't there.

It just had to be done, and done now. He walked quickly through the *place du centre* and took the uphill street, thinking of what to say to Henri. Protestants. Talk about Protestants.

He passed the crest of the hill, not seeing the hills and the woods bright with autumn against the blue sky; only the apple orchard, down there, and the black stone house. The wrought iron gate was shut. The house had a look of silence. Only the wind in the apple trees moving, and a solitary chicken scratching in the dirt. His heart sank.

"Hello?" he called, but his voice died away in the stillness. "Hello!

Hello! Is anyone there? Henri!" Frail echoes shivered back from the surrounding hills, and died. The gate was locked with a chain and padlock. He took hold of it and shook, hard; then stopped and looked quickly around. But there was no one. Just the blank blue sky looking down on him, and the cold wind.

He could almost hear God laughing.

He stood, looking back up the hill toward home. Tears stung behind his eyes. He crouched down on the road, shivering, and the wind whipped the dead leaves past him. He watched them skitter away down the road north to Grandpa's.

After a minute, he stood and followed them.

Grandpa's kitchen was warm, the woodstove glowing. Grandpa welcomed Julien with a *bise* on both cheeks and sat him down at the table. Julien was shaking. "Are you all right, Julien?"

He shook his head.

Grandpa put the kettle on the woodstove and sat down. He gave Julien that look, that quiet, open face that meant Julien could talk, there was no hurry, he was listening. He would hear and would not judge.

But this *deserved* judging.

"Grandpa. I've done something very bad."

Grandpa listened.

"I . . . I . . . Henri . . . Grandpa, I hate him. I really do. Him and his father."

"I don't think that's too surprising," said Grandpa quietly.

"But he hasn't told his father yet. And it's been three days. Mama thinks he could be having second thoughts. And I'm just about the only one who could go talk to him—try to make him understand the truth about them—but he won't listen to me." His fingers dug into his palms. "He knows I hate him, and he hates me too. I've given him lots of reasons to. Good ones."

He risked a look into Grandpa's eyes. They were sober.

"I took over his soccer games that he used to lead. I've practically taken over the class. I mean I am *it* at school right now," he said bitterly. "I'm the latest thing. And then last week, I put him down in front of everybody—his friends, my friends—I almost got him to punch me. He's always the one standing there cool as a cat while you get madder and madder and you look dumb, and I beat him at his own game. Except"—he looked Grandpa in the eye—"it was the wrong game."

Grandpa nodded.

"Do you see? Do you see where this is going? If I hadn't been a hateful, arrogant . . . *fool,* Gustav and Nina could be safe right now. If they arrest her and she dies in some camp, it's my fault."

Grandpa's eyebrows rose very high. He sat back. "Julien," he murmured, "do you really believe that?"

"Don't you?"

Grandpa looked at him for a long moment, then away. "It's impossible to know what would have happened, Julien. There are others whose responsibility is far greater than yours."

They sat not looking at each other for a moment. The kettle began to whistle in the silence.

"Julien, have you talked to God about this?"

He shook his head mutely.

"It might help."

He stared at the table. The kettle began to scream.

"Julien. I want to tell you a story." Grandpa jerked the kettle off the stove and sat back down. "I was in Le Puy, serving my apprenticeship. Or trying to. The son of the people I lived with was my age, and he was a mocker. My clothes, my shoes, the way I talked, everything was ridiculous. I wanted to hide." Grandpa looked away, and swallowed. "He . . . he had a fiancée. She and I talked sometimes. I thought he didn't deserve her. I hated him so much, Julien. I . . . told her something about him. Part of it was true. Part was a lie. She left him."

Julien looked up. Grandpa was looking out the window. He could see the lines etched deep in his face.

"And I went home to my beautiful Régine. Your grandmother. And I had no idea what I'd done until I took her in my arms and felt what it would be to lose her." Grandpa turned and looked him in the eye. "Julien, I did a terrible thing."

Julien swallowed. Outside the window, the trees were swaying in the wind.

"Sin is for real, Julien. In you, in me, in Victor Bernard. We are bad people." Grandpa was looking at him, his eyes deep with sorrow. Julien watched the wind whip the trees.

"Tell me what you believe about Jesus, Julien. What he did."

"He . . ." His voice was a whisper. "He died for our sins."

"Do you believe that?"

Did he? *Jesus died. Jesus died for what I've done.*

"It's true."

It's true.

"He meant to, Julien. Nobody made him do it. He did it for what he wanted the most–for you and me to be able to come to him. After what we've done. It was worth that to him. That's what he wants. Us. To welcome us back."

Behind his eyes, it felt strangely open, as if tears were ready to come; but they did not. "Grandpa," he said quickly. "Grandpa, the Gautier place was my fault too. When the school lost the rental because Monsieur Bernard made this big deal about Benjamin being German? *I* started that. I told Henri. To make him understand the difference between me and Benjamin. He probably went straight home and told his father."

Grandpa looked at him, eyes bright in the weathered face. "Julien," he said, "he forgives you that too."

Outside the window, the trees danced, the wild wind filled the sky with its fierce joy, and they bent and bowed to it, green and supple and free. The knot in his chest was loosening. Desire surged up in him like a sudden spring: he wanted to jump up and dash out into that wind. He almost laughed.

"Yeah," he whispered. "Yeah. I know."

The sun was making great ribbons of scarlet and flaming pink in the west, fading at the edges into cool rose and gray. Julien had eaten: potatoes and cheese, bread and honey and apples, more food than he had had in a month. It felt wonderful. Never try to do a brave deed on an empty stomach, Grandpa had told him; not unless you have to. And he should try to get some sleep too, before he did what he had to do.

What he had to do.

"Julien, it's very, very difficult. To love your enemy."

Julien nodded.

"I think the only reason Jesus asks it is that he loves your enemy too."

Julien looked up.

"Do you see, Julien? He has welcomed you back today. He wants desperately to welcome back Victor Bernard and his son."

Julien sat very straight and looked out the window. Wild red glory hung above the western hills, and the sky was blue and deep above it, and huge. So huge. God probably loved Hitler too. How could God do it and not be torn apart?

Maybe he was.

"I'm going to apologize to Henri."

Grandpa nodded. "That's good."

"What . . . else should I do, Grandpa? I'm not good at this. I'm *terrible* at this."

"That's good, Julien." Julien gave him a look. "No, I mean that. If you thought you were good at this, I'd be worried. I'll tell you what you can do. First, pray for him."

"Pray what?" He'd screwed that one up already with Pierre.

"That God's will be done in him. That's something you can pray without pretending you know what to do about someone else's life. And pray that God will show you what good there is in him. Because it's there, and that good will help you, Julien. That good may save us all."

Julien swallowed.

"And one other thing, Julien. Believe he can change."

Julien said nothing. He looked out at the darkening blue sky.

"You are not God. You cannot change him, and you are not responsible for what you cannot do. Do these things, Julien, and leave him in God's hands. Apologize, know he can change, and tell him the truth as if he wants to know. And then trust God. Because God loves him, and God loves you."

Julien felt his heart lifting. "Are those the weapons of love?"

Grandpa's eyes lit up. "Yes, Julien. Yes. I think you could say they are." His face sobered a little, and he looked out the window at the gathering dark. "Some, at least. Some of them."

"Hey Henri," said Julien, headed out the school gate. "Can I talk to you?"

"About what?" Henri's voice was flat.

"Well. I . . . wanted to say—"

"Hey Lucien!" Henri called. "You walking with me?"

Lucien came up. "Sure. Is *he* walking with us?"

"I just wanted to say something, Henri. I won't bother you after that."

"Great," said Henri. "Say what you wanna say and we can get going."

Julien looked at Henri, whom God wanted back. "I've said some stupid, jerky stuff to you since school started, Henri. And I'm sorry."

Henri recovered very quickly from his double take. "What do you want from me, Julien Losier?"

"I still think that law stinks. That one I showed you in the paper. And the flag salute stinks too. But they're not your fault, and I'm sorry I waved the paper in your face like that, and I want to thank you for coming to me last week to talk about that thing because—because that was the honorable way to do it. And I'd like to talk to you about it some more. If that's okay."

Henri was looking at him. Just looking. Julien looked back. "Could I come over?" Julien said. "Maybe Sunday?"

Henri's eyes flicked to Lucien, and he shrugged. "Nothing better to do on a Sunday. Sure."

"Thanks," said Julien.

Chapter 36

Terms of Surrender

Oh God, please forgive us. Me and Henri. Undo what we have done.

He could feel it now. It was so strange, after all this time, not to feel like he was sending a telegram at all, but more like—like holding hands under a table might feel, or the touch of sunlight on your face when your eyes were closed. Something you were totally aware of but couldn't see.

God, will you show me what's good in Henri?

Still no answer came. He would have to look, he supposed. This was show, not tell.

But today, okay, God? Please?

Today was the day.

"So their father thought it was so dangerous to be Jews that they should leave the country with no adults, no papers, and apparently no money. And you believe that?"

"Yes," said Julien.

"It's insane. No father is that stupid."

Julien sat in the Bernards' kitchen, facing Henri across a pine table. Pale light came through the window; the house was empty except for them, dim and quiet. He lifted his cup of fake coffee to his lips to hide the fact that he had nothing to say. That he had come to talk terms of surrender. That he was scared.

"So they told your mother this ridiculous story, and she believed them, and then they told her the girl is sick?"

Julien put down the coffee and leaned forward. "They didn't 'tell' us the girl was sick. She couldn't stand up. I had to bring her up the street in a wheelbarrow, she was burning up with fever, any fool could have seen she was sick." He tried to stop. "Except, apparently, your father."

Henri's eyes went very cold. "If you and your parents and that sanctimonious pastor want to get taken in by every pickpocket and street performer that comes along, that is no concern of my father's," he said. "When my father saw that girl, she was dressed as a boy and standing on her own two feet."

"You mean on her crutches." Julien closed his eyes for a moment. Then said in a quieter voice, "Your father probably mentioned that."

"No," said Henri. "He didn't."

Julien looked into his eyes; they looked back, pale and unreadable. "Her leg is twisted. My mother examined her and bathed her. I think it would be hard to fake that."

"Hm."

"Ma—someone's taking care of her round the clock. I visited her the other week—she looked awful. Her arms are this big around. She looked like she was dying."

Henri was silent for a moment. Then he said, "Are they at your house?"

Julien's head jerked up. "No." His eyes burned. *He doesn't deserve to be forgiven.* "You can come to my house and search it," he said bitterly.

Henri shook his head quickly. "No. I believe you." He took a sip of coffee. "But listen, Julien, if she's really that sick, I don't see what you're so worried about. We're only talking about informing the authorities so that this can be dealt with in the proper way. Whatever they decide is most appropriate. If they decide to send them to a refugee camp, they won't make the girl travel while she's dangerously ill. They'll wait till she's recovered."

Julien stared. He *trusted* them. *If you were in Paris, would you give them to the Nazis? If you were in . . . in the* désert *. . . would you just hand over the Protestants to the king?*

"Henri, where did your family come from?"

Henri blinked. "From the Rhône Valley, right near Vienne. Village called Saint-Rémy. During the persecution under Louis the Fourteenth."

"*Le désert?*"

"How d'you know what it's called?"

"I'm from here, Henri. My father grew up here, he moved to Paris, he moved back. My grandfather's told me the stories."

Henri looked at him.

"Henri, this is what I wanted to tell you. Persecution is persecution. It was Protestants then, and now it's gonna be Jews. I see it coming. I know government jobs aren't that big a deal, but that's how it starts. Isn't it? In Paris, they've started breaking the windows of Jewish shops. Not *boches*—French people. And then the Marchandeau Law—the papers were already blaming the defeat on Jews before that. Didn't they say stuff like that about Protestants too? That they weakened the nation by being different?" Henri was looking away. "Now that—"

"You can't," Henri interrupted in a low voice, "make a comparison between Marshal Pétain and Louis the Fourteenth."

"I guess I wouldn't compare him to the marshal. I'd compare him to Hitler."

"What's Hitler got to do with it?"

"Well—" *Can't you see?* "We were defeated. I mean, they *let* us set up the Vichy government. The marshal has to give them what they want, because what's to stop them taking the rest of the country?"

Henri's eyes were hard. "You can harp on 'Marshal Pétain is a Nazi puppet' till kingdom come, Julien Losier, if that amuses you. I'm not going to listen."

The doorknob rattled. Julien's heart leapt to his throat, and he half turned, scraping his chair loudly on the floor. Henri lifted his lip.

The door opened. Victor Bernard had come home.

"Hello, boys. Talking politics? Well," said Monsieur Bernard, "I'm sure he hasn't got you promising to stop saluting our flag." And he beamed at his son. Henri gave him a look Julien had never seen in his eyes before; the melting of the ice at last, the clear dance of water in the sun. *So that's what he looks like when he smiles.*

"Um," said Julien. "So. I should probably go."

"Here. Take this to your parents from us." Henri's father pulled a bottle of cider out of the cupboard, smiling, and put it into Julien's hand. Julien had to look at him then, meet the eyes of Victor Bernard, whom God loved, who had tried to send Gustav and Nina away. He took the bottle.

"Thanks," he said, his voice odd in his clogged throat, and he shook Monsieur Bernard's hand. Then Henri's. Then he walked out the door into the dark day.

It had happened all wrong. When his mother asked, he growled, "At least we got a bottle of cider out of it." The falling of her face hurt him so badly he turned away without a word, went to his room, and slammed the door.

On Monday morning, Henri Quatre was in his place, saluting the flag.

Nina slept, and woke, and slept again. Dark figures moved through her dreams. Fräulein Pinatel sat her up in bed and fed her soup, fed her milk, fed her spoonfuls of fishy oil; she lay down and slept again. In the morning, when the sun came in her window, Marita was there, rubbing her back and singing softly in Italian. She spoke to her sometimes. She said her name was Maria not Marita. She said it would be all right, she was safe now, God loved her.

Gustav was here now. She'd woken so many times, and he'd been gone. They'd said he was away working or that he'd be here soon. And he had come and gone again. But now he was here whenever she called for him. He sat by her bed and fed her soup and said she would be all right. He didn't say anything about God. He talked about Father, and the good times, the way he used to swing them round and round in the living room when they were little, and the little white cat he'd brought home one day that he'd found in the rain. And the songs he used to sing while he was working. Gustav sang them to her: "I Had a Little Overcoat" and "Tum Balalaika" or "My Resting Place" if she was sad. But mostly she wasn't. She woke more often now. There seemed to be more light.

"How long have I been sick, Gustav?"

"I don't know, Nina. But I know how long you'll be better."

"How long?"

"A long, long time. All your life!"

She smiled weakly. She remembered lying on her quilt in the Lyon train station, letting herself go, the peace of it. And that peach, like the taste of sunlight. "Will I be happy?" she murmured.

"Yes, Nina. You'll be happy as . . . happy as . . ." He grinned his old Gustav grin. "As a hog in slop!"

"A *hog*, Gustav?" She laughed out loud. It felt good.

And she lay, and felt deep inside herself, and found that maybe she could do it. If it was true, if she could trust them, if the nightmare was ending finally. For Gustav, for herself, for a chance again at the sweetness of life. For the taste of sunlight, on a morning without fear.

She could live.

On Friday, there was another headline, a black banner of shame across the top of the paper. Julien's heart leapt at the sight. "Collaboration!" it read. Above a photo of Hitler and Pétain shaking hands.

Oh Lord, he thought. *You've had mercy.*

They'd had a meeting—Hitler and Pétain—at a place called Montoire, in a train car, and it was official. Collaboration. It was nothing new, nothing he hadn't known already. Yes, it was awful, yes it made him angry, but there it was in black and white, a picture of two men shaking hands, it could never be erased. Henri would have to see it now.

Henri hadn't told his father yet. Mama'd heard nothing. He had come to school all week, saluted the flag, looked past Julien—and said nothing to his father . . .

Julien walked down to school beside Benjamin, hope beating in his heart.

Henri wasn't there. Julien stood by the wall with his friends, who were buzzing about the news, and he watched the flag circle gather and the flag rise, and Henri was not there. Maybe he was sick. Or maybe . . . *oh Lord, tell me it's true.* Henri slipped in through the gate just before the bell. Julien looked at him, wild with hope.

Henri looked back with hatred in his eyes.

Julien drew back, and went into class and copied the Pythagorean triples from the board. All that day, whenever Julien looked at him, Henri turned his face away.

He prayed that night, and he prayed the next morning. He prayed for Nina and Benjamin and Gustav, and Vincent and his family, and Pierre. And for Henri.

He could still feel it. The sunlight on his face, though the sky was drowned in cloud.

On Monday, the schoolyard was in absolute chaos. By the flagpole, Monsieur Ricot called shrilly, but no one listened. No one but

Gaston and Lucien. The rest of the school was gathered by the wall around a stocky figure with a loud, familiar laugh.

Pierre.

Pierre, even bigger than before, and deeply tanned; Pierre, grinning at the *petits sixièmes'* wide-eyed admiration, eating it up. Pierre spotted him. "Hey, Julien, long time!"

"No kidding!" When they reached each other and shook hands, Pierre grinned and added under his breath, "I met your friend. He's pretty cool."

There was so much to hear, so much to tell. So much that was going to have to be told in private . . . the bell rang before they were halfway started, and Pierre went on talking as they filed into class. "So what's with that flag thing? What was Ricot hollering about?"

Lucien answered. "It's this new thing Marshal Pétain instituted—we're renewing a spirit of patriotism in France. You want to join us tomorrow?"

"Wait. Who's this marshal guy?"

Wow. He *had* been gone a long time.

"*You* know. He won the Battle of Verdun. He became head of government after the defeat. Head of Free France. He's given everybody new hope—"

"He's not the guy in the picture who's shaking hands with Hitler, is he?"

"Um . . ."

Julien almost laughed out loud. Pierre was the best.

"And he's supposed to be this *war hero?*"

"Pierre Rostin," said Monsieur Matthias, "*sit down.*"

On Tuesday Henri was there again, saluting the flag, but Julien stopped and stared across the schoolyard at him. Henri's hand was not raised stiffly in the air like the others'.

It was over his heart.

There was a letter. A flimsy, preprinted postcard, and on it Uncle Gino's handwriting:

> Dear *Martin and Maria,*
>
> *All* . . . in good health . . . ~~tired~~ . . . ~~slightly, seriously ill~~ . . . ~~wounded~~ . . . ~~killed~~ . . . ~~prisoner~~ . . . ~~died~~ . . . without news of . . . *family B. K. (evacuated). The family Pirelli* . . . is well . . . back to work . . . ~~in need of~~ . . . ~~supplies~~ . . . ~~money~~. *Vincent* . . . will go back to school at . . . *Paris* . . . ~~is being put up at~~ . . . ~~is going to~~ . . . Best wishes . . . Love . . . *Giovanni Pirelli*

Mama had tears in her eyes. Julien hugged her. *They're all right.* After a moment they looked again at the postcard. "Evacuated," Mama murmured.

They looked at each other. Julien thought of the roads, the bombers, Régis Granjon glancing up in fear.

"We don't tell him," said Papa.

Julien nodded, slowly.

Nina began to walk again.

She could put her feet on the floor. She could stand. Fräulein took her bedpan away, and she hobbled to the bathroom, leaning on Gustav's arm. He brought her crutches, scrubbed clean; she stood leaning on them, holding the handgrips her fingers knew so well. Here it was, waiting for her: her life.

She walked between bookshelves out into a place of windows, and light. A kitchen table laid for three, a steaming bowl of potatoes. Gustav's face lit at the sight of her; on the edge of her memory, she could see Father holding out his arms to her: *Come on,* herzerl*! You can do it!* She leaned her crutches against the table and sat at the place prepared for her. Gustav beamed.

She walked slowly through the apartment that afternoon, her

crutches clicking gently on the floor. Every wall was lined with books. French, English, German, Italian, languages she didn't even recognize. One that looked like Hebrew. Did this woman read Hebrew? She touched the spines of the books gently as she moved down the hall. It had been so long. She wondered if Uncle Yakov had given her books to Heide as she'd asked. If she'd ever see Heide's round friendly face again—if she'd ever see Vienna, and Uncle Yakov, and her cousins—

"I wouldn't start with Kant, if I were you." She jumped and snatched her hand away from the books. It was Fräulein. "Not before you get your strength back." Quiet amusement tinged her voice.

"I wasn't going to . . . I . . . I couldn't—"

"You certainly can and will read my books," said Fräulein firmly. "I merely ask to be allowed to advise." She took down a thick book from the opposite shelf. "Now this is the Torah. Should I presume you've read it before?"

She hadn't read it. She leafed through it in bed that night. She read about the Flood, about a king murdering somebody over a vineyard; she read long poetry she didn't understand, about God punishing and forgiving, full of warriors and chariots, mountains and springs of water, mothers and babies. It sounded familiar somehow. While she read she saw Uncle Yakov's table, and the Shabbat candles.

The Italian woman came, the woman named Maria. Maria showed her the center of the Torah book; the psalms. She couldn't read German, but she told Nina the number of her favorite psalm and quoted lines from it to her in Italian, her eyes closed, her face open: "*When evil men come upon me to devour me, when my enemies and my foes attack me, they will stumble and fall . . . Though my father and mother forsake me, the Lord will take me up . . . I believe I will see the goodness of the Lord in the land of the living.*"

Nina found the psalm in the Torah book that night when Maria was gone. She read it three times. Then she read on. "*The Lord is my strength and my shield; my heart trusts in him, and he helps me. My heart leaps for joy, and with my song I thank him . . . The voice of the Lord is over the waters; the God of glory thunders . . . The voice of the Lord makes the deer to calve, and strips the forests bare, and in his temple everything cries, 'Glory!'*"

She did not believe or disbelieve the beautiful words. She read them. She heard the glory cry. She turned off the lamp and lay in the dark with her eyes closed, feeling strangely quiet, strangely open, as if someone had slipped in when she wasn't looking and unlatched the doors of her spirit, opened them slowly, like the windows of a small and airless room.

When she woke, the wind had blown the whole sky in.

It was blue, bluer than any sky she had seen before, deep and filled to the brim with the sun. The curtains were a clean and brilliant white against the blue, and the sunlight rested on the edge of her bed, touching the tip of her fingers with a sure and gentle warmth. Her heart was buoyed and carried in the warm air, the strange sensation of lightness, the stone weight of fear rolled away.

"Peace," she whispered in surprise. "It's peace, isn't it."

She sat in Fräulein's chair by the window with the Torah book open in her lap, drinking in the sky. Gustav paced behind her: to the kitchen, to the bedroom, to the kitchen again. "You all right, Gustav?" she called, wishing it were warm enough to fling the window open. She pushed the curtains farther aside, and at the sound of rings sliding on the curtain rod, he was there. "Not so wide, please," he begged.

"We need more light in here! They're always shut!"

"Fräulein doesn't like people looking in."

"It's a beautiful day out there, Gustav. You should go out or something. When I'm strong enough—"

Gustav swallowed and twitched the curtain just a little. "When you're strong enough," he said brightly, "you'll step out the door, and all the boys in Tanieux will fall at your feet! Have you looked in a mirror lately?"

"Oh, come off it." But her face felt warm.

Julien had learned to stay out of Henri's way. *I may have my hand over my heart*, his eyes said, *but I still wish you were dead*. Two weeks now, he had lived this way, asking his mother every evening: "Any news?" "No news," she said, and he could breathe again. And sleep, and wake, and face the school day and Henri's burning eyes.

Pierre still talked to Henri. Pierre, the old friend who was slow to understand the new alliances, who stayed out of the flag salute with puzzled disgust on his face and spent the rest of his break moving freely around the schoolyard—under the tree with Henri, by the wall with Julien, by the gate with Léon and Antoine. Pierre didn't care. Julien wished he were Pierre.

Pierre, who had cut through the National Revolution crap so instantly he still thought he could straighten Henri out.

"I don't get it, man," Julien heard Pierre say, putting away his books after math class. "The guy is working with the *boches*. Why do you listen to a word he says?"

Henri clapped his math book shut. "You have to learn to see past appearances, Pierre."

"You mean he just *looked* like he shook Hitler's hand?"

"I mean," said Henri, slowly and with emphasis, "that he was *forced* to shake Hitler's hand."

Gaston shot Henri a look of scorn. "Forced? You sound like Julien Losier."

Henri turned white. "'You sound like Julien Losier,'" he mimicked in a high-pitched voice. "*You* sound like a six-year-old. Go ahead. Tell my friend here why the marshal shook Hitler's hand," he snarled, "and make it good." Henri turned to Julien, who instantly looked away. "And you. Get out of here. Now." He took a trembling breath. "By the way," he added in a quiet, deadly voice, "I know where they are."

Julien's heart stopped. Pierre's eyes went wide. "Where what are?" asked Gaston.

"None of your business," said Henri.

The farmer Gustav had worked for needed his help again, Gustav said, if Nina could spare him. They were putting the garden to bed before the frost, the last big push of the season.

"If I can spare you! You're driving me crazy, pacing around here all day!"

"I'll have to be gone for a couple nights."

"Is it so far?"

He shrugged. "Out of town. I think I might need to leave in the morning early. You might not see me at breakfast."

She lay in bed, wondering. She couldn't sleep. Fräulein had been all strange today; she'd changed Nina's sheets and taken all her little things off the desk—the thermometer, the water glass, the Torah book she was reading—and spent half an hour arranging boxes and tarps under the bed and practically crawling in behind them like she was playing hide-and-seek. But all without smiling. Hardly looking at Nina. It made her nervous. And Gustav—why did he have to work so far away? It didn't make sense. She'd missed him so much while she was sick—hadn't they known she needed him? He'd never been there, and now he always was—but pacing like an animal in a cage, twitchy, being strange about curtains . . . like he was . . .

Hiding.

He hadn't left the house. Ever. In more than two weeks.

She heard the creak of a floorboard outside her door. She breathed deep and slow as a sleeper, her heart racing, her throat tight. Heard the click of a latch, and quiet footsteps on the stairs; she leaned to the window and saw, down below, the downstairs door swing open and a dark figure slip down the street; keeping to the shadows, afraid of the faint light of the moon.

The window was cold and hard against her forehead. None of it was true. The dark was a weight pressing on her, and the ragged moon laughed in her face, and she hardly heard her own dry whisper: *Gustav, you lied to me*. And everywhere there were evil men.

"*Bonjour*?" A head was peering in the barn door.

Gustav squirted the last couple streams of milk into the pail and released the goat. "*Bonjour*," he said back, peering through misty dawn light. It was awfully early for anyone to be out there. Even him. But he'd missed this so much; the milking especially.

"Where is Pierre?" The boy's silhouette was tall and thin.

"He sleep. I tell him I do milking today."

"You're Gustav," said the boy, stepping through the door. Brown hair and a thin face; nobody he knew.

"Yes. You?"

"A friend of Pierre."

"You look for Pierre?"

"I thought I'd help him with the milking. I can help you if you like."

Gustav looked at the boy, considering. Well, he was a friend of Pierre, and he'd known where to find him at six o'clock in the morning. "You can milk?"

"No problem." The stranger pulled the old milking stand out of the corner, took Paquerette by one horn, and with a neat twist got her up on it. "She used to be ours," he told Gustav, beginning with a practiced hand to shoot a hard stream of milk into the pail. "We had three, but my father sold them to the Rostins a couple years ago. Now we just have a cow. Do you like it here?"

Gustav blinked. Nobody had asked him that. *Don't you know, friend-of-Pierre? I'm lucky to be anywhere that's not behind barbed wire.* The goat on his stand tossed her horns, and he grabbed her udder and started milking, feeling the rhythm of it in his hands. He liked this. Even on those farms in the mountains, as a raw kid just learning to work, he'd liked it.

"Yes," he said finally. "Yes. I come from city, you know? My father, he made—" he gestured at his feet.

"Shoes?"

"Yes. But my father die, and we go. In Italy, I learn to work for farmers, and it is good. I like it. But I never can stay. Always there is danger. When we stop, we must go again . . . most time we are in cities, nobody know us, my sister she is very afraid. Here—I work on farm again, this is good family, I hope that now we can stay. This place, it is very, you know?" He couldn't remember the word. "Like woman . . ."

The stranger's hands paused in their motion, and he looked at Gustav. "Beautiful?"

"Yes. Beautiful." There was more light now.

"How is your sister?"

"Better! Every day she is little bit better. I think . . . I think she will live."

"What did she have? What kind of sickness?"

"I don't have name. Fever, and—she need, you know, toilet all the time. Very thin. Before we come here, we are in Lyon. So many people, no food. I tried . . ." It hurt to even remember how he'd tried . . . He blinked fast and kept on milking. "In Lyon a woman beats her. Takes Nina's stick for walking and she beats her, because she thinks we are Germans. Now she have hurt here"—he touched his side—"it breaks, you know? Maybe this make her sick. Maybe because hungry. I don't know. Maybe because—" He released Nanette, and sat at the empty milking stand for a moment, looking into the darkness of the barn. "In Lyon—it is end. We think, now we die. She think that. How you say? I don't know word . . ." He could not think how to say it. The morning sun filtered in through the cracks in the walls; it poured through the open doorway. The other boy looked away, toward the sunlit world.

"In Lyon, she think life no more good. She—I think she want to die. But Samuel bring us here. I make her come, and now she lives. She think safe. She not know about train man. I not tell her. I want she should get better."

"If you tell her about the train man, she won't get better?" The boy was sitting very straight, his hands motionless on Jaunette's udder, his face very still. Gustav looked away.

"I don't know. If she afraid again . . ."

The boy nodded. Abruptly, he began to milk again, harder than before. "This train man is a bad person?"

Gustav stared at him. He was milking furiously. Why would he ask such a thing? "What you think?" he said quietly, hard.

Jaunette bleated. "He told you to go away and die? Is that it?"

"He give us train ticket to go back, he say, because people no want us here. Back to Lyon. In Lyon we die." Gustav looked away, his throat growing tight.

"I should go." The boy untied Jaunette with a quick motion. "We are finished, no?"

Gustav glanced down the row of goats. "Yes," he said, shaking himself. "Yes. Thank you. You stay maybe for—"

"My father will expect me at breakfast."

Gustav held out his hand. "I not know your name—"

The boy looked at the hand for a moment and took it. "Henri," he said. "My name is Henri."

Chapter 37

Life in Their Hands

Nina woke to fear, as she had every morning for the past year. As she always would.

Who was he hiding from? Hiding *her* from? What did they mean to do? He hadn't seen fit to tell her. None of them had. They had left her in the dark.

In Lyon she had been ready. She remembered the hunger, and the way the hunger had faded, the still and heavy peace. Sinking toward sleep at the end of a journey, the end of a long and terrible day. And then Gustav pulling at her, shouting at her—"*Live, live!*" He would never know how hard it had been. But she had done it. She had fought her way back to life; she had found rest. She had found what she thought she would never taste again.

Joy.

She wished she had died.

In Lyon, she had been ready. But *now!* Now after one last taste of freedom, one day with the stone lifted from her heart—to feel the weight of fear again and know it would never go— There was no God. *And if there is.* And if there is he doesn't know what he is doing. He is stark shrieking mad. He's been too long in the dark.

Even this town in the hills, with its kind faces, was a place of danger. All her long-ago hope and her courage had been pretty lies, and Uncle Yakov was right. She knew this now. The world was full of thieves and soldiers who took whatever they could; even women and children had hatred in their eyes. Gustav with his desperate, fierce care had bought her one day of freedom, and this terrible truth. And now she had to do it all over again; to let go of peaches, and sunlight, and all the hopes she had hidden down inside herself for the things she would never have. A sweetheart. A husband. Children.

She lay dry-eyed, looking up at the blank ceiling.

There had been no word from the mayor, nor from Victor Bernard. It had been four days. Julien was beginning to breathe again.

He walked out to the farm Sunday afternoon behind the rented cart to haul wood for the winter. The wild thyme in the woods this year had grown taller than Grandpa had ever seen it. "Did I ever tell you what that means, Julien?" he asked as they stacked wood.

"No."

"It means a hard winter. Maybe the hardest in a very long time."

Julien glanced at the long woodpile, and Grandpa followed his gaze.

"We cut a lot of wood last year, Julien. As much as we could. Beyond that we'll have to trust God." He looked at Julien, his eyes bright. "Julien—" He broke off and smiled and rocked the cart to see if the load would shift. "In the city," he said quietly, "I've seen tarps over woodpiles. As if the rain would rot them. When the rain's what makes them strong. Leaches the sap out, seasons the wood—it's not worth burning till it's been out in the storms for a year."

In the end of the gray log Julien was lifting were little lines. Little dents, the bites of a clumsy maul. He had split this log last year. When he was fifteen.

"You really think we're ready?"

"It's been quite a year for storms, Julien," said Grandpa quietly. "We're as ready as we'll ever be."

News was in the wind, on the radio, news of change. More refugees. Tens of thousands expelled from Lorraine for "disloyalty," which meant, Papa said, not speaking German. A bunch of them from some Protestant boarding school in Lorraine were enrolling in the new school. A few were Jewish. Benjamin was called into the principal's office at lunchtime and came out with a bigger grin than Julien had seen on him in months.

"You'll never guess," he said as they walked home. "I bet you twenty francs."

"If I had twenty francs," said Julien, "I wouldn't waste them on some dumb bet with *you*."

"C'mon. Guess."

Your parents are alive. "Full scholarship to the Sorbonne?"

"They want me up to the new school on Friday. To give a *talk*. On being Jewish."

"Really? They invited you?"

"Yep," said Benjamin. "Me."

"Hey!" Magali was calling to them across the *place du centre*, waving. "Hey," she shouted again, running toward them. "You'll never guess what Rosa and I just saw!"

Julien and Benjamin both rolled their eyes. "Bet us twenty francs?"

"I'm serious, Julien. It was amazing. It was *great*."

"All right, what d'you see?"

"Well, we were watching the twelve-fifteen train come in, and this guy got off. Older guy, real dirty, messy beard. Wearing a coat without any buttons—he had to hold it closed—and the soles of his shoes were coming off, and Monsieur Bernard sees him, right?"

Julien swallowed. *Right.*

"So he steps up to him like he's a *gendarme* or something, like so"—she did a brisk military step, her face right in Julien's—"'What is your business in Tanieux?'" she said crisply. He could just hear the man.

"And the guy mumbles something in this accent, maybe Polish, and the Bernard guy's about to give him his speech and a ticket back out, right? And then"—her eyes grew bright—"then old *père* Soulier steps up from beside this huge crate of cabbages he was shipping. He steps up and says, 'Excuse me, Victor.' Just like that—*Victor*—I didn't know they knew each other that well! 'Excuse me, Victor, he has business with me.'" Her laugh rang across the *place*. "And *Victor* does this complete double take—man, it was beautiful. Best thing I've seen all day."

"Then what happened?" asked Benjamin, a fierce light in his eyes.

"*Père* Soulier says 'He's my guest' and turns to the old Polish guy and says, 'Monsieur, you will come. Come and eat with me today. Cabbage soup!'" She laughed again, happily. "Then he tells Bernard 'Cross off my shipment,' and Bernard says 'How much were you going to get for it?' And *père* Soulier says 'Cross off my shipment,' again. And the old guy's standing there with tears in his eyes."

"Then what happened?" whispered Julien.

"Bernard crossed off the shipment, that's what. I guess he knows he's up against more than just Pastor Alex now." Her grin was fierce. "I saw Monsieur Faure and Monsieur Cholivet giving him dirty looks, and they helped *père* Soulier load up, and Monsieur Raissac took one of the sacks of potatoes he was shipping and just slung it on *père* Soulier's cart without saying a word! Man." She gave a huge sigh of satisfaction. "Let's go have lunch."

"Magali, was Henri there?"

"Yeah." She frowned. "He was there, but I don't know if he saw. I didn't see him till they were all gone, and he was looking the other way. C'mon Julien. Let's go."

Looking the other way. Julien followed them down the street, slowly.

On Wednesday the wind rose; the *burle* come early this year, a promise of terrible cold. The French flag fluttered wildly in the icy wind, and the boys in their circle around it hunched and shivered; Henri's jacket flapped and billowed against the hand he held hard over his heart. When the salute ended and the school doors opened, Julien paused a moment, watching. Henri Quatre had drifted away from his group and stood alone by the black stone wall, his hands in his pockets, looking out over the Tanne in the bitter cold.

"Julien," said Papa, beckoning him into his office and shutting the door behind them. "There's going to be an assembly at school today. I know they didn't announce it. Now I want you to do what I say, Julien. Benjamin won't be there today. And I want you not to tell him what you've heard."

Julien blinked.

"If you have any questions about why, ask me at lunchtime."

Julien nodded slowly. "Yes, sir."

Gustav sat at the table staring at a piece of bread, his heart tight, trying to understand what had happened. Nina wouldn't eat.

She wouldn't *eat*.

She said she wasn't hungry. She said he should eat it, he was going to live.

It was like Samuel hadn't come to them, that terrible day in the train station, like none of it had happened. In her head, she was back in Lyon.

She knew they were hiding her. He told her it was only a precaution because of the stationmaster; she looked at him with flat, empty eyes and looked away.

Fräulein Pinatel had sent for Signora Losier. To talk to her. It was all she could think of. Gustav looked at her as she came in, remembering what she and Frau Alexandre had seemed to him: two mothers standing at the end of the road, with life in their hands for the taking. And saw that he'd been wrong. She was as lost as he was.

Nina did not turn her head when the door opened, but she saw her. The Italian woman. Here to make her eat. Make her live.

Make her die another day.

"Hello, Nina," said Maria. "How are you?"

"Fine." Nina did not move.

"You need to eat."

"Go away."

"I will not go away. You need to eat. You need to grow strong. I know you are afraid, but that is all the more reason why you need to eat."

Nina turned her head and looked Maria full in the face. "You know I am afraid," she said through her teeth. "*You know?*"

"Yes, Nina," said Maria softly. "I know what it is to be afraid."

Nina sat up and leaned toward her, her teeth bared. "You," she spat. "You with your house, with your doors that lock"—she'd broken into Yiddish—"you tell me *you know*? Liar!" she shouted. "*Liar!*" She took a deep, shuddering breath, forcing herself to think of the words. This woman had to know what she had done. "You lie," she said in Italian. "You say *sicura*. You say safe! I am not safe. Nowhere is safe, not for me. Nowhere." *Everywhere there are evil men.*

Maria closed her eyes. "I am sorry. You have a place here, Nina. Here in Tanieux."

"You talk. Easy talk. You do not know."

"I do know, Nina."

"You know hunger? You know fear? Here in your house—with door, food, bed, light—you say you know? You know nothing," she spat. "*You have never been alone.*"

Even the air in the room stopped moving. For a split and silent second their eyes were locked on each other, and the force of Maria's anger hit Nina like a blow. "You do not know me," said Maria between her teeth, and her voice cut the air like a whip. But Nina was already recoiling, as if she had been slapped.

There was silence. Nina looked into the woman's eyes, felt a trembling in her belly.

"I have been alone," said Maria quietly.

Nina dropped her eyes.

"No. Look at me."

She raised them slowly.

"Nobody to help you. You sit on the floor. You don't move. You don't speak. You don't look at anything. There is nobody to help you when the man comes with his gun." Nina's eyes were wide, staring at her. Behind them she felt the sting of tears. They were both shaking.

Their locked gaze broke. They dropped their eyes to the white bedspread. Nina held a fold of it clamped in her fist. Maria sat down on the bed.

"You?" Nina whispered.

"Yes."

They looked at each other. Maria's eyes were wide as if with fear. "In the Great War. The first war. You know *war*?"

Nina nodded.

"I was in Italy. My village. Bassano del Grappa. A small farm. We were poor. It was like now—when the war came, there was no food." Nina was very still. "My two brothers, they were soldiers. My father, my mother, they worked very hard without my brothers, so we could eat. I worked hard too. I was fourteen. You understand my Italian?"

Nina nodded.

"We worked hard, three years; we were hungry. My mother, she made me eat, she always gave me some of her food. We were thin. Then the war came to our village—the Austrian soldiers came."

Nina looked away and looked back; the two women's eyes met, and understanding was in them. "We were afraid. But they did nothing bad to us. Except the worst thing: they took our food."

Maria paused a moment, looking down; then she continued.

"That winter was terrible. Always my mother said, 'I'm not hungry. You eat.'" Of course. Of course she had said that. "I don't know how we lived."

Maria took a deep trembling breath.

"In the spring," she said, "the sun came back. It was warm. We planted an early garden, and we hoped. You know this word, *hope*?"

Nina nodded, her eyes never leaving Maria's face.

"Spring. We start to hope—then we get the news. My brother Tomasso is killed. My mother cries and cries. Then more news. My brother Gino has been killed also—they think he has been killed, they do not know. They cannot find him—you understand? My mother stops crying." *Yes. Yes. You stop crying. And then . . .*

"She doesn't cry, she doesn't talk, she doesn't eat. Soon she is in bed with a fever. She was so thin. So weak—" Maria looked down, her throat laboring. "I was with her," she whispered. "I watched her die."

It came back so vividly—the wet sound in Father's throat, his struggle to breathe. To whisper to her to run, fight, live. She had found him—in the morning—could she have borne it if she'd had to watch him, to hear every breath come harder than the last, feel him growing cold? *Oh, Father.*

She had shut away the pain and obeyed him. She had shut away the pain, because deep inside she had known it would hurt this much.

"There was only me and my father. We worked as hard as we could to stay alive. I guided the plow, and he pulled it; all our animals were gone. He cried sometimes at night when he thought I was asleep. It was terrible to listen to. The soldiers came again, but there was no food for them to take. We should have left, but we didn't know where to go. The soldiers came once more—running away, with the Italian Army after them. We hid in the cellar while the battle went over us. And then the war ended. We had hope again, but so tired. So tired."

Nina could feel it in Maria's voice, that bone weariness; she could feel it in her weary heart.

"We got sick. Both of us. The influenza. It killed more people than the war. I was delirious with fever for days. When I woke up I was alone."

Nina's stomach tightened. Tears were welling in Maria's eyes.

"I ran through the house, calling for him, calling 'Papa, Papa.' It was so quiet. I thought he had left me while I was sick—that hurt so much . . . I ran outside to the chestnut tree where my mother's grave was—you know *grave?*" Nina nodded. The tears made bright tracks down Maria's cheeks. "There were two graves," she whispered.

"All," breathed Nina. "All your family . . ."

Maria nodded. They looked at each other for a moment. Then Maria took a breath.

"I was alone," she said, not looking at Nina, her voice growing harsher. "The neighbors on the next farm came and left food for me. They left it outside the door. They were afraid of the sickness. I sat on the floor, I didn't eat the food, I didn't sleep, I didn't see the light. I wanted to die. And then I looked up and in the doorway there was a man with a gun."

Nina froze. *No.*

"A soldier—Austrian. He was dirty. His uniform was torn. He said something in German, and he pointed his gun at me. I didn't understand." She was gesturing as though she had a gun. But her eyes were looking into the darkness of the barrel. Nina saw it too, that deep blank eye. They were kneeling on that floor, together, in that dark.

"He yelled at me. He took the bowl of soup out of my hands—it was cold; I'd had it for hours. He drank it." She lifted an imaginary bowl, tipped back her head, drinking savagely. Nina could see the soup spilling out the sides of his mouth. She could feel his hunger. "He threw it at the wall, and it broke. He yelled at me again. I was starting to cry."

She grabbed Maria's hand; they were both shaking. "And he—he *looked* at me, Nina. Do you know what I mean?" Maria's face twisted with that look—ugly: lust and scorn and desperation. Nina drew back, shaking her head no, no. "And then he stopped. And he looked around." The nervous eyes of a deer in an open field, the quick turning of the head. "There was nobody. But . . . he looked out the door and then looked at me and"—Nina's mouth was open, she was leaning forward, tears wet on her face—"and then he was gone."

Gone.

"Out the door. I was alone. Nina—I was alone for days. In the empty house. The door was broken. The neighbors who brought the soup had gone. Nobody came," she whispered. "Nobody came for days."

You have never been alone.

Maria's eyes were closed. Her face was very still. Nina reached out a hesitant hand as if to touch her cheek—her throat hurt, she could hardly breathe, the salt taste of tears was in her mouth. Maria spoke, and she drew back. Her voice was very low.

"I escaped. Others didn't. I don't know why he left." *It was pure, blind luck.* "But I learned what I learned, about the world. I have not told my children this story, Nina. I am afraid to tell them what I learned. But I have told you. Because I think you know."

"Yes," whispered Nina. "I know."

"Nina." Maria opened her eyes. They were very dark. "I have told you my story. Will you tell me yours?"

Story. As if it was something with a meaning. An end. She stared at Maria. Maria looked quietly back. Her face was so—open. Open like the door to a firelit house at the end of a long and terrible journey. Story. Nina swallowed, gripped a fold of the cover in her fist, and opened her mouth to speak.

It was bright and bitter cold. The boys in the schoolyard shuffled and stamped their feet to keep warm. Monsieur Astier stood before them with his bullhorn, his face very serious.

"I won't keep you long. But I have something very important to tell you. It's news you won't read in the papers or hear on Radio Vichy. It's news you have a right to know."

Julien rubbed his hands together and wished he were somewhere where none of this was happening.

"I love my country," said the principal. "I know you all do too. So it's difficult for me to tell you this, but you have a right to know. As do your parents. You have a right not to be led blindly where our country seems to be going.

"Before I tell you this story, I want to emphasize that Pastor Alexandre and I heard it directly from an eyewitness."

Julien's throat was dry. *Hurry up.*

"You may know that the Nazis have persecuted the Jews in Germany almost from the day they came into power. It appears that now they want to be rid of them completely. They've been deporting many of them east into occupied Poland. But three weeks ago, they decided to send a trainload of deportees to France. To Lyon."

Lyon! Julien and Roland looked at each other. Were they coming here?

"They didn't tell our government their plans. Not a word. They just packed the train with Jews they had rounded up, and sealed the cars from the outside, and sent them. When the train arrived in Lyon, officials there were shocked to find it packed with people—men, women, children, the elderly—all Jewish.

"You have to understand," said Monsieur Astier slowly, "that the Germans were breaking the armistice by doing this. And that the officials were afraid that there would be more. And you can imagine they asked themselves, what will these people eat?"

The crowd stirred. Everybody understood *that* question.

"Yes," Monsieur Astier said heavily. "What will they eat?" He looked away for a moment. "So our government in Vichy stood firm and refused to accept them. They insisted the Germans take them back. But the Germans didn't take them back." His voice grew heavier. "And that train sat in a corner of the Lyon train station for three days, *shut*. Nobody was let out. Nobody brought them food or water. Nothing."

The schoolyard had gone dead silent.

"After three days, they sent it on to an internment camp, without opening it. When it arrived, some of the people inside were dead."

He would never tell Benjamin.

"Our eyewitness watched the bodies being unloaded. Many of the living were so weak they had to be carried. None of them were taken to a hospital; they all went directly to the camp. Where it's said the conditions are so harsh that even healthy people are at risk."

Julien was light-headed. How many times did he have to say, *I never imagined this*? Was this the future?

There was a long silence.

"We can still be shocked," said Monsieur Astier, "at seeing human beings treated in this way. The Nazis have not finished their work on France. But how long? When does our government start to resist? Do any of us really believe this won't happen again?"

Julien and Roland looked at each other. Roland looked sick.

"I do not believe," said Monsieur Astier slowly, "that our new government is going to resist. They are cooperating with the Nazis. And the Nazis will expect them, and us, to get used to seeing certain people treated this way. To find it normal, to shut up. I felt I had to tell you this, boys, because you as much as your parents have a right to the truth. To make your choices in the light of day. Boys, it's not just our government that has to decide what to do with the people who come in on the train. It's us."

There was silence.

"Let's take a minute to think," said Astier. "The podium is open, if anyone has a response."

A powerful hush settled over the schoolyard. The flag was flying high in the cold bright air, red as blood and blue as Henri's eyes. Julien closed his eyes against it and wondered, for a moment, if there really was a God. When he opened them, someone stood at the front, holding the bullhorn.

Henri Quatre.

"Let me tell you a different story," said Henri in a clear voice. *No,* thought Julien, *no. When does this stop? It doesn't stop. Nina is only the first. This is the future.*

"Old *père* Pallasson, who lived out at Le Chaux some years back," said Henri, and Julien lifted his head. "Have you heard about him? He never set foot out his door all winter for fear of the cold. And then come spring, the snow melted, and *père* Pallasson looked out his window at the sunshine and thought it was summer—and he opened the door and walked out into the *burle* without a coat. May he rest in peace."

There were a few chuckles from the crowd.

"I got up here to tell you," Henri said, and he paused. Julien stared, his heart in his throat. A dark flush was coming over Henri's face. "I got up here to tell you that *père* Pallasson is me." His quiet voice rang into the silence. "When the armistice was signed, I thought we'd be okay. That it was spring, that it was back to normal. And it turns out," he said slowly, "that the *burle* is blowing harder than ever."

No one whispered. No one moved. The entire school was staring at Henri Bernard. Julien was faint, he was light, he would dissolve at any moment into the cold, clear air.

"Monsieur Astier is right," said Henri, loud and clear. "The Vichy government isn't resisting. They are cooperating with the Nazis." His voice was harsh. "I hate to say it, and I hate to think my country is doing this, and I'd put my hand to the fire that if the marshal knew what was going on, he'd stop it. But I've made up my mind. I trusted them. But I can't trust them anymore." Julien was numb. Benjamin would never believe him.

"And we know." Henri's voice began to ring. "We know about persecution here in Tanieux. We know what to do with a government that makes unjust laws, laws that go against the law of God. We haven't forgotten the Huguenots—we still sing their songs; we haven't forgotten how our people came here fleeing the king's soldiers, hounded and driven out because someone thought they were the wrong kind of people. And so we know how it feels. And I'm here to say"—there was the tiniest tremble in his voice, and his fist clenched and he raised it up—"that I have made my choice. I'm here to say—"

There was a pressure in Julien's head, in Julien's heart. He could feel them all around him, the heads thrown back, the faces turned up toward him, toward Henri Bernard. Who knew exactly what he was doing. Who was king of France again just like *that*, and always would be. His eyes burned.

"I'm here to say," said Henri fiercely, "that anyone who wants to put people back on the train and send them somewhere else is not going to get any help from me!" Julien looked at him, at the clear blue sky above his head. *Someone'll tell him. You know that, don't you.* In Roland's eyes was awe.

"We're not going to keep refugees out of Tanieux!" Henri was shouting now. "It's going to be what it was then: *un abri dans la tempête*—a refuge! We did it once, and we can do it again!" He stopped—Julien saw his throat working—and looked around. Monsieur Astier was stepping up to Henri, his hand held out; he was shaking Henri's hand. Henri Quatre.

It should have been me, but it was Henri Quatre. Oh God. You've bested me again.

And Louis beside him began to clap.

And Roland clapped. And Jean-Pierre clapped, and Philippe clapped, and Pierre and Dominique clapped, and then it swelled, and it swept through the crowd, and the boys were cheering and stamping their feet, and Julien threw back his head and laughed out loud.

"Tanieux!" somebody yelled. "*L'abri!*" Someone else took it up, in rhythm, and then they were calling it out on the one-two beat: "Tanieux! *L'abri!* Tanieux! *L'abri!*" And Roland shouted and Louis shouted and Pierre shouted, and Julien shouted, at the top of their lungs.

Nina was crying. Hard sobs that shook her, her head held tight against Maria's chest. Maria, who had heard her, who knew it all now. Who had been with her on the border in the dark; who had wept with her in her cell. Maria, Marita, the arms of a mother, holding her tight. The grief and fear shaking her, and the anger, like waves of the sea: they crashed over her, sucked her down, and lifted her again. Maria's arms gripped her and took the shaking, and the waves washed her clean.

Slowly, the sobs wore themselves out, and she breathed.

The light from the window fell on the white bedspread. It glowed. It fell on Maria's face that bent over her, her cheek bright, her eyes dark.

"Maria," she whispered. "I was right. Wasn't I. About the evil men."

"Yes," said Maria quietly.

"But I think maybe. Maybe." She looked Maria in the eye, hard, searching. There was so much light. "Maria . . . is there a God?"

Maria looked at her, her dark eyes deep and steady. Then she smiled. That glowed too. "I didn't tell you the end of the story," she said. "Gino came home. My brother. One week after the man with the gun, my brother came home alive. We went to France. I got married. I had children."

Tears filled her eyes. They filled her eyes with light.

"Is it–true?" Nina whispered. The light said it might be. The light said this woman would not lie to her, ever, while the earth went round. "Am I . . . safe . . . here?"

Maria bent over her. Her eyes were very dark. "Nina," she said, "I am not God. I cannot say, 'You are safe.' But I can tell you two things: There is a God who loves you. And if they take you, they must take me too."

Outside the window was the sky. She could see up and up, so far, she could see forever into the blue, and the sight amazed her; as though the edge of some huge shadow had passed over her, and was now gone.

It wasn't until lunchtime, on the way out of school, that Henri caught Julien by the sleeve and pulled him aside.

"I wanted to shake your hand, Julien."

Julien looked at him. Henri and his honest blue eyes looking straight back at him. "I'd like to shake yours," he said. And there at the gate, as the boys walked past them on their way home for lunch, Henri Bernard and Julien Losier shook hands.

"You're a real *tanieusard*, Julien. I'm sorry I ever said any different."

"I'm sorry too. You know."

"Yeah. Listen. Tell your friends they don't need to worry about my father."

Julien blinked and was silent a moment. "Are you sure?"

"Would I say it if I wasn't sure?"

And Julien looked at Henri Bernard and saw it, the answer to all his praying. Henri would never lie. Not in any way, not to him, not to his worst enemy. The warmth of an unseen sunlight for a moment touched his face.

"No," he said. "I'll tell them."

Epilogue

The winter of 1940 was the worst Grandpa had ever seen.

The cold was deadly. The ice in the streets turned a dull gray-white, reflecting nothing of the sky. Grandpa looked at the woodpiles with sober, calculating eyes and called the family together to talk.

They went out together into the painful cold, to climb the hillsides and gather *genêts* to burn.

But tonight, it was Christmas Eve, and the fire was piled high and blazing, lighting the circle of faces: Mama and Papa, Magali and Benjamin, Grandpa and his new houseguest, Jacques Bellat, whose real name was Jacob Blumenfeld.

There was no Christmas tree, no presents. But the smells from the kitchen made Julien's stomach ache with longing: a coq au vin from an old rooster of the Rostins', an apple cake topped with real cream. Cups of mint and blackberry tea with real sugar, the mugs reflecting the fire's light; the nativity scene on the mantelpiece; and in the window, three candles glowing warm against the blue evening. Benjamin had put them there for Hanukkah.

"What was Hanukkah like?" asked Grandpa.

Benjamin looked shyly round the circle. "I—it's the only thing I remember from before we left Germany. I was so little. I remember the lights, the whole house filled with them, and all my aunts and uncles and cousins and everyone talking and singing—and my uncle would play the fiddle, and everyone would dance . . ." He looked at the window again, at the candles, and stopped, blinking hard.

"I'm sorry," said Grandpa.

"No," said Benjamin quietly. "No. I'm glad I remember."

It was only five minutes later, they remembered afterward; only five minutes before they heard the sound of boots coming up the stairs. And Pastor Alex came in.

His cheeks were bright pink with the cold when he came in the door, and he didn't take off his boots, and in his gloved hand was a brown paper envelope held out before him like a sword.

"*Bonjour, bonjour,*" he said hurriedly as they rose to greet him. "One of our guests gave us this. It's addressed to me, but I think it's for Benjamin. From his parents."

Benjamin stood up so fast he knocked his chair backward, and it clattered on the floor. He stood breathing quickly, his eyes huge in a white face. "My parents?" he whispered. Then he took the letter Pastor Alex held out to him and ran out the door.

They sat looking after him for a moment. Then made Pastor Alex sit down and gave him tea. As he drank, he told them what he knew.

The Kellers had left Paris before the first wave of refugees; they had found a train that took them to Bordeaux. From there, they'd walked south across country all the way to the Spanish border. But there they found crowds, masses of people trying to cross into Spain, scenes of panic. There had been a rush on the guard post, people trampled, many more arrested. Monsieur Keller had pulled a wad of money out of his pocket, and the policeman had let them go.

They didn't dare try the crossing again. They didn't dare risk anything. Not even mailing a letter to their son. They went into hiding in southern France. Eventually, they made it to Marseille. And there they met a man who knew a man who knew Pastor Alex, and they gave the letter to him.

The door was flung open, and Benjamin was back, his face like a beacon filling the room. He ran at Julien, grabbed him by the shoulders, shouting "They're all right, Julien, they're alive, they're *alive!*" And then he was being whirled around the room, and Magali was whirling with them, laughing, and Papa was beaming, and Mama's face shone with tears. Benjamin was hugging everyone and laughing and saying things they couldn't even understand in every language he knew, and Julien caught only those strange words he had once heard in the dark of Manu's chapel, when Benjamin stopped and spoke them almost too softly to hear, his eyes on the glow of the fire. "*Ribbono Shel Olom,*" he whispered. "*Ribbono Shel Olom.*"

And he understood when Benjamin turned to him, and put a hand on his shoulder. And called him brother.

Nina looked out the window at the town, at the blue twilight that surrounded them. Snow was falling—brilliant white in the pools of light under the streetlamps—swirling, drifting, floating through the light, almost as lightly as her heart.

She was going back to school.

In January she could start, they said. At the *Ecole du Vivarais*—for free, they would stick an extra desk in the back. *School!* And Gustav too. They would both be in *sixième*, a grade below Samuel—a girl of sixteen in a class of twelve-year-olds. She didn't care. She could feel no fear of anything, of anybody's eyes. Not today.

The fire in Miss Fitzgerald's fireplace blazed high, and it was Christmas Eve, and they were drinking Miss Fitzgerald's Irish tea with real milk and sugar. The blond girl across from her grinned shyly. Fräulein Pinatel on the sofa argued with Gustav.

"You're going to need all the time you can get for homework. You're fourteen years old. You don't *need* to earn your keep; what you *need* is an education."

"To help you earn your keep *later*," put in Miss Fitzgerald in her oddly accented German.

"But I already know what I want to do! I like farming, I like livestock, I'm learning *that*. You want me to stop learning what I'm going to use and learn—*geometry*?"

"You'd be surprised at the uses of geometry in farming," said Fräulein drily.

"Gustav," said Nina, "give it a try. For me. Not much is going to grow out there for a while anyway."

He gave her a rueful grin. "I'll try it. Sure I'll try it. But you're the one who's gonna go to college in this family."

"*College?*"

He laughed. They all laughed, throwing their heads back in joy. Her long dark hair fell back over her shoulders, and the sheer feel of it was joy; there was joy in the soft clean cloth of her new dress, in the face of the laughing blond girl, in the memory of her own face, that morning, in the mirror. The color in her cheeks, the way she filled out the green dress now, her first in a long year, the way her eyes looked . . . alive. Like a girl, a normal girl who went to school—read books—made *friends*. She drank joy down like water, even in this rock-hard winter knowing again the taste of sunlight. The taste of having woken, that morning, without fear.

Julien went to the window for a moment, away from the circle of faces, his heart too full, and looked out into the blue and bitter night. The snow was still falling, covering the cracked gray ice, softening the harshness, whitening the cold. He knew it had only begun, this winter; and they would burn *genêts* and shiver; and eat potatoes, not enough. Winter had come to his country, the most terrible of winters, and he knew it could last the rest of his life. He looked up into the deepening sky, and he could barely see them still; the flakes swirling, dancing in the darkening air, falling light as grace onto Tanieux. He watched for one long and quiet moment. Then he turned back to the faces, and the light.

Historical Note

by Heather Munn

It's not true that the Germans killed thirty thousand people in the bombing of Rotterdam.

The Luftwaffe carpet-bombed downtown Rotterdam and killed almost a thousand civilians; but the city had been under attack for four days already, and most people had evacuated. (Good thing they had: a whole square mile of the city was completely leveled.) The Allies inflated the number of victims for propaganda purposes: their news sources reported thirty thousand civilians dead. So Julien would have believed it was true, if he'd existed.

All the other historical information in the book is true: the news that Julien hears on the radio and reads in the paper, the summaries of the invasion of France and its surrender. The title of the editorial Julien reads, "Let us be French!" was the title of a real editorial written after the French defeat, and the ideas it expresses were common at the time. Marshal Pétain's speeches in the novel are direct translations of speeches he really gave. The story the principal tells his students in the last chapter is also true.

The news Julien gets about anti-Jewish laws from Vichy is true, and represents the Vichy government's gradual buildup to the point of full cooperation with the Nazis in rounding up Jews. Most of this news wasn't common knowledge, however; the Nazis ran a cover-up campaign aptly called "Night and Fog," and Vichy's tactics were similar. Julien gets this information because he is surrounded by people who are paying attention—and because he has a Jewish friend. It was very easy in those days not to know what was really going on. Next to no one in France at that time had heard even a rumor about the death camps.

The camps Vichy set up in the unoccupied zone of France, like the one Nina and Gustav might have been sent to, were internment camps, not death camps; their purpose was to isolate Jews, Communists, and other "undesirables" from the rest of the population. But people did die in them. Living conditions were terrible and even healthy people sickened. They were also deadly in another way: just a little later in the war, Vichy began to let the Nazis deport all interned Jews to Germany and the death camps. This is what would have happened to Nina and Gustav, even if Nina had lived. You'll hear more about the French internment camps in our next book.

One of the reasons this period of history fascinates me is choices. In France under the Nazis, people made all kinds of choices. Some got rich off the black market; some through collaboration. Some used the Nazis for revenge, feeding them true or false information against their enemies. Some followed Pétain unquestioningly; some just survived, as *attentistes*, "wait-ists," who chose not to get involved. Some vowed to fight the Germans to the bitter end and started the Resistance, which in those early days seemed completely doomed. And a few, like the people of a village in central France called Le Chambon-sur-Lignon, chose to focus on those in the deepest need and danger, and protect them from harm.

The true story of Le Chambon-sur-Lignon is told in *Lest Innocent*

Blood Be Shed by Philip Hallie and in the documentary *Weapons of the Spirit* made by Pierre Sauvage. I recommend them both if you want to know more. Basically, Le Chambon, a village of 3,000 people in the plateau country of central France, far from everything that mattered, over the course of the war, saved the lives of more than 3,000 Jews.

Tanieux is loosely based on Le Chambon: the landscape is similar, though it's mixed a little with the landscape of my childhood, about an hour's drive away. The people are (I hope) similar too. The real Reformed pastor of Le Chambon, André Trocmé, considered to be the guiding force behind the town's rescue movement, is the inspiration for Pastor Alexandre: like Alex, he was a Christian pacifist who preached resistance through "the weapons of the Spirit." (The sermon in which Alex uses that phrase is a loose translation of a sermon preached by Trocmé. The other sermons are fictional.) The story of Manu is fictional, but Le Chambon really did have the history of the Huguenots and *le désert*, and it was a history they cared about; it probably did have something to do with their choices during the war.

Vichy did hand down an order to use the fascist flag-salute in French schools, and the pastor and principal did deliberately undermine it. A third man also helped: Edouard Théis, principal of the new school (which had actually been started in 1938). Their plan was to have a combined flag ceremony, each school's students making a half circle in their own schoolyard—with a busy street in between. The flag-salute fell apart after a few weeks, just as they hoped it would.

The real stationmaster of Le Chambon never did any such thing as offering refugees a ticket back where they came from. But Magda Trocmé, Andre Trocmé's wife, did go to the mayor and ask for a ration card for a Jewish refugee, and the mayor did tell her angrily that she was endangering Le Chambon and had better get this person out of town immediately. The refugee was a middle-aged woman, and she was not sick, so Magda found a family in a nearby town who would take her in.

At the end of the book, Julien expects his country to be under Nazi domination for the rest of his life. This also is accurate. There was no good reason, then, to think otherwise. It was with no hope in sight that the people of Le Chambon trusted God and did what they could for the people they saw being persecuted. Sixty-five years later what they did is still remembered. I hope it always will be.

Heather Munn was born in Northern Ireland of American parents and grew up in the south of France. She decided to be a writer at the age of five when her mother read Laura Ingalls Wilder's books aloud, but worried that she couldn't write about her childhood since she didn't remember it. When she was young, her favorite time of day was after supper when the family would gather and her father would read a chapter from a novel. Heather went to French school until her teens, and grew up hearing the story of Le Chambon-sur-Lignon, only an hour's drive away. She now lives in rural Illinois with her husband, Paul, where they offer free spiritual retreats to people coming out of homelessness and addiction. She enjoys wandering in the woods, gardening, writing, and splitting wood.

Lydia Munn was homeschooled for five years because there was no school where her family served as missionaries in the savannahs of northern Brazil. There was no public library either, but Lydia read every book she could get her hands on. This led naturally to her choice of an English major at Wheaton College. Her original plan to teach high school English gradually transitioned into a lifelong love of teaching the Bible to both adults and young people as a missionary in France. She and her husband, Jim, have two children: their son, Robin, and their daughter, Heather.